The BLUE GIRL

Books by Charles de Lint

The Riddle of the Wren

Moonheart: A Romance

The Harp of the Grey Rose

Mulenegro: A Romany Tale

Yarrow: An Autumn Tale

Jack, the Giant Killer

Greenmantle

Wolf Moon

Svaha

The Valley of Thunder

Drink Down the Moon

Ghostwood

Angel of Darkness (as Samuel M. Key)

The Dreaming Place

The Little Country

From a Whisper to a Scream (as Samuel M. Key)

Spiritwalk

Dreams Underfoot (collection)

Into the Green

I'll Be Watching You (as Samuel M. Key)

The Wild Wood

Memory and Dream

The Ivory and the Horn (collection)

Jack of Kinrowan

Trader

Someplace to be Flying

Moonlight and Vines (collection)

Forests of the Heart

Triskell Tales: 22 Years of Chapbooks (collection)

The Road to Lisdoonvarna

The Onion Girl

Seven Wild Sisters

A Handful of Coppers (collection)

Waifs and Strays (collection)

Tapping the Dream Tree (collection)

A Circle of Cats (picture book)

Spirits in the Wires

Medicine Road

The Blue Girl

CHARLES de LINT

VIKING

VIKING
Published by Penguin Group
Penguin Young Readers Group, 345 Hudson Street, New York, New York 10014, U.S.A.
Penguin Group (Canada), 10 Alcorn Avenue, Toronto, Ontario, Canada M4V 3B2
(a division of Pearson Penguin Canada Inc.)
Penguin Books Ltd, 80 Strand, London WC2R 0RL, England
Penguin Ireland, 25 St Stephen's Green, Dublin 2, Ireland (a division of Penguin Books Ltd)
Penguin Group (Australia), 250 Camberwell Road, Camberwell, Victoria 3124, Australia
(a division of Pearson Australia Group Pty Ltd)
Penguin Books India Pvt Ltd, 11 Community Centre, Panchsheel Park, New Delhi - 110 017, India
Penguin Group (NZ), Cnr Airborne and Rosedale Roads, Albany, Auckland, New Zealand
(a division of Pearson New Zealand Ltd)
Penguin Books (South Africa) (Pty) Ltd, 24 Sturdee Avenue, Rosebank, Johannesburg 2196, South Africa

Penguin Books Ltd, Registered Offices: 80 Strand, London WC2R 0RL, England

First published in 2004 by Viking, a division of Penguin Young Readers Group

9 10 8

LIBRARY OF CONGRESS CATALOGING-IN-PUBLICATION DATA IS AVAILABLE
ISBN: 0-670-05924-2

Printed in U.S.A.
Set in Bembo
Book design by Jim Hoover

FOR MY NIECES,
CASSIE, JAZ, & KMORÉ

with special thanks
for astute editorial advice to
Julie Bartel, Sharyn November,
and my dear wife MaryAnn

If I can dream

of waking in a dream,

how can I tell

I'm not dreaming now?

—SASKIA MADDING,

FROM "THINKING AFTER MIDNIGHT"

(*SPIRITS AND GHOSTS*, 2000)

NOW: *Imogene*

It starts with this faint sound that pulls me out of sleep: a sort of calliope music played on an ensemble of toy instruments. You know, as though there's a raggedy orchestra playing quietly in some hidden corner of my bedroom, like the echo of a Tom Waits song heard through the walls from the apartment next door. Rinky-dink piano, tinny horns and kazoos, miniature guitars with plastic strings, weird percussion.

I don't really wake up until I hear a creak from inside my closet. I know exactly what it is: the old wooden chest where I store my childhood treasures. I lie there, staring up at the ceiling, straining to hear more over the insistent whisper of the music, because now I know that all these nursery rhymes and fairy tales are creeping out of the books I used to read when I was a kid. A hinge squeaks on the closet door—the one I'm always telling myself I have to oil, but promptly forget before I actually get to it—and out they come, one by one, their feet making little scratchy noises on the wood floor.

I don't know if they're the actual characters from the books or something else again: patchwork creatures made out of words and rags and twigs, of bits of wool and fur, skin and bone. There's too much shadow and spookiness in the room, so I only catch glimpses of them as they emerge, and

I don't want to lean over the side of the bed to have a better look. All I know for sure is that they come from the books. A pack of strange little creatures, shuffling and dancing their way out of the closet and into the shadows around my bed. And in among them, standing a lot taller than the rest, so I can see his features in the light that comes through my window from the streetlamp outside, is my old imaginary friend, Pell-mell.

I used to call him Pelly and stopped playing with him a good seven years ago, when I was ten. I haven't really thought much about him since then, except for that day when I first met Maxine.

He hasn't grown the way I did, so he's still only around four feet tall, this weird, skinny cross between a hedgehog and a boy, with floppy rabbit ears and a monkey's prehensile tale. He used to be so sweet, but now he has all the innocence of a dead child's ghost. It's in those big eyes of his. He knows too much. He's seen too much.

He steps up to the bed and lays his hands on my comforter. The fingers seem too long, like they have an extra joint. I don't remember that from before, either. His face leans close to mine. My gaze lifts, and now all I can see are those big, strange eyes of his. They're deep and luminous, and I feel like I could fall right into them.

"Imogene," he says. His voice is a husky rasp and harmonizes with the faint calliope music. "I've missed you sideways."

His hand lifts from the comforter and reaches for my face.

And then I wake up for real.

THEN: *Imogene*

"You look just like the imaginary friend I had when I was a kid. Only older, you know?"

That was the first thing I ever said to Maxine. We were both sixteen, and it happened midterm on my first lunch break at my new school. I'd just transferred to Redding High, after my mom moved us from Tyson to Newford so that we could "find ourselves." Find *herself,* she really meant. Neither my brother Jared nor I was particularly lost.

The words were a test of sorts, the sort of peculiar thing that's always popping out of my mouth. How people react lets me gauge their possible compatibility. Jared uses music. To register positively on his radar, you have to have the right attitude about the right band at the right point in their career. I think my way's way more fair. Or at least more inventive.

Maxine didn't really look like the imaginary childhood playmate I could barely recall, never mind describe—I remembered there'd been something about ears like a rabbit's and a tail like a monkey's. I was pretty sure that Maxine was completely human, though she could be hiding a tail under that knee-length skirt of hers. It was hard to tell. What couldn't be argued was that she was a slender girl with auburn hair and taller than me. But then most people were. Taller, I mean. And while she was also pretty enough to be popular, when I stepped out into the schoolyard, she was sitting by herself on a bench by the baseball diamond, eating her lunch while she looked out across the playing field.

I'd gotten really tired of the endlessly shifting cliques at my old school, so I'd decided that this time I'd align myself with only one person. A special person, someone who cared as little for the social merry-go-round as I did. Sitting by herself the way she was, Maxine seemed a likely candidate, so that was why I'd walked over to the bench, sat down, and delivered my pronouncement.

Maxine gave me a cool look after I spoke, but the hint of a smile tugged at the corner of her mouth.

"Maybe I am," she said.

I smiled happily. It was the perfect response. Playing along, but not committing, so there was still some mystery. Not, "Go away." Not, "Yes, what took you so long to find me again?"—although that might have proved interesting.

"I don't know," I said. "It's all hazy, but I seem to remember something about floppy ears and a tail."

Maxine shrugged. "People change."

"Even when they're imaginary?"

"Probably more so then."

"You're probably right."

"My name's Maxine."

"Mine's Imogene."

"For real?"

I nodded. Considering the way my imagination tends to spill out of my mouth, it was a fair question, not to mention an astute one on Maxine's part, her having just met me and all.

"My mother got it from this book she bought while she was pregnant with me. It's about this irrepressible little girl who wakes up one morning with antlers."

"So, in other words, you grew into the name."

I beamed at her. "This," I said, "feels like the beginning of a great friendship."

Maxine shook her head.

"Why ever not?"

"The best thing you could do right now is to say something mean to me and then walk away. And never talk to me again—unless it's to say more mean things."

"Don't be stupid."

"You don't understand. I'm like a pariah around here."

I tilted my head. "I've never heard that word used in a conversation before."

"I'm serious."

"So am I. It's weird how certain words are really just book words and hardly ever get used in regular conversations. I wonder why that is. And *pariah* is one of those interesting ones that sounds like it means. There's a word for that, too, isn't there?"

"Onomatopoeia."

"Which, in itself, is an interesting word."

Maxine could only shake her head. "Are you always like this?"

"Pretty much. So what's so bad about you?"

"Oh, who knows? I suppose it started because I was too smart and showed it."

I gave her a slow nod of understanding.

"Have you ever noticed," I said, "how everyone says they want to be different, but as soon as they meet someone who really is different, they ostracize them?"

"Exactly. And now it's just a habit—the making fun of me, I mean."

"I don't care. I'd still rather be your friend."

"But you haven't met anybody else. They could be wonderfully interesting."

"Not to mention mean. Why would I want to be friends with people like that?"

Maxine shrugged. "I don't know. Most people just do. I did once, but they never gave me the chance."

"And besides," I went on. "I'm sure I'm weirder than you. So being your friend is like a preventative measure."

"How's that?"

I grinned. "This way I'm sure of having one friend."

"You *are* weirder than me."

"And besides all of that, our names have a nice rhythm when they're put together. Maxine and Imogene."

"Except yours has one more syllable than mine does."

"So you'll just have to catch up."

Maxine shook her head and really smiled for the first time. "I'm not sure I ever could."

* * *

Later than afternoon, a girl named Valerie Clarke approached me at my locker between classes. She was very cute, blonde, and had obviously taken her fashion tips from an MTV video—one by a boy band, mind you, not some slinky rap one. Short little skirt, perky shoes, sleevcless top, all of them just right. I didn't know what clique she was with, exactly, but I knew she belonged to one from the little gaggle of clones that stood in a cluster behind her, listening in.

"So you're the new girl," she said.

It wasn't a particularly endearing opening line—not at all like the one I'd used with Maxine—but then I don't think it was supposed to be.

"Apparently," I said and offered her a low-watt smile.

I was willing to be amicable so long as it didn't take a lot of work on my part, nor entail my having to join her clique. Not that I thought an invitation was forthcoming, but you never know. Little Bob, a hillbilly kid back at my old school, swore it once rained snails up in the mountains where he lives, so stranger things have happened.

"Where did you transfer from?" Valerie asked.

"It wasn't in the newspaper? I was sure it made all the gossip sections."

"What?"

From the confused expression on her perfectly made-up face, she obviously didn't get that I was joking. And okay, I wasn't trying too hard to make nice. But kids like that have always rubbed me the wrong way, all intimidation and cooler-than-thou. Please. Still, I relented.

"I went to Willingham High," I told her. "In Tyson."

"Ah."

Already I didn't much like Valerie—look, I never said I was particularly tolerant, and she was obviously the sort of person who was naturally annoying—but I was impressed with how much she was able to put into that one simple sound: disdain, false sympathy, a smidgen of mockery. It takes talent to be that subtly expressive with nonverbal sounds, and I told her as much.

"Well, you're about what I expected," she said.

"I'm flattered. I had no idea that anyone would have any expectations whatsoever."

Her perfect lips made a perfect *moue*. She was quite amazing really. A living, breathing stereotype of an in-crowd teenage girl. I wondered if she practiced expressions in front of her mirror at home.

"You think you're so smart," she said, "but you're no different than Chancy. You're both just dumb."

Wow. Great with the image, but not so big in the eloquency department. Though maybe I was missing something, because all her clones began to giggle. As if.

"Who's Chancy?" I asked.

"Your loser lunch buddy."

"Oh, you mean Maxine."

"You deserve each other."

"Good. I like her."

"What are you—gay?"

"What are you—homophobic?"

"Jesus, you're weird."

I nodded. "I'm definitely more weird than gay. Unless you meant cheerful. Then sometimes I'm more gay than weird."

"Just stay out of our way."

"I'll try, princess."

"Don't call me that."

"Why not?"

"God, you are so lame."

And with that last witty rejoinder, off she went, the heels of those perky shoes of hers clicking on the marble floor, her clones bunched in a group around her. I turned back to my locker.

* * *

Jared was waiting for me after school, because Mom had asked him to walk home with me. She was afraid that I'd get lost in the few blocks to our new apartment, but that was just her projecting again. She had actually gotten lost going to the corner store over the weekend. I have a great sense of direction.

"I can't believe it," Jared said as we headed off. "We're not here for more than a day, and you've already got a reputation for being weird."

"What have I done?"

"So far? Befriended a nerd. Sexually propositioned a cheerleader."

"Really?

"You didn't?"

"Well, I befriended a girl named Maxine who apparently people don't like because she's smart, but I don't remember the propositioning part. You'd think I'd remember something like that."

Jared laughed. "You'd think."

"So how was your day?"

He shrugged. "Oh, you know. Not so much boring as—" He gave me another laugh. "Well, boring. Did you hear the lame-ass music they were playing in the cafeteria at lunch? Real cutting-edge. Not."

"But you, of course, made a wonderful impression on everyone you met."

He gave me another shrug. "I don't know. I wasn't paying much attention. I met a couple of okay guys, and the girls are definitely way hotter than they were in our old school. But it doesn't look like I've got much chance of starting a decent band here. It's all pap and rap and headbanger crap."

Decent, for Jared, meant retro. You know, hippie music, jangly and psychedelic, and loaded with words.

"Don't worry," I told him. "We're in the big city now—you'll find players."

"I suppose."

"It's lucky you're so charming that no one cares how weird your sister is."

It was true—even back in our old school. But how could you not like Jared? He was handsome and smart and kind. Sure, he was weird, too, but not deliberately and confrontationally so, like me. With him it was mostly this obsession he had with music—all kinds, but especially the old stuff. And that just added to his cool.

No, that's only partly true. He got along so well with people because he looked the way he did, handsome but not a pretty boy. Because he was good at sports *and* the arts. Because he didn't exactly toe the line, but he didn't step way over it the way I did. And he was so easygoing that you'd really have to work at disliking him.

"So are you going to stick it out?" he asked.

He was talking about my habit of skipping school. I only ever spent a couple of days a week in classes when we were going to Willingham. I could have aced my exams by studying, but why bother?

"We'll see," I told him.

* * *

I called Maxine that evening after supper. I lay on the couch with the TV on at a low volume, flipping through channels while I waited for someone to answer. I thought it was going to go to an answering machine, but Maxine picked up on the sixth ring.

"Hello?"

She sounded a little hesitant, like she was expecting a telemarketer or a wrong number. I guess she didn't get many calls.

"Hello, yourself," I said.

"Imogene?"

"In the flesh—no, actually on the phone, if we're going to be specific. I just thought I'd try your number to make sure it worked."

"Why wouldn't it work?"

"Well, you could have given me the number for a pizza

joint because you thought I was too weird and pushy."

I could feel her smiling.

"You're definitely weird," she said, "*and* a little pushy, but that's okay. My life is so not-weird it could use some of your fantasies to spruce it up."

"Fantasies? I'll have you know that I'll take whimsy over fantasy any day of the week."

"What do you mean?"

"I'd just always rather meet a talking spoon than an elf."

Maxine laughed. "Do you have to practice to be like this?"

"No. Unfortunately, it comes naturally."

"Don't say that. I like the way your mind works."

"'Work' being a subjective term. Just think how much easier I'd get along in the world if I could be more normal."

"I got the feeling that you don't like normal."

"Well, no," I said. "Not being who I am right now. But if I was normal, then I probably would like it."

"I'm pretty normal. It's not all it's cracked up to be."

"No," I assured her. "You're extraordinary."

That got me another laugh. "Yeah, right."

"No, really."

"How can you be so sure of that? We only just met this afternoon."

"A spoon told me."

"Of course."

"So are you watching TV?" I asked.

"No. Are you?"

"Mm-hmm. Switch to channel twenty-two."

"Just a sec. I'm going into the other room."

"You have a cordless phone, don't you? I'm so jealous. Mom won't let us have one because she thinks it'll give us brain cancer."

"She's probably thinking of a cell phone, which is what I'm on. And nothing's been proven one way or another. What channel did you say?"

"Twenty-two."

"That's just the weather channel."

"I know. Can you believe that woman's hair? It doesn't move."

"Oh, my god, you're right. It's just like a helmet."

"We should send her a letter. Maybe she doesn't know."

"How could she not know?"

We spent a while channel flipping, keeping up a running commentary on everything we saw. Maxine might have thought she was normal, but she had me giggling hysterically more than a few times with her observations, and that's something normal people never seem to do. At least not intentionally.

"I should go," she finally said when we landed back on the weather channel for maybe the fifth time. The weather woman's hair still wasn't moving. "I need to study."

"I thought you were naturally smart."

"Mensa material, apparently. But you still have to stick information in your head so that the big brain has something to work with."

"So that's the step I've been missing. See you tomorrow in school?"

"Of course," she said. "It's not like we could just blow it off."

I let that go. Just because I had bad habits was no reason to share them. One of the teachers at my old school used to call me a virus because of how the trouble I got into always spilled over onto whoever happened to hang around with me. I was going to make a valiant effort to not let that happen with Maxine.

"I wish we had some of the same classes," I said. "Or at least the same homeroom."

"No, you don't. Your friend Valerie's in my homeroom."

"God, does everybody know *everybody's* business in this school?"

"Why are you surprised? You're the new girl, and she's the captain of the cheerleader squad."

When Jared told me she was a cheerleader, I should have realized she'd be the captain. No rank-and-file for that girl.

"You might want to be careful around her," Maxine added. "She can be pretty mean, and people tend to follow her lead. Trust me, I know."

"I'll be the very model of a careful, well-behaved mouse and stay out of her way."

Maxine laughed. "I think this is going to be a very interesting year."

"Good night, Maxine."

"Good night, Imogene."

We hung up. After I cradled the receiver, I lay my head back on the arm of the couch and smiled happily. This felt so much better than it had been back in Tyson, where for some reason I'd always had a chip on my shoulder. Maxine made everything seem so different. Better.

I loved Jared, but I needed a girl in my life. Someone my own age. Mom liked to act like she was our sibling, but while I loved her too, it just wasn't the same because, at the end of the day, there'd always come a point where she'd feel the need to play the mother card.

And who knew? Maybe if I hung around with Maxine enough I'd get smart, too. But it'd have to be by osmosis, because it wasn't something I could ever see myself actually working on. Do as much as you need to get by—that was my motto. I'd leave it to somebody else to put in all the effort to become valedictorian.

* * *

Of course, keeping out of Valerie Clarke's way proved to be impossible. I don't know if it was some holdover of the way I was this trouble magnet back in Tyson, or if she'd just decided to make a project out of giving me a hard time, but I seemed to run into her everywhere. At first I managed to keep my mouth shut when she made her snide little comments, but that got old fast, and being a mouse was never really a big part of my repertoire.

I'd tried dressing normally the first few days at the new school in hopes of not standing out—jeans or slacks, a simple top, one of Jared's jackets that was only a little long on me and looked okay with the sleeves rolled up—but Valerie made that impossible. With her on my case, the last thing I could be was invisible, so by the end of the week, I was back to my old no-style style. I showed up Friday morning in a plaid skirt with striped socks, clunky shoes, a black T-shirt, and my old Army surplus olive green jacket. I'd used a veritable militia of barrettes to transform my black pageboy into a thicket of little hair tufts that stuck up every which way.

And you know, I didn't really stand out *that* much. This being a high school, fashion went from one end of the spectrum to the other, holdover punks and hippies to skateboarders, preppies, headbangers, and everything in between. Just an endless array of cliques and small gangs with as little mixing as possible except when actually in class.

But my punk-grrl-cum-thrift-shop look still gave Valerie plenty of fuel. As soon as she saw me that morning, she started right in on me—at least until I took her aside, just far enough from her little coterie of clones so that they couldn't listen in. I have no idea why she even stepped out of their hearing, because half the satisfaction for someone like her is playing to an audience. I guess she was curious.

"You're having your fun," I told her, "and so long as we're on school grounds, I'm going to let you say any damn thing you want."

"Oh, like you could stop—"

"Because I just don't need the grief of detention and visits to the office and crap like that. But here's the thing, princess."

"I told you not to call me—"

I leaned in close, a friendly smile on my lips.

"Keep this up," I told her, "and you don't *ever* want to see me out of school because I will so beat the crap out of you."

"You wouldn't—"

"Princess, you don't know the first damn thing about what I would or wouldn't do. So you just think on that."

"You are so—"

"Now go tell your little friends how you really put me in my place, and I'll look suitably chastised, and we can get on with our respective days."

She got this look in her eyes that I couldn't figure out. Some weird mix of anger, fear, and relief. But she didn't say anything. She just went off with her little friends, their giggles trailing behind them, and I figured that was that.

But then she had to go sic her boyfriend on me.

* * *

His name was Brent Calder, and of course he was the football team's quarterback. Who else would the captain of the cheerleader squad be going out with? I suppose somebody, somewhere, might have considered him to be a lovely young man, but I pegged him for a big dumb jock the moment I saw him. What can I say? I can be as guilty of stereotyping as the next person.

He was taller than me, naturally, and good-looking in the same plasticky way that Valerie was, except he had this whole boy thing going for him. You know, rugged, while she was soft. His hair was short and brushed back, and he filled out his shirt the way a guy does when he exercises regularly. Seeing him made me realize I had to change my personal nickname for Valerie. I was forever going to think of them as Barbie and Ken.

He stopped me on the west stairwell, giving me a little push that banged me up against the wall. One of his teammates, a dark-haired guy named Jerry Fielder, stood a couple of stairs up from us, arms folded, a little smile of anticipation playing on his lips. The other students just went by, looking away, nobody wanting to get involved.

"I've heard all about you, Yuck," he said.

Like making that joke with my surname, Yeck, was even remotely original.

"And I don't like what I'm hearing," he added.

I started to straighten up from the wall, but he stepped in close, totally invading my personal space. I knew I had to talk my way out of this, but I've never been able to stop from being a smart aleck.

"Gee, I'm sorry to hear that, Ken," I told him.

"The name's Brent."

"Whatever you say."

Sarcasm obviously went right over his head. Smart, just like his girlfriend.

"You got it," he said. "That's the way it works around here—just whatever I say. And what I'm saying right now is, keep out of Valerie's way."

"Or?"

"What do you mean 'or'?"

"Well, what are you going to do if I don't? Are you going to beat me up? That'll look really good, won't it? Smacking around a little thing like me, half your size and a girl in the bargain. That's going to impress just about everybody with what a big, tough guy you are."

I was talking way braver than I felt, but talking was all I had. His face went dark, and for a moment I thought he was going to hit me. I knew a couple of tricks for taking down a guy his size—I had to, hanging around with the crowd I had back in Tyson—but none of them were foolproof, and standing on the stairs like we were wasn't exactly the best place to implement any of them.

"Anyway, I'm trying to stay out of your girlfriend's way," I went on. "But for some reason, every time I turn around, there she is."

"You've got a smart mouth, Yuck."

"I know. And the rest of me's not so dumb either."

He grabbed my arm and squeezed hard enough to bruise. I didn't pretend it didn't hurt, but I wasn't going to let it cow me either.

"That bruise'll make an interesting photograph," I told him.

"What's that supposed to mean?"

"As evidence."

He laughed, but he let me go.

"You're a real piece of work, aren't you?" he said. "You actually think the principal would take the word of some loser reject like you over that of his star quarterback?"

"I have no idea," I told him. "I'm thinking more judge, lawyers, civil lawsuit, that kind of thing."

"Like that would ever happen. Just stay off my radar, Yuck. You don't want to get on my bad side."

"Or you'll . . . ?"

"Or I'll squash you like the weird little bug that you are."

Then he laughed and gave me another shove, banging me back up against the wall once more. Turning away, he went on up the stairs with his friend Jerry. Throughout our little encounter, no one else ever stopped or looked once in our direction. They continued to just go by as I leaned against the wall, but I knew they'd taken it all in. Knew they were all as scared of him as I was supposed to be.

I rubbed my arm where he'd bruised it. All kinds of little revenge scenarios played through my head Road Runner cartoon style, except Brent and Valerie took turns being the coyote, and they didn't bounce back the way Wile E. did.

It was dumb, but they were comforting to consider as I continued on down the stairs, still rubbing my upper arm, and I knew I wouldn't put even one of them into practice. I wouldn't say boo to either of them.

Unless they got on my case again.

Then maybe I wouldn't be able to stop myself, and the next time, I'd probably get beat up for real, instead of just pushed around the way I'd been today.

THEN: *Adrian*

I know exactly the moment that I fell in love with Imogene Yeck. It was that Friday afternoon on the stairwell—the first time she ran into Brent Calder. Standing up to him didn't help her any more than it had ever helped me with Woody and Trevor and Mac and all those guys who were always on *my* case. Brent still pushed her around. He was still in control. But she wasn't intimidated. She looked him right in the eye, even when he was hurting her.

I knew I could never be that brave. It was like she was daring him to do his worst, but whatever that was, it wouldn't make her cry.

I wanted to go up to her once Brent and Jerry finally walked away, but when she looked my way, I just stared at the floor. I couldn't even meet her eyes, and she just looked right through me, the way everybody else does.

But I fell in love with her all the same.

* * *

I took to following her around when she was at school. I'd always make sure she was in my line of sight in the cafeteria. I'd find someplace to stand in the halls or out in the schoolyard where I could look at her, but she wouldn't notice me. Not that I had to worry. For all that was special about her, she paid no more attention to me than anyone else ever did.

I know—it sounds so creepy. But I just wanted to look at her. I'd have *liked* there to be more. I had a hundred scenarios worked out in my head as to how we'd meet and she'd realize how we were meant for each other and how she couldn't live without me. Sometimes I stepped in and saved her from Brent or one of the other guys who was bothering her. Sometimes we just happened to be in the library at the same time, reaching for the same book. Sometimes we just bumped into each other in the halls.

But it was all perfectly innocent.

Well, not totally innocent. Once she realized how much she wanted me, we'd *do* things. We'd have sex everywhere. In the girls' bathroom. In a pile of blankets by the furnace in the basement. Under the bleachers.

But that was only in my head, and I knew it wasn't something that would ever really happen.

When I say my following her around was innocent, I just mean nothing was ever supposed to happen.

Whatever else, you have to believe this: I never meant to hurt her.

THEN: *Imogene*

"God, I heard about you and Brent," Maxine said at the end of the day.

She'd told her mom that morning that she had to do some research at the library after school, so we had a little time to hang out. I tried to get her to go to one of the coffee shops further down Williamson Street—I was totally getting the scoop on the neighborhood by now—but she felt uncomfortable about not going where she'd said she would. I couldn't imagine living in such a strict environment, but I didn't try to push her into doing something that would distress her. Besides, when we got there, I discovered the Crowsea Public Library was pretty cool, too.

The only thing that came close back in Tyson was the old courthouse, and who'd want to spend time there? I knew too many people who walked in there and then ended up in juvie.

The library was a nice old building, all stone and ivy, with gargoyles on the cornices and big, beautiful leaded windows that were arched at the top and had seats built into the deep sills at the bottom. The steps going up were wide and welcoming, and there were stone lions sitting on their haunches on either side of the door. Inside, it was all polished, natural wood—the bookcases, the floors, the crown moldings—and it smelled like books, old, but not musty. A friendly smell.

Maxine led me upstairs to the nonfiction floor, and we got comfortable in one of the window seats that looked out on Lee Street. Outside, we could see the wind blowing the last leaves from the trees and then chasing them up and down the pavement. People were already walking with a cold-weather hunch in their shoulders. Here, where we were, it was cozy and warm.

"I'm sure it sounded worse than it really was," I told her.

"You're not scared of anything, are you?"

"Are you kidding? I'm scared of everything. I just try not to show it. Bullies sense weakness—if they think you'll back down, that's when they really move in for the kill. I should know. We had enough of them at my old school."

"Well, you should still be careful around Brent. He can be really mean, especially when the team loses a game. Everybody tries to keep out of his way then, even Valerie."

"Why, does he beat on her or something?"

Maxine shook her head. "I don't think so. I mean, why would she keep hanging around with him if he did?"

For a hundred reasons, I thought, and none of them good.

"But I've heard he's said some really mean things to her," Maxine added.

I could hear Brent's voice in my head.

I'll squash you like the weird little bug that you are.

"Been there," I said. "Didn't impress me."

"How'd you get to be so brave?" Maxine asked.

"Or stupid."

"I didn't say that."

"I know. But they almost go hand in hand, don't they? I guess it's because I've been beat up before, so it doesn't scare me as much as it probably should. Or I'm just too ornery to let it scare me."

Maxine smiled. "*Ornery*'s a good word."

"It is, isn't it?"

Maxine's smile faltered. "I got hit once—really hard, right in the chest. Jerry Fielder punched me, and it really hurt. Enough to make me cry, which I *so* didn't want to do in front of everybody. I stayed sore for a long time and I had a bruise for a couple of weeks after."

"I met him. He was with Brent on the stairs today."

"It's just," Maxine went on, "getting hit like that didn't make me brave. Instead, it made me more scared. I do everything I can to keep out of the way of that crowd. It doesn't work though, because I've got classes with some of them, and they're always knocking down my books or pushing me in the hall. But I'm too scared to do anything."

"Which was the whole point of him hitting you."

"So how do you get brave?"

"You have to not care."

"But how can you not care?"

I shrugged. "It's only pain. Here, look."

I turned and pulled the edge of my sleeveless T-shirt up enough so that she could see the tattoo of a blue swan on my shoulder.

"I've got a couple of others, too," I told her. "It hurts a little when you're getting them done, but once you're past the pain, you've got these cool tats to show for it. It's the same thing with bullies. It hurts when they hit you, but if you stand up to them, afterward you have the satisfaction of not having let them cow you. Mind you, you'll have to nurse your bruises . . . "

"It shouldn't have to be like that."

"Of course it shouldn't. But what can we do? 'Zero tolerance' policies never seem to do anything to stop the bullies."

"So were you like this in your old school?" Maxine asked.

"Pretty much. I guess Jared got all the peace, love, and flowers in our genes."

"What do you mean?"

"We grew up on a hippie commune outside of Hazard, and the whole vibe of the place just took—with him."

Maxine was looking a little wide-eyed. I forgot sometimes how exotic my family could be to people who'd lived their whole lives walking the straight and narrow.

"We lived there until I was eleven," I said. "But then it all kind of fell apart because everybody was doing their own thing and nobody was really taking care of upkeep and taxes and basic stuff like that. And some of them started growing dope back in the hills and smoking too much of it. Anyway, before we had the bailiffs knocking on our door, my parents smartened up enough to move us into a little apartment in Tyson."

"Was that strange for you?"

"Well, it was a big change, all right, but Jared and I were so ready to be living in a place where we could get cable, eat fast food, and go to music stores and thrift shops and that kind of thing. Our parents weren't any more together than they'd been on the commune, but somehow they managed to keep the apartment. Jared and I did odd jobs. We collected bottles for their deposit and went curb crawling—anything to make a buck."

"What's curb crawling?"

I grinned. "You go out on garbage day and check out what's been left at the curb. You wouldn't believe the stuff people throw away that can be resold to junk shops and antique stores. I mean, the stores ripped us off, because they'd go on to sell it for way more than they ever gave us, but it wasn't like we paid for the stuff in the first place."

"Really?"

"Sure. We're going to do it here, too, as soon as we figure out the pick-up schedules and suss out the right shops to sell to. You can come if you want."

"I don't know . . . "

"It's not as bad as it sounds."

"No, it's not that. It's just—my mom'd kill me if she ever found out I was doing something like that."

"She doesn't have to find out, but if you're not comfortable keeping secrets from her, you shouldn't do it."

"There's nothing comfortable in our house, not like you think a family should be. You know, close and loving. I mean, I know Mom loves me, but she's always on my case about something or other."

"What about your dad?"

"They separated last year. I stay with him on weekends sometimes, but he's pretty busy."

"Yeah, we've got the dadless household, too."

"So you just live with your mom and Jared?"

I nodded. "Like I said, Mom and Dad were both hippies—second generation, if you can believe it—but Mom decided to make the big change in her life: go back to school, get her life back on track."

"What about your dad?"

"Oh, he's sweet, but he's almost always stoned. I don't think marijuana's particularly bad for you—except for all the tar in it—but it sure does make you stupid when you do enough of it on a daily basis. If they really wanted to stop kids from smoking, they should bring in guys like my dad to talk to them. *Nobody's* going to want to get high if they figure they'll end up like him."

"Is that why your mom left him?"

"Partly. They still get along great, except she's finally getting on with her life. Thirty years too late, maybe, but better late than never."

"I guess it was weird for you."

"I suppose in some ways. But it's funny: they might have been spaced out most of the time, and I guess Jared and I ran a little wild, but they also gave us a real sense of our own worth. I know, that sounds kind of weird, considering how totally untogether they were. But it's true. All the freedom they gave us made us more determined to do something with ourselves."

"I wish my mom would give me a little more freedom," Maxine said.

"How so?"

"Well, she's totally focused on my having good grades and getting into a good university and just basically not having any fun. Forget boys." She fingered the knee-length skirt she was wearing. "And look at these clothes."

"You don't like them?"

"Do you?"

"Well, they're not me," I had to admit.

"They're not me either. But anytime I try to pick something I like, she tells me it'll just make me look like a whore or a bum."

"Oh, dear."

"I *love* the way you dress. At least," she added with a smile, "since you stopped trying to pretend you were a nerd like me."

I'd told her how I'd been trying to be invisible when I started classes earlier in the week, and we all know how well that worked out.

"First of all," I said, "you're not a nerd."

"No, I just act and dress like one."

"And secondly, we can fix this."

"What do you mean?"

"I'll take you shopping."

"You don't understand. My mom won't let me wear anything except what she picks out."

"We'll keep your new clothes at my place."

"And how could I ever afford them?"

"Your mom gives you *some* money, right?"

"Well, sure."

"So, you'll do like me and shop the thrift stores. You won't believe the stuff you can find in there—like designer jeans for under five bucks."

Maxine shook her head. "You've got an answer for everything."

"Not really. All the big questions still have me guessing."

"You know what I mean."

I shrugged. "Anyway, if we go to hang out somewhere—she does let you hang out, right?"

"Some."

"You can just come over to my place and change first."

"But if we're going to do that," Maxine said, "my mom's going to want to meet you. And, well, you know. Once she sees you . . . "

"Don't worry. I clean up really well."

"I don't know . . . "

"Trust me with this," I told her. "It'll all work out."

* * *

Meeting Maxine's mom for the first time entailed my trawling through a number of thrift shops for just the right costume. I had lots of plain blouses, but nothing in the way of the skirts or shoes or jackets that a serious student would wear. I could've worn some of the pants I'd had on earlier in the week, but judging from the fact that I'd only ever seen Maxine in a skirt or dress, I got the sense her mom didn't really approve of pants.

It took me a while, but eventually I found everything I

needed, and for under ten bucks, too. I'm just *so* good.

"Please tell me you're not going out like that," Mom said as I was about to step out the door.

She was lying on the couch, hippie-casual in a tie-dyed T-shirt and faded, frayed jeans, one of her textbooks open on her lap. She looked over the top of her reading glasses so that she could check me out in sharper focus.

"God, you look like my grandmother," she said.

"Oh, come on. Don't you keep up on *anything*? The goody-two-shoes look is all the rage."

She shook her head, sad rather than disapproving. "I just really thought I'd brought you up better than to slavishly follow the trends laid down by the fashionistas. And you know as well as I do that they get their marching orders from Big Business."

That's my mom for you. Every little thing's a part of the big conspiracy picture.

I crossed over to the couch and kissed her on the cheek.

"I love you, too, Mom," I said, then headed out on my mission.

It was a little like dressing up for Halloween, except nobody was handing out treats. But the best part of all of this was seeing Maxine's face when she opened the door and found me standing in the hallway outside her apartment.

I wasn't wearing any makeup and my hair was neatly brushed, the sides held back behind my ears with barrettes. I had on a three-quarter-length conservative wool coat and sensible oxfords; a dark, pleated skirt that decorously covered my knees; and a white top with a bit of lacy frill around the collar, pinned at the throat with a cameo.

"Imogene?" she said.

I gave her a wink and put a finger to my lips when I saw she was going to bring up the obvious question of what I thought I was doing.

"So's your mom home?" I asked.

She gave a slow nod and stepped aside so I could come in.

Her mom wasn't the fierce dragon I'd built up in my mind. Instead, she was that most insidious creature: a nice, ordinary woman who went through life with the quiet assurance that she knew better than anybody else How Things Should Be. I could tell within the first few minutes of meeting her that while she might be pleasant, and even kind—in her own way, on her own terms—no one was ever going to change her mind once she had it made up about something. How'd I know? It's hard to say. Maybe it was the set of her shoulders, or the steel I saw in her eyes.

I just hoped she couldn't read minds.

"It's very good to meet you, Mrs. Chancy," I said when we were introduced.

"It's Ms. Tattrie," she corrected me. "Maxine might have decided to keep her father's name, but I most certainly have not."

Ho-kay.

"I'm sorry, Ms. Tattrie," I said. "I had no idea . . . "

"Of course you didn't. Would you like some tea before you girls begin your study session?"

"Yes, please. Thank you."

Ms. Tattrie turned to Maxine. "Why don't you see to it, dear? That will give me the chance to get to know your friend a little better."

Here comes the third degree, I thought, but Ms. Tattrie surprised me.

"I'm so happy that Maxine has finally found a friend," she said once Maxine was out of the room.

Unspoken, but tangled there in her words if you were looking for it, was the relief that the friend was as obviously prim and tidy as she thought her daughter was. But hey, that's the image I was trying to project, so I couldn't complain.

"She rarely goes out, unless it's to the library or the bookstore," Ms. Tattrie went on, "and I can't remember the last time she had someone over. This past year's been the worst. I think losing her father has been particularly hard on her."

I guess Mr. Chancy had been the buffer between his wife and his daughter, making it a little harder for Ms. Tattrie to run completely roughshod over Maxine. But it sure was weird the way she made it sound like Mr. Chancy had died. My own mom said that happens when some couples break up, when it's really messy and bitter. It wasn't at all like that with Mom and Dad—they still had long talks on the phone every couple of days.

"Well, I just feel so lucky to have met her," I said.

We sat in the living room while Maxine made the tea—no hanging around the kitchen table in this house, I guess. It was one of those sterile spaces that made you wonder why they'd call it a living room because, for all intents and purposes, no one actually lived in here. The furniture was all tasteful—sleek, polished wood tables; white couch and armchairs. The walls had generic landscapes, one per wall, no more, no less. On the mantel, flanked by silver candlesticks, was a formal portrait of Ms. Tattrie and Maxine. The coffee table had a fan of magazines—*Time, InStyle, Life, National Geographic,* and the like—spread just so.

I didn't have to work to remember my posture and keep my knees together. I wasn't likely to relax in here—not in this room, or under Ms. Tattrie's watchful eye.

"I don't know how I'd ever catch up with my studies if it wasn't for her help," I went on. "I have to admit feeling a little guilty, taking up her time the way I have, because I certainly wouldn't want her grades to suffer, but she's assured me that helping me keeps the material fresh for her as well."

Her mother nodded. "There's nothing like teaching to help you learn better yourself."

"That's *exactly* what she said. And she's obviously so smart that she doesn't need my help, but she seems to think I can be useful quizzing her on what we're learning."

"Well, I'm just glad that she's finally found herself a friend with some *decent* values."

I smiled at her, my hands folded primly on my lap. Oh, I really am good, I thought. But then it helps when the other person is seeing what they hope to see, rather than what they fear.

Maxine arrived with the tea, and we made small talk while we drank. I think I was the only one who was even remotely relaxed and I was tense—well, at least tense for me.

* * *

"I can't believe you," Maxine said later when we were in her room. "You should be an actress."

It was such a girly room, all frills and lace—straight out of the Proper Girl Handbook, chapter four, "The Bedroom." The lower part of the walls was a dark, dusty rose, the upper a lighter shade, the edging a border of vines and roses. The comforter had the same pattern, and so did the lace bedskirt and the pillows heaped at the headboard. The furniture was all white—bed, night table, dresser, bookcase, and a desk and chair set—while a rose throw rug picked up the color from the walls.

Lined up on the back of the dresser, with a few more on the windowsill, was a collection of what I could only call prissy dolls. You know the kind, all ringlets and lacy dresses and too-perfect porcelain faces. They were immaculate, as though they'd just come out of their packaging and had never been played with. Though I guess I was being unfair. Just because I like scruffy things, doesn't mean everyone has to.

"I didn't know you collected dolls," I said.

Maxine pulled a face. "I don't. This whole room's my mom's creation."

She went to a corner of the room and pried up a loose floorboard. Reaching into the space that was revealed, she pulled out a battered plush toy cat, all lanky, droopy limbs. I could see it had been a calico once, but the plush was so worn away that only the memory of color remained.

"This was my only real toy," she added.

"God, that's so sad."

She got a hurt look.

"Not the cat," I said. "I mean what your mom's done to your room."

"It happened the first weekend I went to stay with my dad. I came back and it looked like this. She'd even boxed my books and put them in the basement storage, but I managed to convince her I needed them for my studies."

I looked at the bookcase and could see how the mismatched spines of the books would drive her mom crazy.

"So I guess it wasn't like this when your dad was here," I said.

"Just not as much. She talks about him like he's dead."

"I noticed. Why don't you live with him?"

"He's always out of town for work, or I would. It's not that I hate my mom, it's just . . . hard."

"It'd sure drive me crazy."

I picked up one of the dolls from the dresser, then put it back down.

"You don't mind me snooping?" I asked.

She shook her head.

"I just have this insatiable curiosity about other people's stuff," I said. I sat beside her on the floor. "So what else do you have stashed away?"

"Nothing much. Pictures of my dad. Some CDs that Mom'd hate. My journal."

I made no move to take a closer look and got up when she returned the plush cat to its hiding place, sliding the floorboard back into place. I liked the idea of a hidden stash but would hate *having* to use it like she did.

"That's one of the doors into hell," she said when I wandered over to her closet.

I laughed. "What do you mean?"

"Just take a look."

I opened the door to an array of clothes, all neatly arranged on their hangers, blouses on one end, dresses on the other, skirts in the middle. I fingered the nearest skirt. Of course, it was good quality material. I tried to think of something nice to say about them, but we'd already been through the whole business about her clothes.

"I hate that everything I own has been picked out for me," she said.

"That bad, huh?"

She nodded. "Except for my books and what I've got stashed away. But the rest of my life is all focused on making me into the dork I already look like."

"I don't think you look like a dork."

"How can you say that? If we're going to be friends, you have to be honest with me."

I shrugged. "I don't judge my friends by the clothes they wear."

"Oh, come on. You do the casual punk thing, but you have to be spending time planning it out."

"I do. But clothes are only for fun. They don't say who I am—not really, not inside. I don't think I've ever had an original look. I just see somebody wearing something I like—in a magazine, on the street—and I think, that'd be fun."

"Fun."

"Mm-hmm. And my idea of fun changes from day to day. For instance," I added, giving my pleated skirl a swirl, "today, this is fun."

Maxine shook her head. "God, I wish I could be like you. You are *so* sure of yourself."

"It just seems like that," I told her.

"How'd you ever get to be that way?"

"That's kind of a long story."

"I suppose," she said with a glum look, "you're going to tell me it's the same way you got to be brave."

"Not really."

I came and sat on the bed with her. Opening one of the textbooks I'd brought, I laid it on the comforter between us, just in case her mom came to check up.

"There was this girl back at my old school," I said. "Her name was Emmy Jean Haggerty, and she was this real hillbilly who got bussed in from the hills up around the old coal mines north of town. People'd rag on her mercilessly because of her raggedy hand-me-down clothes and her thick hill-country drawl, but she'd just ignore them all.

"I was getting my own fair share of hard times and bullying in those days—I mean, I was the little hippie chick who grew up on a commune, and everybody knew it. It didn't matter how much I tried to dress like them and be like them. So one afternoon I went up to Emmy Jean in the library, where she was sitting by herself as usual, and asked her how she coped so well. You know what she told me?"

Maxine shook her head.

"She said, 'My granny told me to be happy inside myself. That while I can't do the first damn thing about what other folks think on me, leastways I can be whatever I want to be, inside me. So I choose to be happy. I know the other kids call me "the Hag" and think I'm simple in the head, but I don't care. I don't even hear them anymore. Time was, they'd make me cry every day, but not no more.'

"'How can you be that strong?' I asked her, because I couldn't imagine being able to do that.

"'Well, you think on it,' she said. 'Do you really want to count folks like that as your friends? Do you *really* care 'bout what they think?'

"That's when I realized that I did. I wanted to be just like them, but maybe I didn't have to. But I also wanted to be just like Emmy Jean, and I told her so.

"'Oh, you don't want that, neither,' she said in that slow drawl of hers. 'What you want is to be yourself, hard as that can seem.' Then she smiled. 'But let me tell you something else Granny told me 'round 'bout the same time. She said it didn't matter how good I got at being myself, for myself, because sooner or later I was going to meet me some boy and I'd be throwing all my hard-earned considerations out the window, just for a smile from that boy's handsome lips.'

"'You think?' I said.

"Emmy Jean laughed. 'Well, I'm sure not letting it happen to me,' she told me. 'Not after spending all this time learning how to be happy with myself. You think on that, Imogene, when they come courting you.'"

I gave Maxine a grin. "Like they ever would, I thought.

But the rest of the stuff she was telling me made sense. Maybe it was because she was just repeating what I heard all the time at home. Like I said, Jared and I grew up in the original laid-back household, where we were taught from the moment we could sit up in our high chair not to care what 'the Man' or anybody else thought about us."

"So why was it different coming from her?" Maxine asked.

"I don't know. I guess because she wasn't some stoned old hippie, and I could see how it worked. She was by herself pretty much all the time, but she wasn't unhappy. And the mean things the other kids said just rolled right off her. So I taught myself to be like that, too. And you know what the funny thing is? Once they saw I didn't carc, I started having all these little cliques wanting me to be their friend."

"And did you?"

I shook my head. "No, I ended up hanging with the dropouts and punks who didn't bother going to school."

"But you still did."

I nodded. "Which is funny, because of all the kids going to Willingham, I probably had the only parents who would have supported my dropping out to 'do my own thing.'" I made quotation marks with my fingers. "And I guess that's why I stuck it out—because I didn't have to. I skipped a lot of days, but I didn't totally blow my tests and exams."

"You make it all sound so simple," Maxine said. "Especially the part about not caring what other people think."

"It's not," I told her. "But it gets easier. And the thing is, people like Valerie and Brent really can't hurt me anymore. Only someone like you could. Or Jared. Because I really care about what you guys think."

That was more than I'd meant to say, so I shut up. I'd barely known her a week and I didn't want to scare her off by being too intense. I really wanted a best friend, a sister. And I wanted it to be her. I couldn't even tell you why, exactly. It just snuck up on me that first time we talked and now it felt like anything else wouldn't be right.

But maybe I'd already scared her off, because Maxine went silent as well. The two of us sat there, staring down at the open textbook for a while, neither of us turning the page, but neither of us really seeing it either. Or at least I know I didn't.

"So did the thing with the boy happen to you?" Maxine asked after a while. "Because I know I just want to crawl into a crack in the floor every time I see Jimmy Meron walking down the hall."

"Who's he?"

"I pointed him out to you on Friday. The guy on the track team."

"Oh, right. He *is* cute. Have you talked to him?"

"God, no. He doesn't even know I exist." She paused a moment, then said, "You never answered me."

"About the boy thing?"

She nodded.

"Not really," I lied.

I wasn't sure why, exactly. I guess I just wanted her to like me and I figured the best way for that to happen was for me to pretend that most of the stuff I'd done in Tyson had just never happened.

Before she could press me on it, I asked her, "So have you ever been kissed—like for real?"

She shook her head. "Have you?"

I nodded. This I could talk about.

"Sure," I said. "The first time was by Johnny Tait. I was twelve, and we were at a bonfire near the sand pits outside of Tyson. It was nice, but I didn't love him or anything."

But that didn't matter to Maxine. She still had to know everything about it.

NOW: *Maxine*

We're sitting on the library steps on a spring morning, sharing an apple and watching the pigeons, when Imogene turns to me.

"Do you remember the first day we met?" she asks.

"Of course. You were determined to make friends with someone no one else liked so that you could be sure of at least one friend in your new school."

"Is that how it seemed?"

I smile and shake my head. "No. I'm just teasing." I have another bite of the apple and pass it back to her. "Why were you asking?"

"Remember I told you about my imaginary friend?"

I nod. "It was the first thing you said. He had a monkey face or something."

"Tail, actually. With rabbit ears and a body like a skinny hedgehog."

"I can't imagine a skinny hedgehog."

"Many people can't."

"So what about him?"

"Well, he's back."

"What do you mean 'he's back'?"

She shrugs. "I keep dreaming about him and these . . . other things. Little root-and-twig creatures made up out of fairy tales and nursery rhymes."

I look for the smile that's usually in her eyes when she's spinning one of her stories, but it's not there.

"And he keeps saying these weird things to me," she says. "Like 'I've missed you sideways' and 'Be careful. Once you open the door, it can't be closed.'"

"What's that supposed to mean?"

"I don't know. Maybe that once you've imagined an imaginary friend, you can't unimagine him again."

"Okay, that's creepy."

"I *know*."

"But it's just a dream, right?"

She nods. "Except it's freaking me out a little because first, I never remember my dreams, and second, I keep having it. There's even a soundtrack."

"Trust you to have a soundtrack."

"I guess. Except it's not a very good one."

"Dream soundtracks never are," I say, trying to lighten her mood.

It doesn't work.

"The funny thing is," she says, "in my head he *is* real."

"I'm not following you."

"I mean, the memories I have of him and the memories I have of things that really happened are all mixed up. Like they're all real. But I know they can't be. Like the time we went chasing the Clock Man to try and get back some of Jared's spare time."

I smile. "Because everybody knows that the very concept of spare time is a made-up thing."

That got me the smallest twitch of a smile in the corner of her mouth.

"Some people do have it," Imogene says.

I nod. "Except none of them have a dragon mom like I do, overseeing every part of their life except when I get away with you."

"Point taken."

"Thank you."

"But I was talking about Pelly and the Clock Man," she says. "Things like them can't be real. The Clock Man was . . . well, he was all made of clocks. A big old-fashioned alarm clock for a head, and then the rest of him was cobbled together from all sorts of bits and pieces of other kinds of clocks."

"And Pelly?" I ask.

"That was my imaginary friend. It's short for Pell-mell."

"That figures."

She gives me a look. "What do you mean?"

"Well, being who you are, he'd have to have a name like that. Or Chaos. Maybe Pandemonium."

"But the *real* thing that's so weird," she says, "is that it's all scary now. Pelly never scared me before, but he does now."

It's so odd seeing her like this. She's a great listener—she really is, especially for someone who talks as much as she does. But she's also kind of like a boy who has an answer for everything. She told me once that it was because of the way she and Jared grew up, wild and free on the commune, gender traits mixing. She was always a tomboy, and Jared ended up being way more sensitive than a lot of guys are.

That tomboy part of her is what makes her so sure of herself and so fearless. It's what makes her Imogene. So to see her like this, nervous and so at a loss, it's . . . well, just weird. It makes me feel like I should have the answers for her, the way she always does for me.

I think back to something she said near the beginning of this very strange conversation we're having.

"Maybe he's here to warn you," I say.

"By scaring me."

"I don't know about that. Sometimes things that don't scare us at all as kids totally freak us out when we get older. And vice versa."

"Well, what would he be warning me about?"

"Didn't you say that he said something about doors? About how once they're open, they can't be closed? Maybe the door's got nothing to do with him coming back. Maybe it's something else you did—some other door you opened back when you knew him."

Imogene shakes her head. "Now you're getting as bad as me. Talking about him like he really exists. Like he *ever* existed."

"It's just . . . "

"I know. I'm making him sound like he's real."

I nod, but don't bother saying that she's always like this. She's forever making the implausible seem real. I'm not saying she lies to me—at least I don't think she does, though she does get evasive sometimes about parts of her life before she met me. She just likes to make sure that life stays interesting. Whenever it's not, she seems compelled to say or do something to get it back on an oddball track.

"By the time I was nine or ten," she says now, "I realized what he was. I wasn't *playing* with him anymore. I *knew* he wasn't real. But I'd tell stories in my head—mostly at night, staring up at the ceiling as I was falling asleep—and he'd be in all of them."

"Your point being?"

"That I used to know the difference. I'm not so sure anymore." She gives me a look that's as much amused as unhappy. "I've even got *you* half believing in him. Or at least talking like you do."

I shake my head. "I'm just going with the flow like I always do."

"Well, I need you to be the hardheaded, rational-brain part of our friendship right now."

I give her a slow nod. "Okay. Except, even big brainy me

isn't entirely unconvinced that dreams aren't messages of some sort, if only from our subconscious."

"So what's the message I'm supposed to be getting?"

"Who knows? It's about as clear as any fairy-tale riddle. But I'd say there's something you're supposed to be remembering. Some door you thought you'd closed, but it turns out you forgot to turn the key."

"The key," she repeats.

"I mean, there's unfinished business happening here," I say.

"I guess . . . "

She sounds unconvinced, and I don't blame her. I'm not so convinced either.

We sit there on the steps for a while, watching the people go by on the sidewalk below, the pigeons doing their synchronized air show. We finish the apple we've been sharing. Imogene sets the core on the ground by her knapsack.

"What if it's the dead kid?" she finally says.

THEN: *Imogene*

I'd been going to my new school for a little over three weeks when I realized that someone was watching me—and it wasn't Ken or Barbie, or any of that crowd of theirs.

Well, really, why would they bother? Sure, they liked to rag on people like me, but it was only when we invaded their sphere of influence. It wasn't like they needed to go stalking the people they considered to be losers. One or another of us was forever stumbling into their proximity to be tripped or mocked.

No, this was someone else, and I wasn't imagining it. I have a sixth sense for that kind of thing. I just know where people are, if they're checking me out, and I never get lost. It's one of the reasons Jared always hated playing games like hide-and-seek with me. He felt I had an unfair advantage—which, let's face it, I did.

So anyway, I knew I was being spied on, but for the longest time, I couldn't get a fix on who it was. That feeling would come to me and I'd turn to look, fast, but there was never anyone there. Or at least no one who seemed to be paying any particular attention to me.

I thought I was losing my touch until, a week or so later, I finally spotted him not too far from my locker, right near the hall to the gym and auditorium.

He was this pale, nerdy guy—sort of like a tall Harry Potter, the way the character is pictured on the books and in the films, you know, with the black glasses and the kind of messy hair, but gawkier and with a narrower face. Actually, Jared insists the image was stolen from a Neil Gaiman comic book, the one about the kid who discovers he's this great magician—wait a minute, that's the basic plot of the Harry Potter books, too, isn't it?

But I digress.

I dumped my math book in my locker and grabbed what I needed for my next class. Closing the door, I gave the combination lock a spin, acted like I was going to go the other way, then quickly turned and headed for my stalker.

He ducked down the hall, and by the time I got to the corner, he'd disappeared. Not *poof*, disappeared. He just managed to slip off before I could see where he'd gone.

I wanted to ask Maxine about him, but I didn't see that much of her during the day except for lunch and after school.

It took another week before I spotted him again—while Maxine was with me, I mean. I'd caught glimpses of him, but he always managed to duck away before I could confront him.

"Who's that?" I asked.

I nodded to where a line of kids were waiting to be served what passed for food in the cafeteria. And Jared was right. The music they piped in here really did suck. But the Barbie girls really seemed to like the old Backstreet Boys song that was playing, at least judging from the way they bobbed their heads to the beat.

"Who's who?" Maxine replied.

"The tall, pale guy with the Harry Potter glasses?"

"I don't see a tall, pale guy, with or without glasses."

I glanced at her, then looked back, but he wasn't there anymore.

"Though I'm surprised," she went on. "I would have thought you'd reference Buddy Holly. Or at least Elvis Costello."

"That's funny."

"It wasn't that funny."

"No, I mean, funny-strange," I said. "He's gone. But where could he have gone? He was right by the end of that line, and it's too far to the door for him to have slipped out. I only looked away for a second."

Maxine got an odd look. "You must have seen Ghost."

This was good, I thought. A nickname was a start.

"How'd he get the name?" I asked, though I could guess from the way he kept disappearing on me.

"Because he really is a ghost. People have been seeing him for years."

I waited for a punch line, but it didn't come.

"You're kidding," I said.

"Why would I joke about something like that?"

"I don't know."

"If you don't believe me," she said, "ask somebody else. Though I should warn you, popular wisdom has it that only losers ever see him."

"Oh, great."

Maxine smiled. "I've seen him, too."

"Really?"

"But only once. It was last year."

"Well, I see him all the time. He's always lurking around, spying on me." I sighed. "And now you're telling me my stalker is a ghost."

"Sorry."

"Not your fault."

I looked around the cafeteria, but I still couldn't spot him.

"So how'd he die?" I asked when I turned back to Maxine.

"I don't know the whole story," she said. "I suppose nobody except Ghost really does."

"What's his real name?"

Maxine shook her head. "I've never heard him called anything but Ghost."

"That's okay," I said. I could find out. "So what happened?"

"I heard he was like us—got pushed around by other kids—except it was worse for him because *everybody* ragged on him. Even some of the teachers."

* * *

That night, while we were making supper—Mom was staying late at the university again—I asked Jared if he'd heard about the ghost haunting our school.

"Yeah, Ben told me about him."

Ben Sweetland was on the football team, and that didn't particularly endear him to me at first. But apparently he loved music as much as he did sports, which explained how he and Jared had hooked up. And to be honest, once I got to know him a little bit through Jared, I found myself liking him. He didn't fit my jock stereotype, but then most people don't fit their stereotypes. Oh, he had the look, all right, big and strong, but he had a good mind and a sharp, sly wit.

When I asked him how he put up with guys like Brent and Jerry, he just shrugged and said, "There's always going to be assholes. When I'm around them, I just focus on the team and the game."

"They piss me off."

He nodded. "Yeah, I can see how that would happen when you get on the wrong side of them."

"I don't want to be on any side of them."

"So avoid them," Ben told me. "They're on the top of the heap right now, but that's only going to last another couple of years. Then we're all going to be out of school, and while your life is going to get way better, all they'll have while they work at some dead-end job is memories of their glory days."

"They'll probably all get scholarships."

Ben shook his head. "We have an okay team, but no one on it's going to get picked up by any colleges. Why do you think Brent loses his temper so much when we lose a game? He *knows* football's his only shot at something better, but he also knows it's never going to happen for him. Or if he doesn't, he should."

You've got to admit that's a pretty astute summing-up for a supposedly dumb jock. But Ben's always like that. He doesn't ever seem to have much to say, but when he does, it's worth a listen. So I was interested in what he knew about Ghost.

"So what'd Ben say about Ghost?" I asked Jared.

He shrugged. "Just that he was this kid who got a really rough time from pretty much everybody at the school. He either jumped or fell off the roof way back in 1998."

That was pretty much what Maxine had told me.

"What does Ben think really happened?" I asked.

"It happened before he started here, so he didn't know the kid."

Jared was cutting up vegetables for the salad we were making. I was in charge of the paella and the dressing for the salad. When he fell silent, I glanced over to see him looking out the kitchen window, but I didn't think he was taking in the view of the alley that ran behind our building.

"It must've been tough on that kid," he said finally. "Being ragged that badly."

"And it hasn't stopped for lots of us."

He glanced at me. "Is Brent still on your case?"

I shook my head. "Only if I happen to run into him, but I've been getting pretty good at avoiding all of his crowd."

"That sucks. Having to tiptoe around people like that. Maybe I should go have a talk with them."

I shook my head again. We had an agreement: out of the house, we each dealt with our own troubles. We couldn't interfere unless we were specifically asked. He'd had a "talk" with some bullies back at our old school—this was before I hooked up with Frankie Lee's crowd and people knew better than to mess with me—and while it had stopped the bullying for that day, a bunch of them got hold of Jared after school and beat him up really badly. They wouldn't have done that to me—it's one of the benefits of being a girl. So long as your bullies aren't other girls, of course, but that's a whole other story.

Anyway, to keep it short—or at least shortish—that's when I made him promise not to get involved in my problems unless I specifically asked him to.

"I can deal with it," I told him.

"Yeah, but you shouldn't have to."

"Well, I could always call in some of my old crowd from Tyson to put them in their place."

Jared got a worried look, not realizing I was joking. But if I were really going to do that, he would have had a reason to be worried. Frankie's crowd was a rough bunch. I'd been younger than all of them—kind of their mascot is the way Frankie put it—but that didn't mean they'd let anyone mess with me. With those guys you were either in the gang, or you were against them. If you were in, they'd literally defend you to the death.

"You're not really thinking of—" Jared began.

I didn't let him finish. "I was joking."

"Good."

"Not that Brent doesn't deserve being taken down a notch or two."

"Yeah, but . . . "

"I know. Frankie's idea of a warning is to put you in the hospital."

"I don't understand what you ever saw in those guys," Jared said.

"They treated me like a person."

He started to say something, then shook his head.

"You're right," he said. "I'll give them that much. They were bad news, but they never walked all over anybody just because that person was weaker than them."

* * *

When I finally spotted Ghost again, he saw my gaze find him, and this time he made no pretense at being normal. He was standing by a door. Turning toward it, he simply stepped right through and disappeared.

Not this time, I thought.

I hurried over and saw that it was one of the custodian's storerooms. I gave a quick look around, but no one was paying any particular attention to me, so I tried the knob. When it turned, I opened the door and stepped inside. I closed the door behind me and leaned against it.

It was impossible to see anything in the dark.

"I know you're in here," I said, "so you might as well stop hiding."

I knew no such thing, of course. I'd only seen him come in. If he could walk through solid objects, he could have walked right out the other end of the storeroom and be anywhere by now.

"This is just stupid," I went on. "Why are you spying on me? What do you want from me?"

Nothing.

"Well, I'm not impressed. I thought it might be interesting to talk to a dead person, but this is about as interesting as watching paint dry. I guess I'll just—"

I didn't get to finish.

The door opened behind me and I went sprawling backward, landing hard on the marble floor, my textbooks flying. But that wasn't the worst of it.

"See?" I heard Jerry Fielder say. "I told you I saw her go in there."

I looked up to see the crowd I was usually trying to avoid standing around me. Jerry and Brent and some other guys from the team. Valerie and a coterie of her followers.

Brent stepped past me and looked into the storeroom.

By the light cast from the hallway, it was easy to see that there was no one in there. There were just shelves of cleaning supplies, buckets, mops, brooms—pretty much what you'd expect for a custodian's storeroom.

I sat up and started gathering my books.

"So what were you doing in there, Yuck?" Brent asked.

"Talking to herself," Jerry said.

"Jeez, what's a girl have to do to get a little privacy around here?" I said, standing up.

I was trying to play it cool, but I had about as much chance of pulling that off as becoming a supermodel.

"Maybe she was practicing how to dance with a broom," someone said.

Brent grinned. "Hell, maybe she was *riding* the broom. Did it feel good, Yuck?"

"Oh, for god's sake—" I started.

Brent knocked my books out of my hands.

"Keep your smart mouth shut," he told me. "Remember: better seen than heard."

I started to collect my books, but one of the guys kicked them further down the hall.

"And better not seen, either," Brent went on.

Then, laughing, he headed off, the others behind him.

I sighed and collected my books. This was so humiliating. I don't mind people thinking I'm weird. I'd just rather be the one to decide when I'm being weird.

* * *

Jared came up behind Maxine and me as we were heading home after school.

"So now you're talking to yourself in broom closets?" Jared asked when he fell in step beside me.

Redding High was a big school, but it never ceased to amaze me how quickly the gossip got around. I'd seen *those* looks all day—you know, amused at what had happened to me, glad they weren't at the center of it. I couldn't get away from it. Maxine had already heard when she joined me at my locker before we left for home. I guess the student body must really have had nothing much going on in their own lives if the graceless doings of a nobody like me could make the rounds so quickly.

"I wasn't talking to myself," I told Jared.

"I heard there was no one in there."

"There wasn't. I mean, there was, but he vanished."

Jared gave me a worried look. "What do you mean, 'he vanished'?"

"I was chasing Ghost," I said. "Trying to find out why he's always spying on me."

"Oh, Imogene," Maxine said. "Do you think you should?"

And Jared added, "I can't believe you think he's for real."

I shrugged. "I've seen him. Or at least I see someone spying on me, someone who's very good at pulling the vanishing act and fits the description of the late, unlamented Ghost. And today I saw him walk right through a closed door—without having to stop to open it," I added, directing the last comment at Jared.

"Really."

"Yes, really."

"So this is like one of those tall tales like Little Bob used to tell back home?"

"I suppose. Except this time *I've* seen the unnatural goings-on."

"Really."

"Will you stop saying 'really,'" I told him.

"I'm just trying to—"

"Oh, crap," I said, spotting a familiar figure coming around the block up ahead. "Keep walking, Maxine, and don't look back. You don't know us. You're not with us."

"But—"

"Just *do* it."

And then she saw what I'd seen: her mother. And here was I, gloriously decked out in plaid skirt, combat boots, and a raggedy sweater—all visible because I hadn't closed my calf-length army jacket. But I only had about ten barrettes in my hair. Yeah, like that would make a difference.

Luckily, I don't think her mother had seen Maxine with us, and Maxine walked briskly toward her, leaving us well behind because I'd stooped to retie a shoelace that hadn't needed it.

When I stood up, I linked my arm in Jared's and turned him around so that we were going the other way.

"What's going on?" he asked, though he did let me lead him away.

"I spotted Maxine's mom coming around the corner."

"Oh. Do you think she saw you?"

He knew the whole story of how I was working on

letting Maxine have another life than just the one her mother had planned out for her.

"It doesn't matter," I told him. "I'm sure I was too far away for her to make out my features, and it's not like these clothes are the kind she'd expect to see me in."

"Good save," he said.

"I hope so."

When I called Maxine later, she assured me that we'd gotten away with it.

"What was she doing there?" I asked.

"She thought I might be studying at the school library, so she was coming to get me. She'd forgotten to tell me this morning that we were having dinner at my grandparents' house."

"How was that?"

"Like it always is. My mom and Grandma staring daggers at each other while talking like they're not just family but best friends. Grandpa and I pretending not to notice the tension."

"Sounds horrible."

"I guess. But I like seeing my grandparents, and at least nobody was yelling or anything." Before I could think of something to say to that, she added, "You've got to stop chasing after Ghost."

"Why?"

"Well, look what happened to you today."

"That wasn't Ghost's fault. At least not directly."

"No, but it's just . . . weird."

"I'm weird."

"No kidding. I guess it's like a dog chasing a car."

"What breed do you see me as?"

"The question you have to ask yourself," she said as she continued to ignore me, "is, once you catch the car, what do you do with it?"

"Good point. And it'd probably be enough to stop me, except I've been cursed with an insatiable curiosity."

"Which killed the cat."

I laughed. "You have to make up your mind. Am I a dog or a cat in this analogy of yours?"

"You know what I mean."

"Don't obsess."

"Exactly."

"So can you get out tomorrow night?"

"What's happening tomorrow night?"

"Curb crawling in the Beaches."

Maxine had told us about the area a few weeks back, and it turned out to be prime real estate for what Jared and I did. Big houses, old money, and lots of turnaround on furniture and other neat stuff. Last week we'd scored a small oak desk that we sold for seventy-five dollars to one of the antique shops in the Market. I saw it in their window for twice the price the next day, but I didn't care. It's not like it cost us anything.

"I don't know . . . " Maxine said.

She'd yet to come out with us. I don't know if it was that she didn't trust the old junker of Mom's that we used on our rounds, or if she was too afraid her mom would find out. Probably both.

"That's okay," I told her, not wanting to put her on the spot. "Just so long as you'll help us bring the stuff to the stores later."

That, she didn't mind doing. I gave her a cut out of my half of the profits, which every week she tried to give back to me, but eventually accepted. I mean, how could she resist money that didn't need to be accounted for to her mother? And I had to make sure she had some cash for when we made the rounds of thrift stores.

Oh, I'm a wicked little thing, but it was doing wonders for her self-esteem, having stuff she picked out on her own. She kept most of it at my place, but some went into her locker at school. She didn't go for anything drastic—once she'd changed in the girls' washroom in the morning, you'd see her in jeans more often than not. And they looked good on her, too.

"So tell me," she said. "Did you really know a guy named Little Bob back at your old school?"

I laughed. "Oh, sure. Little Bob MacElwee. As opposed to his brother, Big Bob. And then there was his sister, Bertie—short for Roberta."

"That's just weird. Why would their parents name them all pretty much the same?"

"Beats me."

"Considering their surname, I'm surprised Little Bob didn't up being called Wee Bob."

"They couldn't. That's his dad's name."

"Now I know you're having me on."

"I swear it's true."

"If you say so." She paused a moment, then asked, "And he told stories about ghosts?"

"He had stories about every damn thing you could imagine living back in those hills. Ghosts were the smallest part of it. According to him there were talking frogs, girls that could change into crows, rains of snails and tadpoles, headless turkeys, a black panther that you were supposed to treat as royalty, fairies made of roots and vines . . . you name it."

"Were any of them true?"

I had to laugh. "What do you think?"

"Of course, it's just . . . it'd be cool."

"I suppose. But come on. Think about it for a moment."

"We've both seen a ghost," she said. "You more often than me."

That stopped me—but only for a moment.

"Well, all I can say, Maxine, is that just because one weird thing turns out to be true, doesn't mean every weird thing is."

"But it'd be cool."

"So would winning the lottery," I said, "and what are the chances of that ever happening?"

"You don't even buy tickets."

"But even if I did . . . "

And on we went.

THEN: *Adrian*

When I was a kid, I couldn't wait to get into high school. I just knew that somehow, all the humiliation and embarrassments I'd suffered in the lower grades would be a thing of the past. I didn't have any false hopes of suddenly becoming cool, but I did believe I'd finally make some friends and that my tormentors from the first eight years of my scholastic life would move on to other pursuits and forget about me. And if nothing else, Redding High was so much bigger than South Foxville Elementary. Surely, I'd just get lost in the crowds.

Wrong on all accounts.

Not even the other nerds would have anything to do with me. Apparently, I carried my stigma of loser so prominently that no one dared to be seen with me for fear of dropping even lower on the social totem pole. As for me, well, I was already at the bottom. Even the teachers weren't above making fun of me, especially Mr. Crawford in gym and weird Mr. Vanderspank in biology. Is it my fault that dissecting frogs makes me throw up?

But the teachers just used verbal barbs to mock me. My fellow students added physical abuse to their vocal harassment.

I was tripped. My books were always being knocked from my hands. My glasses were stepped on. I got my head dunked in the toilet. I got creamed during dodgeball. I got wedgies. You name it and it happened to me, with a constant chorus of "Hey, Ding-a-ling!"—the oh-so-clever elementary school play on my surname, Dumbrell—following me through the school halls.

The hours I had to spend at school, as well as the long blocks I had to navigate to get there and go home, were a time of perpetual tension for me as I walked with hunched shoulders, forever anticipating the next disaster to befall me. My nerves were getting on my nerves, as it says in some old song.

I know. Could I be more of a poster boy for losers? And is it any wonder I started seeing things?

The first time it happened I was sure that one of the stoners had slipped some kind of hallucinogenic drug into the can of pop I'd bought to go with my brown bag lunch. I had a spare for my last period that day and was trying to decide if I'd be better off leaving school early, thereby forestalling some new torment on the way home, or going to the school library to get in some research on a history essay that was due early next week. I opted to do the research—yet one more mistake in the endless parade of mistakes that made up my life.

If I hadn't gone to the library . . .

Though in retrospect, if they hadn't got to me that day, they would have got to me later, seeing how I became a special project of theirs. But I'm getting ahead of myself.

I went to the library, and of course Eric Woodrow was

there, "studying" with some of his buddies. Woody was one of those pretty boys—"too good-looking for his own good," my mother would say when she saw a guy like him on TV. He had short, curly blond hair and a charming smile, and was well built—by which I mean he had arms with actual muscles, unlike the twigs attached to my shoulders. The girls all liked him, and he was never without a girlfriend even though—and I know this for a fact—he cheated on each and every one of them. But none of them seemed to care. No one did, no matter what kind of trouble he got into. Woody seemed to be able to do any damn thing he wanted, and people would just smile.

I'd known him since grade school—or rather I'd been trying to avoid him since grade school because, whatever else might be going on in his life, he always had time to rag on me.

I ducked down an aisle between the bookshelves as soon as I saw him—hoping he hadn't seen me—and then I stopped dead in my tracks. Directly in front of me was one of the many study areas scattered through the library, and sitting at the closest desk was Doreen Smithers. Maybe she wasn't the most beautiful girl in school, but she came close, and she was certainly the best endowed.

Seeing Doreen was always stop-worthy, but she wasn't what had brought me to such a sudden halt. No, that was the little brown-skinned man on top of the bookshelf in front of her, looking down the front of her blouse. Not that I blamed him. Every guy in school had probably wanted to. But we didn't do it.

We weren't one foot high and dressed in rags, either. We didn't have matted hair, or sharp, pointy features or big, scary dark eyes.

That dark feral gaze chose that moment to turn in my direction, big eyes widening further with . . . I don't know. Surprise, I guess.

I could feel myself going weak, and my books fell from my hands. The thump of them hitting the floor startled Doreen, and she turned to me, then looked up at the little man when she saw me staring at the top of the bookshelf. But she didn't see anything. I know, because if she had, she'd be like me, completely stunned.

The little man grinned, waved at me, then swung up to the top of the bookshelf and scampered out of sight. Doreen turned back to me.

"What are *you* staring at?" she asked.

"Yes," came a sharp voice behind me that I recognized as belonging to Mrs. Edelson, the school librarian. "What *are* you staring at, Adrian Dumbrell?"

I shot her a guilty look, then got down to fumble with my books.

"Nothing," I mumbled. "I . . . I just felt a little dizzy . . ."

"Then perhaps you should go see the school nurse."

I gave a quick nod. Gathering my books, I stole another glance at the top of the bookshelf, but the creature wasn't there. I mean, *of course,* he wouldn't be there. That kind of thing didn't exist outside the CGI effects in a movie.

Doreen shook her head and turned back to her books while Mrs. Edelson walked me to the door of the library. We had to go by Woody's table, and he put out a foot that made me stumble again. This time I kept hold of my books. Just.

"Honestly," Mrs. Edelson said, not having seen what Woody'd done, "do you practice at being so clumsy?"

"No, ma'am," I muttered, and escaped out into the hall.

But I didn't go see the school nurse. Instead I went outside and ducked underneath the bleachers by the football field, where I knew no one would come looking for me. I sat down on a cement footing and set my books beside me. I put my head in my hands.

This was bad, I thought. My life was messed up enough without me starting to imagine things.

That was when it occurred to me that someone had spiked my drink. It was the kind of thing one of them would do to me. Anything for a laugh at the Ding-a-ling's expense.

"So there you are," an unfamiliar voice said.

I turned so fast that I almost fell off the footing. I grabbed the support beam to keep my balance.

There was no one there.

Great. Now I was hallucinating disembodied voices as well as weird little creatures.

"Up here," the voice said.

I looked up, and there was my hallucination from the library, hanging from a crossbeam. When he dropped from his perch I shrank back, but he wasn't attacking me. He landed in the dirt and grinned up at me from his one-foot height. This close to him, I realized that while he was the same kind of creature I'd imagined in the library, he wasn't the *same* one. I suppose a lot of people wouldn't have seen the difference, but I always do. Like when people say all the Asian kids look the same, I have no idea what they're talking about because they all look different to me.

Of course that didn't change the fact that . . .

"Yuh . . . " I cleared my throat. "You're not real."

"Of course not." He jabbed my knee with a stiff finger. "Entirely imaginary."

"But . . . but . . . "

"I know," he said. "When Quinty told me you'd seen him, I was as surprised to hear it as he was to see you."

"I wish I didn't."

"Didn't what?"

"See you—any of you."

"Oh, that's polite. That's friendly."

"No, I meant, I . . . "

I didn't know what I meant, really. I didn't want to be seeing things, but on the other hand it was such an *interesting* hallucination. This little man was even scruffier than the one I'd first seen hanging above Doreen's desk in the library. His hair was a mat of dreadlocks, festooned with colored bottle caps and the silvery pulls from pop cans. There were feathers in there, too, and strings of colored beads and little shells. Also what looked like old dried vines.

The raggedy clothes, I realized, had been artfully ripped and then restitched with red and green threads. Not so much old and torn as a fashion statement. The shirt was decorated with beadwork and feathers in a haphazard arrangement. The pants were plain with frayed cuffs. He was shoeless and I half expected to see hairy hobbit feet, but the brown skin on them, while gnarly like some old root, was as hairless as his hands and face.

"Finished yet?" he asked.

"What?"

"Staring at me."

"No, I mean, yes. I was just . . . I don't know. Trying to figure out what you are, I guess."

"I'm a fairy."

"A fairy."

"Well, that's the easiest description. The first of you big folks to come here called us *manidókwens,* but that's a mouthful, isn't it?"

This whole thing was a brainful was what it was. It had to be some kind of trick, but I couldn't begin to figure out how it was being pulled off. And whoever was pulling it on me had forgotten one important thing.

See, I've always known what I was.

Let's run down the list: I was tall and skinny and seriously uncoordinated. My hair was invariably an unruly thatch no matter how much I combed it, even right after a haircut. I had acne and was half blind without the black horn-rims my parents insisted I wear, I guess to go with the geeky clothes they picked out for me, though to be fair, even a tailored suit would hang on me like it would on a scarecrow. No, that's not fair to scarecrows.

I was the last one to be chosen for any kind of sports activity and the first one to be mocked for the slightest transgression of coolness. I was so far from cool that I was combustible. I was an embarrassment to myself and my family, though not to my friends. But that's only because I never had any.

And if all that wasn't bad enough, there was my name. Adrian Dumbrell. Say it with me: Dumbrell. Would *you* keep a name like that? But my parents and their parents and their parents, ad nauseam, were proud of it.

But I wasn't stupid.

I was all of the above—I won't argue with any of it—but I wasn't stupid.

So I knew that whatever this creature was, he wasn't a fairy. He wasn't real in the first place, but even if he was, he wasn't a fairy.

Fairies were cute and had little wings and fluttered around flowers and stuff like that. They didn't stare down girls' blouses. No, only a weird little creature that I'd hallucinate would do something like that.

"You're still trying to figure out if I'm real or not, aren't you?" the little man said.

"Well, it's just . . . "

Just what? Where did you even start in a situation like this?

He shook his head. "It's amazing that people like you can be so big and yet have such little brains."

"What's that supposed to mean?"

He shrugged. "You have the whole world figured out and so conveniently distrust your own senses whenever you run across something that doesn't fit in with your view of how things are supposed to be."

"Right. Little people like you are just all over the place."

"We are, actually. There aren't as many of us as there once were, it's true, but you can't go very far in this city without tripping over one or another of us."

"I've never seen anything like you before."

"We aren't all as handsome as I am."

Handsome, right. That was like me telling people I was cool.

"I mean, I've never even heard of you before," I said. "Just in storybooks—you know, the kind you read when you're a kid—and then the descriptions were pretty different from the way you look."

"We come in all shapes and sizes. You might try looking us up under *hob* or *brownie.*"

"What I'm trying to say is, nowhere does it say that you're real."

"That's only because you people don't pay attention. You simply don't see us."

"So how come I can?" I asked, coming back to the Big Question.

He shrugged. "Why am I supposed to have all the answers? Maybe you have the gift of the *sight.*"

"The sight."

"The ability to see beyond the narrow confines of the agreed-upon worldview," he explained. "Few of your kind do anymore."

Great. So not only was I a complete loser, but now I had some "special" way of seeing the world as well. If this kept up I'd soon be booking into the Zeb for extended psychiatric care.

"You speak well," I said.

I was just saying something to keep the conversation going, but as soon as the words were out of my mouth, I realized how condescending that must have sounded. But he didn't seem to take offense.

"Thank you," he said. "So do you."

"Well, I read a lot. Books don't beat you up."

"For me it's a natural gift."

Like humility, I thought, but this time I kept it to myself.

I sat there for a while, half expecting him to just fade away, but he continued to stand there, big eyes looking up at me, a little smile pulling at the corner of his mouth.

Great. Even fairies thought I was worth a laugh.

"I don't suppose there's a way I can learn to unsee you?" I asked.

He laid a hand on his chest and let his eyes go all soft and deerlike.

"Now I'm hurt," he said.

I almost apologized. I'm such a wimp.

"So what's your name?" I asked instead.

"That's a rather personal question."

"What's that supposed to mean?"

He shrugged. "We're not as free with our names as you big folk. But you can call me Tommery."

I thought about that for a moment. If I could *call* him Tommery, that didn't necessarily mean it was his name.

"So what's that?" I asked. "A nickname?"

"Like I said—"

"I know. You're not as free with your names as we are. Why's that?"

"When you know the true name of a thing, it gives you a certain measure of power over it."

"Do things include people?"

"It includes *everything,* Adrian Dumbrell."

"How do you know my name?" I demanded, trying to cover up the nervousness I felt that he *did* know it.

"It's in your school record, right beside your picture."

"You go through the school's records?"

"Fairies go through everything."

"But why?"

He shrugged. "We like to know what's going on. The world's not much of a story if you don't know who the characters are."

I wasn't sure what he meant by that, so I decided to ignore it.

"So what happens now?" I asked.

He cocked his head, reminding me of a bird—especially with those big eyes of his—that and the fact that he was looking up at me.

"I'm not sure I understand the question," he said.

"What happens to me? You know—now that I know you exist."

"Oh that." He shrugged. "You can do whatever you want. Tell your fellow students—"

"Right, like that would go over so well."

"—or do nothing at all—though I'd hope that you might at least give me a friendly nod the next time we happen to run into each other."

"Well, sure. That's if I ever, you know . . . "

"Oh, you'll see me again. Once you encounter one of us like this, you'll never be blind again. Not unless you work at it."

With that, he swung back up into the support beams under the stands. I watched him go, scurrying like he was equal parts monkey and squirrel, until he was lost from sight. Then I put my head in my hands and stared at the ground again.

I wasn't sure how I felt about this. The only thing I knew for sure was that everything had changed.

* * *

So that's how I got my first friends, like, *ever*.

There were four or five of the little men living in the school. Tommery was the one I saw the most, or at least the one I talked to the most. The others were just around, like the way that Quinty was forever hanging around the girls' bathrooms, which just gave me the creeps.

Tommery said I shouldn't let it bother me, that everybody has their quirks, and the thing that friends do is put up with each others' quirks. He said they had to have something to amuse themselves with since people didn't do what they were supposed to anymore, which was basically be respectful to the house spirits of a building—you know, leave them little cakes and saucers of milk, and thank them for their help in keeping the place tidy, though the thanking part you should only do verbally. Leave a gift other than food, and they're out of the place like a shot; don't ask me why.

See, that's what Tommery and Quinty and the others were—a kind of house spirit, like in that story about the elves and the shoemaker, which is weird when you think about it—to have little fairy people for friends—but a lot easier to take than having people laugh at you all the time or stuff your head into a toilet.

And life did improve for me after I met them. I don't mean that the kids at school started treating me any nicer, or that Mr. Crawford or Mr. Vanderspank stopped ragging on me in class. It just made a difference, having someone I could talk to and hang with—even if they were only a foot high.

And they showed me all kinds of cool things, like hidden places in the school where *no one* can see you, but you can see *them*. Or secret passageways—invisible to the human eye, or at least the eye of most humans—that let you move quickly from one place to another. They called both of these things elf bolts.

But what they didn't tell me—well, they wouldn't, would they?—was that something happens to house spirits when they're left on their own too long. It turned out that Tommery and his gang probably really were like the fairies you see in the old storybooks—at least they were once.

I read all about it in some picture book about the fairies in England.

They start out handsome and pretty, but they can get kind of rough looking when they live in the wilds, away from men. Then you can have trouble telling them apart from the roots and leaves. And if they were originally house spirits, but abandoned by the people using the house—and for fairies, Redding High's like some big house—they get to looking like Tommery does. And they can turn mean.

Not that they were ever mean to me. Like I said, they treated me like a special project, constantly trying to make life a little better for me. So as far as I was concerned, that stuff about them going mean was all just words in some kids' book.

That is, until the day they thought it would be a lark to teach me how to fly.

* * *

"Come on, you'll like it," Oshtin said.

"Yeah, Addy," Sairs put in. They'd taken to calling me "Addy," which—since I'd never had a nickname before that wasn't abusive—pleased me no end. "Or are you scared?"

"No, I'm not scared. It's just . . . I mean, flying . . . "

It was one of those rare occasions when all the fairies were with me at the same time. We were in an elf bolt that looked out on the main hall of the school near the principal's office, drinking herbal tea that Krew had made with water from a kettle that didn't appear to need a power source, and munching on crackers Quinty had stolen from the cafeteria.

"It would be like *Peter Pan,*" Tommery said.

"That's the problem," I told them. "I just don't know that I believe enough."

Tommery laughed. "Don't talk rubbish. You don't have

to believe for it to work. You just need our magic."

"But—"

"You never believed in us, but you saw us all the same, didn't you?"

"I suppose . . . "

We settled on a test run, a short flight down the stairs in the main hall. We couldn't do it when anyone was around, of course, so I had to hide out until the school was empty except for the janitor. We waited until he was asleep on the cot he had stashed away in the basement, then tumbled out of the elf bolt and went up the stairs. I counted the risers as we ascended. Twenty-two.

Once we'd reached the landing, I looked back down. It was higher than I had thought it would be, especially considering I went up and down it a dozen times or more a day. But that was on my own two feet. Right now it seemed way too high, and I got a touch of vertigo.

"So . . . what do I do?" I asked.

The fairies clustered around me.

"Nothing," Tommery said. "Just relax."

Easy for him to say, I thought, looking down at the end of the stairs that still seemed way too far away at this moment.

But then I felt the strangest sensation. The fairies stood by me, two to a side, with Tommery perched on the banister, directing the operation. The others laid their hands on my legs and then I was . . . not flying, but floating. I could feel all the weight of my body disappear, or maybe it was just gravity losing its hold, but up

I went, flanked by the fairies on either side of me.

We hovered for a long moment above the landing, then Tommery cried, "Go!" and we swooped down the stairs. Right at the bottom, we came to a stop and slowly sank through the air until my feet were on the ground again.

I had a moment of wobbliness when we touched down. My body had never seemed to weigh so much as it did at that moment.

I looked back up the stairs, and Tommery came sliding down the banister.

"That wasn't so bad, was it?" he said, landing at my feet.

"Are you kidding? It was great. It was totally amazing. When can we do it again?"

"Right now, if you want."

"Oh, I do," I told him. "And I want to go higher—like from the roof."

Tommery smiled. "What happened to your not believing enough?"

"Who cares about believing? The magic works whether I believe in it or not, right?"

"Just so," Tommery said.

* * *

I led the way as we trooped up the stairs. We knew where the entrance to the rooftop access was—the fairies knew where *everything* was in the school, and by this time, so did I.

The moon was up when we stepped out onto the roof. Tommery told me that he and the others came up here all the time to have picnics and spy on the world at large and just generally hang out. I'd never been up here myself, probably because I'd always had this bit of a thing about heights. I couldn't approach any kind of a high drop-off without a vague whirly feeling starting up in the bottom of my stomach. And then I'd get a pulling sensation from the edge, like I needed to step right off and go tumbling down.

But tonight I wasn't nervous as we crunched across the gravel to the edge of the roof. I wasn't nervous looking down the two-story drop to the ground below, either. My usual height fears and earlier anxiety had been replaced with anticipation. I could still remember the way my body had felt as I lifted from the landing earlier, but it was only in my memory now. I wanted to actually experience it again.

"Coast's clear," Sairs said, leaning over the edge to look around.

"Are you ready?" Tommery asked me.

The other fairies paired up on either side of me again when I nodded. When they laid their hands on my legs, I felt all my weight disappear once more, and we began to rise from the rooftop.

I'd had dreams of flying before and they were much like this: I'd suddenly remember that I didn't have any weight and I could just lift up from the ground if I wanted to. I'd rise up and up, a foot, another, a yard, two yards. Finally, I'd be above the treetops, and off I'd go, soaring. Free.

I can't begin to tell you what it's like to have it happen for real.

We drifted away from the rooftop, and there was only air below us now, with the ground two stories down. I wanted to go higher. I wanted to fly among the stars and touch the moon.

I wanted to do it on my own.

"Well, sure," Quinty said when I told them as much. "Everybody let go."

"No!" Tommery cried from where he was floating beside us.

But it was too late. The fairies pulled their hands away, and down I went.

I don't think I even had time to realize what was happening before I hit the ground.

There was this awful, wet sound. There was a shock of pain like I'd never felt before.

And then everything went black.

* * *

" . . . for a laugh," I heard Quinty saying as I came swirling back out of the darkness.

"Oh, yes," Tommery said. "Very humorous."

"Well, it was kind of funny when he hit the pavement." That was Krew.

Sairs snickered. "Did you see his face?"

"Oh, very funny," Tommery said, his voice tight with anger. "And look at him now. Hilarious. And dead."

I blinked my eyes open to find them all standing around me and forced myself to sit up. I wasn't dead. I felt perfectly fine.

"I'm okay," I said.

Tommery turned to look at me. "No, you're not."

"No, really."

"*Look* at yourself."

I looked down and saw that my hips disappeared into another pair of hips. I turned to look behind me, and there I was. Lying on the pavement, neck at a weird angle, blood pooling around my body. Except I was *here* as well, looking down at my dead self.

I couldn't seem to focus on what I saw. It made no sense.

"But . . . but . . . "

I couldn't get any more words out.

A huge wave of sadness went through me. That connection we all take for granted—the way we're part of our body, the way our body is a part of the world around us—it was gone. I felt alone and lost, and this gibbering panic rose up inside me, swelling until I thought my head would burst.

Then everything went black again.

THEN: *Imogene*

So I survived that first year at Redding High, no thanks to Ken and Barbie and their cooler-than-thou posse. I stopped trying to avoid them, but I gave them absolutely no reaction when they ragged on me, so they tended to focus on easier targets most of the time. Or at least more reactive ones. We sure didn't become friends or anything. They still had something to say about each day's outfit and they tagged Maxine and me as "the homo girls" because we were always together, but I could live with that.

As I get old and wise, moving into my seventeenth year, I find it gets easier to ignore stupid people.

* * *

The funny thing is, I got the best marks I've ever had on my report card that year. I actually *knew* the answers in the exams, so it looks like all that studying I did with Maxine actually rubbed off. Because the thing with Maxine is, she really does like school and studying. It's not just because her mother's always on her case about it. Maxine likes doing well. So lots of times when we said we were going to be studying, we actually were.

I also attended more classes than I ever did back at Willingham, mostly because the first few times I did skip, Maxine was so disappointed in me, I decided to see if I could stick it out. Jared was totally wondering if I was okay.

"You on tranks or something?" he asked.

"Yeah, as if," I told him.

I don't do drugs or alcohol—not for moral reasons, but because I've got this serious thing about always being in control of myself.

"So is there something wrong with doing well at school?" I asked him.

He shook his head. "It's just . . . different."

"The new and improved kid sister."

"Well, new, anyway," he said, so I punched him in the shoulder.

* * *

Maxine and I actually went to the big spring dance in April—and no, not as a couple. It took some seriously complicated maneuvering on my part to get her mom to agree, and she never did know that Maxine went with a boy. Finding dates wasn't a problem. We'd met a couple of boys from Fuller High at a used record store on Williamson in January, Pat Haines and Jeremy Nash. They were both so cute—a little straight, but they scruffed up well. I ended up with Jeremy, and it was the first time in ages that I'd been out with a guy who had fewer piercings and tattoos than me. But he was a good kisser, and that's what's important, right?

So anyway, getting dates to take us to the dance was easy. Convincing Maxine's mother, on the other hand . . .

I swear it was like setting up a military campaign to invade a small country to get it to all work out. But it did, and we had a great time, even though we had to do a whole Cinderella thing to get Maxine out of her makeup and fancy dress and back home on time.

* * *

And then there was Ghost.

I caught glimpses of him on and off through the rest of the school year, but couldn't get close to him, never mind have a conversation. I'd spot him somewhere and before I could even start in his direction, he'd pull his disappearing shtick: stepping through some wall, or just doing this—I have to admit, pretty cool—slow fade from sight.

I had to settle for research. I went through the newspaper files at the Crowsea Public Library, but there wasn't much. Just a small piece in the City section of *The Newford Journal* the day after he died and an obit in the death notices. But I got his name, and in the school library I found a small "in memoriam" notice in the 1998 yearbook. It didn't tell me anything except that he wasn't very popular, and that was only by inference. See, a couple of other kids had also died that year—one of cancer, one in a car crash—and there was a whole pile of reminiscences about them from their friends and the faculty.

But for Adrian Dumbrell, nothing.

Just that he'd been a student and that he'd died.

I knew there had to be more to it than that, but I couldn't seem to get any details. It wasn't like some big secret; just no one knew him at school. Any kids who'd been attending when he was here had already graduated. Everyone had heard the story of Ghost, that he haunted the school, and some of them even knew he was this kid who'd jumped from the roof of the school because everybody was always ragging on him.

I suppose I would have let the whole thing go if he hadn't kept spying on me. There had to be a reason why he was doing the stalking thing—some kind of unfinished business, though what it would have to do with me, I had no idea. I guessed it was something I was supposed to figure out.

So one Sunday in July, while Maxine was away for the month on a trip with her dad and I was seriously bored, I went back to the school, determined to track him down. It was all locked up—no summer courses here, or at least not today—but I'd learned my lessons well from Frankie Lee and jimmied the lock on one of the back doors. Moments later I was inside, out of the sweltering July heat.

It was so nice and cool in here, and quiet. The only sound was that of my clunky platform sandals echoing on the marble floors. I had the normally crowded halls to myself, which was kind of weird, but kind of neat, too. I hadn't done anything like this—what Frankie called creeping a joint—in what seemed like forever.

"Okay," I said. "I know you're in here somewhere, Adrian. So let's talk."

Nothing.

Well, I hadn't thought it would be easy. He'd already shown that he had this whole avoidance thing going for him. Maybe it came with the territory when you were dead. I mean, ghosts are always hard to pin down in the stories, aren't they?—never just coming right out and saying what they want. Instead they have to rattle their chains and beat around the bush with riddles and crap.

"C'mon, spooky boy! It's time for us to get acquainted."

I walked up and down the halls for over an hour before I finally heard a voice behind me.

"You're going to wake the janitor."

I turned, and there he was. Adrian Dumbrell, deceased. Also known as Ghost.

He didn't look like a ghost—not like I had any great familiarity with them other than his stalking me. I just mean he seemed very solid and *here*. Tall and gawky, Harry Potter glasses, acne scars, and all.

"The janitor's asleep?" I said.

Ghost nodded. "He's got a cot set up in the basement where he sneaks off and naps."

"Why's he so tired?"

"He drinks too much."

"He never looks drunk—I mean, when I've seen him."

"He's good at hiding it."

This was very weird. I had a hundred more important things to ask him, but here we were, talking about the school custodian's drinking problem. I guess it was because things suddenly had all the awkwardness of a first date, with neither of us quite sure what to say.

But I couldn't leave it at that.

I cleared my throat.

"So . . . why've you been following me around?" I asked.

He shrugged. "I just . . . you know . . . like you, I guess."

"You like me." Was that all this was, some horny ghost had the hots for me? Right. "You don't even know me."

"I know you're pretty—"

"Oh, yeah. Real runway material."

"Well, you are. And I like the way you stand up for yourself."

"Which is why people have been crapping on me all year."

He shook his head. "I saw you stand up to Brent Calder

your first week here. I heard what you said to Valerie. I think the only reason you let them rag on you is that you can't be bothered caring about what they think."

"I care," I found myself saying, "but I'm trying to stay out of trouble."

Now why had I told him that?

He smiled. "You see? You took the moral high ground—another commendable character trait."

"Mmm."

I've never been good at compliments, but it was especially weird getting them like this, when I was being hit on by a ghost. Or at least it felt like he was hitting on me. I wonder where he thought a relationship could go?

"You're taking this all pretty well," he said. "I mean, considering . . . "

"What? You think other people don't have nice things to say about me?"

"Of course not. I meant, me being dead and all."

He put his hand toward the nearest wall, and it went right through so that it looked like his arm was cut off at the wrist. But when he pulled his arm back, his hand reappeared, inch by inch, good as new.

"You don't seem at all scared," he said.

Okay, that was a little freaky, but I already *knew* he was a ghost, so I could deal with it.

"Should I be?" I asked.

"Well, no . . . "

"Because you *have* been stalking me for months, and I have to say, that's not particularly endearing."

"I wasn't stalking you."

I raised my eyebrows. "What do you call spying on someone from a distance and disappearing when the person tries to talk to you?"

"I just . . . I don't know. I didn't know what I'd say to you. I didn't know you'd be so easy to talk to."

"Oh."

Neither of us said anything for a few moments. I slid down and sat with my back against a locker. After a moment, he came over from the stretch of wall where he'd been standing and sat beside me.

"What's it like to be dead?" I asked.

"I don't know what it's like for anybody else, but I'm always sort of scared."

"Sounds just like life."

"I guess."

"So are there other ghosts around?"

He nodded. "All kinds."

"That's kind of creepy—from the perspective of someone who's still alive, I mean. Knowing that there's all these dead people around, checking out everything you're doing, and you can't see them. And when you think of how many people have died over the centuries . . . " I looked around. "It must be really crowded in Ghostworld."

"Most of us go on."

"Go on where?"

"I don't know. I just never went."

"Did you ever think it might be better than here?"

"Yeah, but what if it's worse?"

"So we get a choice?"

"I don't know that either, but I guess I did."

"Because you have unfinished business?"

"What's that supposed to mean?" He sounded a little defensive.

"Well, isn't that why ghosts usually don't go on?" I asked. "They've got stuff they still have to deal with, here in the world of the living."

"I never thought about it."

"So what happened to you? I looked you up in the newspaper, but they didn't have much to say."

"It's kind of a long story."

I laughed. "It's the middle of the summer and here I am, sitting in school—which is not my favorite place, as you can probably imagine—talking to a ghost. Don't you think I'd be anywhere else if I had something better to do?"

"Then why are you here?"

"I wanted to figure you out. So give. Tell me what happened."

He didn't say anything for such a long time that I thought he wasn't going to tell me anything. But then he sighed.

"When I was a kid," he finally began, "I couldn't wait to get into high school . . . "

* * *

" . . . and so I've been hanging around here ever since."

We were still sitting in one of the school's side halls, our backs against the lockers, legs splayed out in front of us. I knocked the toes of my sandals together and turned to look at him.

"That's a pretty amazing story," I said.

"It's true."

"Of course it is."

"You don't believe me. What part don't you believe?"

"Well, c'mon . . . fairies?"

"Says the girl talking to a ghost."

"Okay, that's a good point. But you being a ghost doesn't automatically make fairies real."

He looked across the hall.

"They think you're rude," he said.

"They're here?"

"Oshtin and Sairs are."

I studied the other side of the hall, but I couldn't see anyone or anything. Not even when I squinted.

"I don't see anybody," I said.

"Not everybody can see them."

"Not everybody can see *you*, either, but I do. So what's the deal with that?"

"I don't know."

I kept checking out the area around us, but there was just me and the ghost. Otherwise, the hall was deserted. Just like you'd expect on a Sunday afternoon in the middle of the summer.

"So why don't they show themselves?" I asked.

For a few moments, he seemed to be listening to someone. Then he said, "They say it's either a gift you're born with or something you have to earn."

"How convenient."

"You shouldn't make them angry."

"Whatever. I don't really care what invisible people think of me."

"Now they're leaving." I watched his eyes track something that I couldn't see. "And now they're gone."

"And the difference is?"

He shook his head. "You really shouldn't be like that. They can be mean, if you get on the wrong side of them."

"Like saying they can teach you how to fly."

"I suppose. But I don't think that they meant for that to happen."

I shrugged. "So where did they go?"

"Into one of those elf bolts I told you about earlier. Do you want to see one? They'd be really useful for you in the new school year if you want to get away from someone."

"I don't think so. Maybe another time."

He gave me a goofy grin. "So there's going to be another time?"

I laughed. "Well, I'm not going to marry you or anything, but yeah, I'll drop by again."

I stood up and brushed some nonexistent dirt from my legs. He scrambled soundlessly to his feet beside me.

"When are you coming back?" he asked.

"Oh, I don't know. Next week, I guess. When the school's empty again."

"There's no one here after around nine or so most evenings—except for the janitor, and he just heads down to his cot after he's checked the doors."

"We'll see."

I started walking toward the door at the end of the hall.

"So can you and your fairies leave this place?" I asked when we got to the door.

It had one of those bars across it that let you open it from the inside and would then automatically lock when it closed behind you.

"They're not 'my' fairies," he said.

"Whatever. Can you?"

He nodded. "But I don't like to go out much."

"Why not? People can't see you if you don't want them to, right? Or at least most people can't."

"Most people can't," he agreed. "But there are . . . other things out there that I'd just as soon avoid."

Now he had my curiosity piqued.

"What kinds of things?" I asked.

"Well, there's the . . . I don't know what you'd call them, actually. Angels, I suppose."

"Like with wings and harps?"

Why not? If he was going to try to convince me that there were fairies running around, he might as well throw in angels. But he shook his head.

"They're just these people," he said, "who try to coax ghosts like me to move on. They can be very persistent."

"They don't sound very scary."

"They're not. But there's also the darkness."

"So go out during the day."

"No, not that kind of darkness. This is something else. I don't know what they look like, but I've felt them." He turned to look at me with an earnest expression. "You know that feeling of helplessness you get when a bunch of guys grab you in the boys' room, and the next thing you know you're being pushed out into the hall wearing your own underwear over your head?"

I couldn't believe he was asking me this, but I guess it had happened to him, so I cut him some slack.

"Not really," I said.

"No, of course you wouldn't. You'd put up too big a fight for them to be able to do that."

I shrugged. He seemed to think I was a lot braver that I thought I was. Who was I to disillusion him?

"Anyway, trust me. It's an awful feeling. It's like you don't have any control over your life and anybody can come along and just do whatever the hell they want to you, any time they want."

"Okay, that I can understand."

"Well," he said, "whatever lives in the darkness leaves you feeling like that, only a hundred times worse."

"But what do they *do*?"

"I don't know for sure. Tommery says they eat souls."

"Anybody's?"

"No, just those that are ghosts. And sometimes those of people . . . "

"Who talk to ghosts," I finished for him when his voice trailed off.

He shook his head. "No. I was going to say, those of people who walk at the edges of how the world's supposed to be. You know, people who don't take what they see around them at face value. Tommery says they carry a kind of shine that attracts the darkness."

"Well, that lets me off the hook," I said, "because the only impossible thing I can see is you."

He got kind of an annoyed look. "Why are you so insistent on the world being just the way you've decided it is?"

I shrugged. "Because it's never shown me to be any different?"

Before he could reply, I pushed on the bar and stepped out into the July heat. I half expected him to follow me, but when I turned around, there was no one there.

* * *

But that wasn't the strangest thing to happen to me over the summer.

Because Maxine was away for a whole month, and I knew I wouldn't be seeing her mother, I took the opportunity to dye my hair a nice dark blue. I used to love playing with hair dyes, back in Tyson. Some weeks I had a different color for each day, like my underwear. I got a new tat as well: a blue-black crow in flight on the nape of my neck that I could hide with a shirt collar if I had to. But I was wearing a tank top and a pair of low-rise cutoffs when I ran into Ms. Tattrie the next day.

So not only could you see my new tat, you could also see the one on my shoulder, the one on my thigh, the ones on each ankle, and half of the knotwork design at the small of my back. I had all my earrings in—six to an ear—my eyebrow piercing, and a little bell hanging from the one in my navel. In other words, I was definitely not her daughter's straight little study partner.

"Imogene," she said as pleasantly as always. "I've missed seeing you since Maxine's been away."

The first thing I thought is, that's some strong medication she must be on.

"Umm," was all I could manage, my brain whirling as I tried to come up with some explanation for my looking the way I did. It wasn't close enough for Halloween and—

"I was hoping you might call," she went on, "but I understand how it can be. It's not like you didn't work hard enough all year to deserve some downtime that doesn't include the stodgy old parents of your friends."

"You're not that old," I said.

Whoops. Maybe I should have lied, and said she wasn't stodgy either.

"Do you have time to go for a coffee or a cup of tea?" she asked.

Everything about this chance meeting had caught me so off-guard that I found myself agreeing, and let her lead me into a nearby café. She got herself chai tea and a plain black coffee for me, smiling the whole time. It wasn't until we were finally sitting at a window table that I took a deep breath.

"I just want to say," I began, "that if you're going to be mad at anybody, be mad at me, because this is all my doing. Maxine's just as good a kid as you want her to be."

"Why should I be mad?"

"Well . . . c'mon."

She shook her head. "Did you really think I didn't know?"

"You . . . but . . . "

Okay, it's not often I'm left speechless, but this was too much.

"As soon as I saw that you and Maxine were becoming friends," she said, "I called the school's guidance counselor, and she put me in touch with the counselor at your old school. I'll admit that what I learned didn't exactly thrill me."

"They can tell you personal stuff like that?"

"When you're determined, and you know the right people, anything is possible."

Well, duh. What was I thinking? Like old Mr. Ford back at Willingham wouldn't jump at the chance to dis me.

"But . . . I know the stuff they would've told you," I said. "Why would you still let Maxine hang with me?"

"My therapist suggested that I give it a few weeks before making any decisions."

"Your therapist."

She nodded. "I know I have issues, particularly when it comes to Maxine. I want the best for my daughter, but I also know that I have to give her some freedom or all I'll do is push her even further away from me. But . . . it's just very hard for me."

I didn't know what to say.

"And then an interesting thing happened," Ms. Tattrie said. "This hellion that I'd been told I shouldn't let my daughter associate with turned out to be a rather charming young lady. She didn't skip school. She didn't run with a bad crowd. Her marks were very good on her final exams. When I spoke again to Ms. Kluge at the end of the school year, she told me that while your sense of fashion was certainly eccentric, none of the behavioral problems on your permanent record appeared to have carried over from your old school to the new one."

I still didn't have anything to say, so I just shrugged.

"So it appears," she went on, "that, in some ways, Maxine has been as much of an influence upon you as you've been on her."

"She's never done anything wrong," I said, ready to defend Maxine where I couldn't—or at least wouldn't—defend myself.

"I know. Your influence has been positive, as well. Before you came into our lives, Maxine barely spoke to me. She went to school; she did homework. She read her books. She watched TV. And that was all she did."

"And now?" I had to ask.

"Now she's more outgoing. We have actual conversations rather than my having to pull monosyllabic responses from her. She . . . she glows."

I couldn't help smiling. "Yeah, she does, doesn't she."

"And that, I know, is your doing."

I started to shake my head, but Ms. Tattrie would have nothing of it.

"I'm not saying you've transformed her," she told me. "You've simply allowed her to be more herself. She was a very unhappy girl before you came along, but she wasn't always that way."

I was good and didn't say anything about how maybe Maxine's unhappiness could have, in a large part, come from how Ms. Tattrie had been treating her.

We fell silent for a moment, and she looked me over.

"So this is the real you," she finally said. I could have said the same to her.

"Well, sort of. It's hot today, and I'm kind of slumming."

"I meant more . . . all the tattoos and piercings. And that hair."

I shrugged. "I just like to play with how I look. You'll be happy to know that Maxine doesn't go for this kind of thing at all."

"Thankfully," she said, but she smiled to take the sting out of it.

I knew what she meant. And the funny thing is, when she smiled, she got this whole other look about her—more like Maxine. She got that same glow.

"So what happens now?" I asked.

"Nothing. I'm glad we had this chance to talk—to get it all out in the open."

"I guess."

"I don't suppose you'd be willing to keep this from Maxine?"

I shook my head. "Not and be a friend. But I'll figure out a way to tell her so that you don't come out looking bad. I'm good at that kind of thing."

"Yes, you are, aren't you?" She finished her tea. "Thank

you for that, Imogene. Thank you for everything."

We stayed a little longer, but then she went off, back into her life, and I was left sitting at the table just trying to figure it all out. I mean, was this weird or what? Maxine's mother was actually kind of cool.

THEN: *Adrian*

I was of two minds about the afternoon I'd just spent with Imogene. Happy to have spent it with her, naturally—to have finally had an actual conversation with her without me blathering on like some idiot—but annoyed at how she could be so infuriatingly stubborn about not believing in the fairies. Though, now that I thought of it, maybe talking about the fairies *had* been blathering on like some idiot—at least it could be construed that way from her point of view. And I guess, to be fair, at first I hadn't exactly believed in fairies either, not even when I had one standing right in front of me.

I sighed, staring out the door, and watched her walk away, across the scraggly lawn fronting the school and onto the sidewalk running along Grasso Street.

Why was it that whatever I did was the act of the village idiot?

"Had your first tiff?"

Turning, I found Tommery perched on the garbage can across the hall. He lounged like a cat, utterly at ease, as though he'd been there for hours, though I knew there'd been no one on the garbage can a moment ago. There was a big grin on his face, the kind that makes me uneasy around the fairies because I never know if it's them being friendly, or laughing at me. It's hard to tell with them. Fairies really are impossible to read. They can laugh at a joke, just like you or I would, but they'll laugh just as heartily when they're doing something horribly mean.

So I did what I always did around them and tried to ignore the uneasy feeling that I was the brunt of some joke rather than in on it.

"I guess," I said. "It just bugs me that she won't believe me about you—that you're real. It's so ridiculous. She's *talking* to a ghost, but she still can't accept the idea that fairies exist as well."

"Perhaps I could convince her."

"I don't know." I was remembering what Imogene had said when I'd told her about how I'd fallen from the school's rooftop. "You're not thinking of teaching her how to fly, are you?"

Tommery got this serious, sad look.

"Of course not, Addy. I'd teach her how to *see*."

That was exactly what was needed. Once she saw the fairies with her own eyes, like I had, how could she *not* accept them?

"How will you do it?" I asked.

"It's a matter of catching her when her mind's not so calm. Humans are more open to the hidden world when they're in a higher emotional state." I must have looked a little blank. "When they're very sad," he went on to explain, "or very happy. Also, when they've been drinking or doing drugs—particularly some of the more potent chemical concoctions."

I tried to get my head around the idea of fairies talking knowledgeably about drugs—it made me wonder: Were there crack fairies? Heroin hobgoblins?—but Tommery was forever surprising me with the depth of his knowledge concerning the human world.

"When it comes to your girlfriend . . . " Tommery began.

"Girlfriend! I wish."

"Yes, well, when it comes to her, I've never seen a human with such a level emotional state."

"She seems animated to me."

Tommery nodded. "But there's no inner turmoil. No cracks in the calmness that magic can slip into."

"So what can you do?"

"Keep an eye on her until the opportunity does appear."

"I don't know if she'll like being followed around."

Tommery smiled. "But she won't know, will she? She can't see us."

Except *I'd* know. And I wasn't sure I liked the idea. I knew for sure that Imogene wouldn't, considering her remarks about me stalking her. And where would Tommery draw the line? I imagined him checking her out while she was getting undressed or having a shower. Or worse, what if he assigned the job to horny little Quinty?

"Oh, don't worry, Addy," Tommery said, as though he could read my mind. "We're not going to invade her precious privacy. We have our own lives to live and, trust me, they're far more appealing than the twenty-four-hour surveillance of any human could be. We'll simply keep an eye on her, check in on her emotional state from time to time. Perhaps send her a dream or two to get her thinking the right way."

"What about the stuff that Oshtin was saying?" I asked. "He told me that this sight business is something that comes to you naturally, or it's a gift that needs to be earned. How does that fit in with what you're planning to do?"

"Both are true. But the ability for us to be seen by humans is also discretionary."

That took me a moment to work through.

"So you can just appear to her if you want to?" I asked.

Tommery nodded. "But it's better that she discovers us on her own."

Which wasn't an answer at all, except that it spoke to some undercurrent that I always sensed around the fairies, but never understood. It was a mystery they played up, some secret with dark edges that I could never see into.

"I don't get it," I said. "Why don't you just show yourself to her and save all the skulking around?"

Tommery shrugged. "We could. It's just not as . . . interesting."

"Interesting."

"Exactly. And trust me, her slowly becoming aware of us over time will leave a much more lasting impression."

"I just want her to know you're real. That I wasn't making it up."

"She will. But if it's not done right, she'll forget, and then you'll be right back where you started." He cocked his head, giving me a considering look. "The only problem is, doing it this way takes some time. But you can be patient, can't you?"

I laughed without humor.

"What's time to me?" I said. "I'm dead."

Tommery sighed and gave me a slow, sad nod.

"There's that," he said.

His voice was soft. If I tried, I could pretend I heard genuine regret in it. I just had to forget the cruel tricks he was capable of, like the year after I died when they gave half the school food poisoning on the last day of classes.

That little incident had the fairies laughing for days.

THEN: *Imogene*

I didn't realize how much I'd missed Maxine until she finally got back and showed up at my front door on the first Saturday in August. No, that's not true. I'd missed her terribly and knew it the whole time she was gone. I'd just tried not to think about it. Maybe I was her first best friend, but she was mine, too. Not having her around to talk to every day was like having a big black hole in the middle of my life, and the postcards she'd sent couldn't come close to filling it, though I had appreciated them.

I let her talk about the trip. Her dad had rented a condo in Fort Lauderdale, close to the beach, so while he went off to do his meetings and work during the day, Maxine got to turn into a beach bunny. She was, like, totally brown when she got back. It made me feel like I'd spent the month in a basement, but then I don't tan well anyway.

The important thing was she'd had a great time, and I was glad for her. Nobody had the preconception that she was this loser from Redding High, so they saw her the way I did: cute and smart and funny. She made some friends; she had boys trying to pick her up. Life was good for her. But I noticed she didn't talk much about the time she'd spent with her dad.

"So," I said, "are you still thinking of living with your dad for your final year?"

He lived up in the 'burbs, when he wasn't away on business, but Maxine had assured me that she'd bus in to Redding.

"I don't know," she said. "I . . . it was a little weird. My dad's great about not talking about why they got divorced, even though we all know the reason, and he doesn't dis Mom, either."

"So what was the problem?"

She shrugged. "I guess just the way he'd look at what I was wearing. He didn't say anything about how sucky my clothes were—not directly—but I could tell he was worried about me getting to be too much like my mother. 'It's okay to be a kid,' he'd tell me. 'Everything doesn't have to be so serious.'"

"But you brought your cool clothes, too, right?"

"Some, but mostly what my mom's bought for me. I mean, she'd think it was weird if she looked in my closet and it looked like I hadn't taken anything. And we both know she'd look in my closet—if only to make sure the skirts were still hung separate from the dresses."

I had to smile. It was sadly true.

"The stuff we got at the thrift stores I wore mostly when I was on my own, at the beach. When my dad was home . . . I don't know. I felt like I'd be betraying Mom if I wore stuff she hadn't picked out for me. Is that messed up or what?"

I shook my head. "You love them both, even with your mom's weird quirks. It makes perfect sense. And maybe your mom's not as tightly wound as we think she is."

That's when I told her about the conversation I'd had with her mother.

"You want weird," I said as I finished up, "how's that?"

Maxine shook her head. "I know exactly what's going on. It's because before I left I told her that I was thinking of living with Dad for my final year."

"But this checking-up-on-me business happened last year, not this summer."

"So?"

"So her deciding to let us be friends," I said, "even when she knew my history, happened long before you told her that."

Maxine looked as puzzled as I'd been that day in the café.

"God, you're right," she said. "That *is* weird. Are you sure it was my mom?"

I nodded. "Unless she's got an identical, nonevil twin."

"So you can just come over looking however you want?"

"Apparently. But I won't. I mean, I won't be all sucky either, but, you know." I gave her a considering look. "So she didn't say anything to you when you got back?"

Maxine shook her head.

"Because I told her I'd tell you."

"I wonder what this means for me?" she said. "Does it mean I can start dressing the way I want and seeing boys and stuff?"

"Only one way to find out."

I could see the uneasiness rise in her, and she got this shy, nervous look that was so Maxine.

"Oh, I don't know . . . "

"This from the popular beach bunny of Fort Lauderdale?"

"It's just too strange. Plus, it really makes me kind of mad."

For Maxine to say she was kind of mad meant that she was furious.

"Don't go all postal on her," I said.

"But all these years . . . obviously she knew she was

messing up, so why couldn't she just let me be me? I mean, you said she was seeing a therapist about it."

"You didn't know that either?"

"I knew she was seeing a therapist, but I thought it was about the breakup with Dad." She sighed. "How hard would it have been for her to cut her daughter some slack?"

"Obviously, way hard."

"I guess." She gave me an unhappy look. "What am I going to do about this? Just walking back into the apartment with her there is going to be so weird, knowing what I know."

"You want weird?" I asked. "I've got way more weird for you."

And then I told her about finally meeting Adrian, how I'd talked to him three or four times now since she'd been gone. That was enough to put the whole problem with her mother on the back burner.

"Oh, my god! You really met Ghost?"

"Well, it's not so exciting when you get past the ghost part."

"That's easy for you to say."

"No, it's true. You know what he looks like, right?"

"Mm-hmm."

"Well, that's pretty much what you get. He's basically just this nerdy guy—smart, nice enough, but he talks like someone who's read way too many books and doesn't have any friends. The ghostliness is about all he's got going for him."

Typically, Maxine ignored that. "I think he's got a crush

on you. Why else would he have been checking you out all year?"

I laughed. "The crush is big-time. But I don't know what he thinks'll come of it. I mean, he's dead. We couldn't even touch each other."

"Would you want to?"

"Not really."

"Tell me more about the fairies," Maxine said.

I shrugged. "What's to tell? I've never seen any, though he pretends to. Personally, I think all this talk about fairies and crap—that's just covering up how messed up he was when he was alive. I'll bet he stepped off the roof all on his own, and then, when he found he was still stuck here, he made up a story about how fairies had tricked him into thinking he could fly."

"You think he just made it up?"

"Well, duh, of course. Though you'd think he'd come up with something more plausible."

"But you said he talks to them."

"He's talking to empty space. There's nothing there. Well, at least nothing I can see. Though I guess to be fair to him, maybe he's told the story to himself so many times now, he really believes it."

"But why can't fairies be real?"

I laughed. "Oh, please. Look, we know he had a shitty life. Only one tiny memoriam in the school yearbook, and while people don't remember his name, they know Ghost is what's left over of a kid that everybody ragged on, teachers and students. No, he did this himself, but now he can't deal with it. And until he deals with it, he's stuck here, haunting the school."

"So is that why you keep going to see him?"

"What do you mean?"

"Are you trying to get him to face up to the truth so that he can move on?"

I shook my head. "God, no. It's none of my business. It's just that, for all his nerdiness, I still find him interesting to talk to."

"Even when that talk turns to fairies?"

I smiled. "Even then. Just because I don't believe in them doesn't make them uninteresting. Remember, I used to listen to Little Bob's stories all the time."

"I'd like to meet him."

"Who? Little Bob?"

She whacked my arm. "No. Ghost."

"No problem."

* * *

But it was.

Maxine called her mother to say she was staying for dinner and that we were going to watch a movie after, which maybe we would, though first we planned to go by the school and then check out Jared's band, which had an all-ages gig. Dinner was pizza from the place down at the corner, because Mom was at the university. She'd taken this whole going-back-to-school thing very seriously and signed up for summer classes, so we hardly ever saw her. Gino's didn't have the best pizza in the neighborhood, but I liked teasing their skateboarder delivery boy.

Over dinner, Jared waxed enthusiastic about the gig, going on and on about the set list and this new tube amp he'd picked up and I don't know what all. I love him, but that stuff gets old after a while. Maxine was totally interested, though, hanging on his every word, which made me think she'd either developed a jones for sixties music and music gear or a crush on Jared.

We begged off helping the band set up—I mean, I've lugged too many amps and then hung around through even more sound checks for it to be a thrill anymore. We let Jared go off on his own, promising to hook up later at the club, and then set off to follow our own agenda.

"So you're really starting to get into that sixties music, aren't you?" I said as Maxine and I walked toward the school.

"I guess. It's fun."

"Yeah, it is. And so's Jared."

She got this cute guilty look. "What do you mean?"

"Well, I think you're finding him pretty interesting, too."

"No, I just . . . it's that he's . . . "

"It's okay," I said. "I like that you're into him."

She looked relieved, but what did she think I was going to do, totally freak out on her or something? Why *wouldn't* she be into Jared? *I* think he's cool, and I'm his *sister.*

"So," Maxine said, "does he ever, you know . . . "

"Talk about you?"

She nodded.

"Yeah, but not in a Potential Girlfriend way. But before

you get all depressed," I added as her face fell, "he needs to have you taken out of the Little Sister's Best Friend context and put into a Potential Girlfriend one."

"How's that supposed to happen?"

"You could tell him."

"God, no. I could never do that."

I shrugged. "Or I could do it for you."

"I don't know. That seems weird."

"It's just a day for weirdness," I said. "And to top it all off, there's the school, a veritable hotbed of fairies and ghosts. Well, one ghost anyway."

We stopped across the street and looked at the building. It looked kind of foreboding, hunched there like some deserted warehouse, dark and squat in the fading light. Maxine put a hand on my arm.

"It looks spooky," she said.

I nodded. "And haunted, too."

Maxine shot me a worried look, and I had to laugh.

"That's because it is," I said, and led the way across the street.

As I jimmied the lock to get us in, Maxine was suitably impressed with my break-and-entry skills and full of questions about where I'd learned them. I felt a little guilty as I shrugged them off.

The thing was, I'd still never really talked to Maxine about my old life in Tyson. I'd only told her bits and pieces, the ones that cast me in a good light. I didn't tell her that I first had sex when I was thirteen. That by the time I was fourteen I'd tried every drug there was to try—which is why I wouldn't touch any now. That I stood watch when Frankie and the boys broke into houses. That I was the best shoplifter in the gang. Stuff like that.

I had no reason to become the way I did. I hadn't had a crappy life. But when we moved off the commune and into the city, it was like someone flicked a switch. I just went wild. It started at school, with me reacting to all those smart-ass, cooler-than-thou kids putting me down, and escalated from there.

How could I tell Maxine any of that?

I felt horrible about holding back when we exchanged confidences, but all I could seem to do was tell her the things I knew she'd like: My first kiss. Little Bob's stories. Emmy Jean's advice. Life on the commune.

Or problems we shared, like the bullying we'd both had to endure at school.

I didn't want her to think the life I'd had back then was cool—the way I had at the time. And I couldn't talk about it like it wasn't, even though I no longer believed it myself. Does that make any sense?

"Hey, Adrian," I called out softly as we walked down the dark hallway. "You've got company."

There was no reply except for the soft echo of my voice going down the empty hall.

"It's weird being in here when there's no one else around," Maxine said.

I nodded, remembering that first Sunday afternoon that I'd snuck in. Now it was old hat, and wasn't that an odd expression? I'd have to look it up in my *Brewer's* when I got home.

"Especially at night," Maxine went on. I could hear the nervousness in her voice and wondered if we'd have to leave, but then she added in a lighter tone, "Hey, here's my old locker. I wonder if there's a way for us to get lockers beside each other this year."

I laughed. "Your mom could probably make it happen."

"My *mom*?"

"Remember I told you how she got Ms. Kluge to cough up my old school records?"

Maxine nodded. "Yeah, Mom doesn't take the word *no* well. But I don't think I'll ask her all the same." She looked down the shadowy hall. "So where's the ghost?"

"I don't know. Except for that first time when I had to wander around for an hour or so, he usually shows up pretty quickly."

"Maybe he went out—he can go out, right?"

"Yeah, but he doesn't like to."

"Why not?"

I shrugged. "Something about angels and the darkness."

"The darkness?" Maxine repeated. "That doesn't sound good."

"Relax. Whatever it is, it's only dangerous to spirits like Adrian."

"And the angels?"

"I don't know what they are either. That's just what he calls them."

We were well into the school by now, and there was still no sign of Adrian. I found myself wondering if I should have taken him up on one of his offers to show me those elf bolts he kept talking about. Maybe he was in one of them right now, fast asleep or something. That's if ghosts slept. I'd have to ask him about that the next time I saw him. But tonight was a bust.

I was just about to say as much to Maxine when we both heard a noise down the hall from where we were walking. We stopped, listening hard, and then heard the echoing sound of footsteps. They were definitely approaching us.

"So . . . " Maxine said in a whisper, the nervousness back in her voice. "If Adrian's a ghost, and ghosts don't have bodies, then who—"

Before she could finish, Mr. Sanderson, the janitor, stepped out of a side hall.

"Hey, you girls!" he cried. "What do you think you're doing in here?"

"Oh, crap," I said.

I grabbed Maxine's hand and started to run in the opposite direction.

"You get your asses back here!" Mr. Sanderson called after us.

Oh right, as if.

The empty hall was suddenly filled with the sound of our running and the janitor's yelling. I doubt he'd have caught us, but before we got a chance to find out, I heard him stumble and fall down.

I shot a glance over my shoulder, then skidded to a halt, hauling Maxine to a stop beside me. Looking back, we saw the janitor backed against some lockers, arms scrabbling in the air.

"Get off me, get off me!" he cried.

"What's the matter with him?" Maxine asked.

"D.T.'s," I said. "Come on. Let's get out of here."

We burst out the side door and kept running until we were by the big cedar hedge that separated the school from the sunken parking lot of the apartment building next door. It was a place kids came to smoke dope during recess—a perfect spot because, once you got into it, you could see out, but no one could see you in the shadows.

I pushed in through the branches, Maxine on my heels, only stopping when I came up to the cement wall of the parking lot. We stood there, holding onto the hedge and each other as we caught our breaths. Finally, I was able to peer out into the schoolyard without feeling like my gasps for air would be heard a block away. I was just in time to see Mr. Sanderson bang open the door and stand there swaying as he glared into the schoolyard.

Maxine and I held our breaths.

The janitor muttered something I couldn't quite make out as he finally turned away and let the door clang shut behind him.

"That was close," I said.

"Do you always have to—"

"Run from a drunk janitor?" I finished. "No, but I do try to avoid him. He's usually in the basement, either drinking, or sleeping off a drunk on this little cot he's got down there."

"We're lucky he didn't call the cops."

"He still might, so we should get out of here."

Which was a great idea except that as soon as we pushed our way out of the hedge, a familiar voice spoke out of the darkness.

"Imogene. What are you doing here?"

I turned and there he was: Adrian in all his ghostly glory, which was basically Adrian standing there all tall and gawky with a puzzled look on his face. I heard Maxine's sharp intake of breath and put a hand on her arm.

"It's okay," I said. "It's just Adrian."

"I . . . I figured as much. It's just . . . he's so real . . . "

"But he won't bite, right, Adrian?"

He shook his head. "Nope. I'm a ghost, not one of the undead."

"There *are* undead?" Maxine asked, moving closer to me so that our hips bumped. "Like, vampires?"

"There's anything you can imagine and then some," he told her. "They just live at the edges of the world that you know, so you don't usually see them."

"Right," I said. "Amp up the spooky factor."

He turned back to me. "I'm only telling the truth. So what *are* you doing out here, hiding in a hedge?"

"I brought Maxine around so that you could meet her, but you weren't at the school."

"I was out, just, you know, walking . . . "

"Whatever. We got caught by Mr. Sanderson, and he chased us out. If he hadn't been so drunk and hallucinating bats or spiders or whatever, he might even have caught us."

"What do you mean?"

"Oh, it was weird. I heard him trip and when I looked back, he was on the floor with his back up against the wall, hands scrabbling in the air like he was trying to get something off of himself."

"That was probably the fairies."

I shook my head. "Right. Tell that to Maxine. She wants to hear all about them."

"I just think it's interesting," she said.

"At least *someone* has an open mind," he said, and smiled at her.

It was an open, endearing smile that I hadn't seen before. It took me a moment to realize why: he could be comfortable with Maxine because he wasn't trying to impress her the way he was me.

"So you're really a ghost?" Maxine asked.

He nodded.

"Can I . . . ?"

She reached out a hand. He lifted his own, and when they should have banged into each other, her hand just went through his. Maxine shivered and pulled her hand back, holding it to her chest.

"That . . . that was the strangest sensation," she said. "Chilly, but kind of, I don't know, warm and staticky, all at the same time."

I was impressed with her. I'd never tried touching him myself, but it wasn't because it made me nervous. I just didn't want to give Adrian any ideas.

"Well, we should get going," I said. "My brother's band is playing at the Keystone and they're going to be starting soon." I waited a beat, then added, "Maybe you want to come?"

Adrian shook his head. "I don't do well in crowds. I don't much like it when people walk right through me."

"No prob. We'll see you later."

"Nice meeting you, Maxine," he said. "I'll tell you more about the fairies another time."

Maxine smiled and then we were off, leaving him standing by the hedge while we made our way back to the street.

"So you see what I mean?" I asked when we were out of his hearing range. "There's nothing really all that spooky about him."

"Except when you touch him."

"Yeah, well, *that* won't be happening any time soon."

"But he seemed nice."

"He is. But he's also a ghost, so this is never going to be more than a 'Hi, how're you doing? Oh, wait, you're dead' kind of a relationship. Which suits me just fine, by the way."

Maxine nodded. "But it's kind of sad, isn't it? The way he's just all by himself like that."

"You're forgetting the fairies."

"Which you don't believe in."

I shrugged. "I don't believe in anything I can't see for myself."

* * *

We had a great time at the club. Jared's band was called the Everlasting First, after a song by some sixties band. They were the middle act, but the best, as far as both Maxine and I were concerned. But then we each had our own reasons to be biased. We left after about the third song of the third band to get Maxine home on time, but not before I got the two of them dancing. As we were going out the door, I glanced back and saw that Jared had this cute, considering look on his face, like he was seeing Maxine for the first time. I told her about it as we walked to her apartment building, and she couldn't stop talking about him the whole way back.

It made me happy, thinking of my two favorite people as a couple, and I told her so, which just made her beam more.

* * *

So things went swimmingly the rest of the month.

Maxine's mom kept treating me nicely, even if I showed up looking a little less decorous than I had before our chat at the café. I could tell she had to bite her tongue at some of the stuff I wore, but I kept it toned down, even if she didn't realize it.

Maxine and Jared were kind of circling around each other now, which was sweet and frustrating at the same time. I kept wanting to grab the pair of them and just bang them up against each other.

As for my own romantic front, Jeremy had come back from the camp where he and Pat had been working as counselors, but I now had this other guy, Thomas, interested in me, who was very cool and worked in a used record shop. He kind of reminded me of Frankie, but without the criminal bent, and said I should be fronting a band, which just made Jared laugh.

"It's all about the attitude," Thomas argued.

"Oh, she's got attitude, all right," Jared said.

Which I guess is kind of a compliment, or at least as much of a one as I'd get from Jared when music and me get mentioned in the same breath.

* * *

Anyway, between the two of us, Maxine and I had pulled off an okay summer. And with the confidence that being Miss Beach Bunny in Florida had instilled in Maxine, I even thought we might have an easier time at school this year.

But then I started having these weird-ass dreams.

NOW: *Maxine*

It's funny, but after I learned about Mom's conversation with Imogene, I got the sense that she thought everything would suddenly be different between us. That we'd become pals instead of just mother and daughter. But I can hardly speak to her at all. My head's filled with Jared and Ghost and this huge resentment for all the years she's made me leave the house looking like such a geek. That's when she even *let* me leave the house.

How am I supposed to talk about any of that?

And then Imogene tells me about the dreams she's having, and *that* totally fills my head. We both agree that Adrian might have something to do with them. I also believe that there might be a connection between her dreams and those fairies of Adrian's, but she doesn't even want to discuss that because she doesn't believe that they exist in the first place.

I can't explain why I don't question the idea of fairies like Imogene does. Intellectually—and before I met Adrian—I always knew that they couldn't exist. Neither could unicorns, vampires, ghosts, talking rabbits, or little spacemen with sleek spaceships and anal probes. But in my heart, I believed. In fairies, at least. Maybe it's because I *had* to believe in them. For so long I had to believe in something more than what this world had to offer: my parents' divorce, the horror that was high school, the loneliness that hung like a shroud over me every day until Imogene stepped up and tore it away.

And that was just when you looked at my sorry little life. When you took in the big picture, the world itself seemed to be falling apart, what with terrorist attacks and wars and weird diseases and poverty and environmental pollution . . .

I'd heard about adopted kids who'd have this fantasy that their real parents were going to show up one day and whisk them away to some kind of paradise. I guess my fantasy was that there really were fairies and that, while maybe they wouldn't whisk me away to Fairyland, at least the idea of something so magical actually existing made everything else more tolerable—don't ask me why.

I've never told Imogene that I truly believed in fairies. I've never told anyone, when it comes right down to it, but it's only odd that I never told Imogene, considering the way her mind works, how it will soar on flights of fancy at the slightest whim, not to mention her relationship with a dead boy. You'd think she'd be the obvious choice.

I've even had the perfect opportunity a few times, like when she talks about that Little Bob guy back at her old school and all the stories he had, and then when she introduced me to Adrian. But something holds me back.

I suppose it's because she so obviously *doesn't* believe in them, and my whole life has been pretty much geared to making nice and getting along. I have my small rebellions, but mostly I've always done what I'm told to do. By my mother. By my teachers. By anyone bigger and stronger and cooler than me.

I tried to follow suit with Imogene, but she wouldn't let me. Like the first time she took me to the thrift stores to buy some new clothes. I asked her to pick out what I should get, and she just gave me a funny look. Then she said, "No, you have to choose your own. You have to pick what *you* want to wear."

And I had no idea.

But I learned. I learned to the point where, if Imogene didn't think I should get something I liked, I was brave enough to get it anyway. So maybe I can learn to stand up about fairies, too, except this seems far different from whether or not I should buy a certain top. It feels like it goes deeper, that it taps into the things that really make us who we are, and I don't know that I want to be different from Imogene in that way. Or maybe what I mean is that I don't want for her to know we're that different. But here we are, regardless: me believing, and Imogene with her mind still firmly closed on the issue, even when she's friends with an honest-to-god ghost.

Mind you, I didn't grow up believing in fairies—or at least I got huge mixed signals about how I was supposed to feel about them. My dad read me fairy tales and would earnestly explain how they lived in hollow trees and sometimes even behind the wainscoting and under the floorboards, but that didn't make Mom very happy. She's always been against any kind of frivolity. Even when I was just a little kid, she argued that I should only experience things I would find useful later on in my academic career.

I know. It sounds horrible. But nothing she's ever done has been out of meanness or spite. She really, truly wants the best for me. The problem is, she doesn't think I should get any say in it. She has my whole life mapped out. What she doesn't see—what she doesn't *want* to see—are the uncharted territories that lie inside my head.

I do understand why she is the way she is. She grew up poor, and her parents made her drop out of high school and go to work. Then she met my dad. He was the one who convinced her to finish her schooling and go on to university. She forgets this, how he supported her for all those years. He was so proud of her when she got her degree. Prouder still when she got a job in human resources at Turner Industries, rising rapidly up the corporate chain until she was a vice president. That's a long haul from the girl who used to work as a waitress in a diner.

Because of how hard her life had been, she was determined to make sure that things were better for me. That I'd be prepared for anything that life had to offer. I was going to learn my manners and dress well and do well in school. Fairy tales weren't going to be part of my life. Neither were boys, dressing like anything but a geek, having a mind of my own . . . Well, you get the picture.

So the pieces of my life that I could live for myself went underground.

The first book I hid from my mom was a copy of *Touch and Go: The Collected Stories of Katharine Mully,* with those wonderful illustrations by Isabelle Copley. I was shattered when I found out Mully'd killed herself and there were never going to be any more new stories. But I had these and I reread that book until the pages came loose and started to fall out.

They were fairy tales, but set in the here and now, in this city, in Newford, one of them just a few blocks over from where we lived. When I read these stories—like "Junkyard Angel" where the wild girl Cosette disappears in the junkyard, or "The Goatgirl's Mercedes" with the old crotchety wizard Hempley who's always trying to steal the goatgirl's car keys—for days I'd carry around the belief that those kinds of things really could exist. When kids made fun of me at school for the way I was dressed, I'd just go my own way and imagine I had someone like the butterfly girl Enodia waiting for me at home.

From the biographical material in the introduction, I found out about Mully's artist friend Jilly Coppercorn and totally fell in love with her fairy paintings. I even snuck into one of her gallery shows once when I was supposed to be going to the library, and got to see a whole roomful of originals. I was drunk on those paintings for days and stashed the postcard advertising the show with my growing treasure hoard under the floorboards of my room.

And then I started reading Christy Riddell, because he was supposed to be a friend of both Mully and Coppercorn.

I liked his stories, but I especially liked his true-account books of encounters that people have had with things that can't be explained. They didn't really have much in the way of beginnings or endings. They were just these mysterious anecdotal vignettes that seemed all the more real because of their lack of traditional story structure.

By the third book of his, he'd bumped Katharine Mully as my favorite writer, and best of all, he was still alive and I could get a new book by him every year or so.

I guess the high point of my life up until I met Imogene was the day he came and gave a talk at the school. It was held in the library and was supposed to be a writers' workshop as much as a talk about writing, but most of the kids who signed up were just looking for a way to get out of class and weren't very cooperative. After the second exercise, Christy gave up and just talked to us instead. For most of the scheduled two hours, the other students sat there and rolled their eyes. The rest of the time they stared bored out the window, or whispered and giggled with each other.

The only people actually paying attention to him were me; Ms. Giles, the librarian; and Andrea Joseph, another student, who obviously totally hated the subject matter of his books, but tried to ingratiate herself with him anyway because he was a real published author.

I don't know where I got the nerve to go up to him with my dog-eared copy of *How to Make the Wind Blow,* but I did. I guess it helped that he was so friendly and unassuming during his talk. He didn't seem to be so much this big-shot writer, full of himself and the importance of his work, as this sort of older guy with kind eyes who was obviously passionate about his writing, and generous in how he was willing to share his craft with others.

I waited until all the other students were gone and there was just me and Ms. Giles left in the library. She was all hovering at his elbow, like being near him would cause something to rub off on her: talent, fame, I don't know. It was just weird, and I wished she'd go away. As though reading my mind, Christy looked up to see me hesitate in my approach, then he turned to Ms. Giles.

"Could you give us a couple of moments, please," he said to her.

"What? Oh, yes. Of course."

She retreated. Reluctantly, but she went.

"I want to apologize for the other students," I began, stopping when he shook his head.

"Don't ever apologize for anyone else," he said. "You're only responsible for what you yourself put out into the world."

"But—"

He smiled. "Don't worry. My ego's not so fragile that something like this will leave some great debilitating scar. I do these kinds of talks quite often, and half the time, this is pretty much the way it goes."

"Then why do you do it?"

"To meet students like you, who do seem interested. On the chance that what I've got to share will make a difference to one person."

That seemed too far beyond the call of duty.

"So do you plan to be a writer?" he asked as he took my copy of *How to Make the Wind Blow* from me.

"I don't know. I've always liked stories, but I feel like I should learn a little bit more about the world before I actually try to write anything."

"I'm not sure I agree," he said. "There's nothing wrong with a youthful perspective. Don't forget—no else sees the world the way you do, so no one else can tell the stories that you have to tell."

"I guess."

"But remember what I said earlier about listening to advice."

I nodded. "'Consider it, but question everything,'" I quoted.

"Exactly," he said. Then he leaned a little closer to add, "Though the one thing that's an absolute truth is that writing requires practice, just like any other art or craft. So the sooner you start, the better you'll be when you do feel you have stories to tell. Write in a journal, if nothing else. Try to do a little bit every day instead of just when you feel like it."

I nodded again. At that moment, having an actual conversation with this man I'd idolized for ages, I'd agree to anything he said. So much for questioning everything.

And then I did the one thing I'd promised myself I would *definitely* not do if I got the chance to talk to him.

"Mr. Riddell," I asked, "do you really believe the stories in your books?"

I could have sunk into the floor as those words came out of my mouth. But he only smiled.

"I could give you the pat answer that I normally offer when I'm interviewed," he said. "It goes something like, 'It depends on the source. I know for certain that the world's a strange and mysterious place with more in it than most of us will ever see or experience, so I can't immediately dismiss elements that are out of the ordinary simply because I haven't experienced them. But by the same token, I also don't immediately accept every odd and unusual occurrence when it's presented to me because the world's also filled with a lot of weird people with very active imaginations. The trouble is, unless I experience what they have, and for all my predilection toward the whimsical and surreal, the lack of empirical evidence makes a strong argument against belief.'

"But the true answer is yes. I've experienced things that can't be explained, and more than once. And the other important thing to remember is that just because something isn't necessarily true for you or me, it doesn't mean it isn't true for someone else."

I guess I had a dumb look on my face, because he gave me another smile.

"The thing to remember when you're writing," he said, "is, it's not whether or not what you put on paper is true. It's whether it wakes a truth in your reader. I don't care what literary devices you might use, or belief systems you tap into—if you can make a story true for a reader, if you can give them a glimpse into another way of seeing the world, or another way that they can cope with their problems, then that story is a success. Does that make sense?"

I nodded. "I don't really believe in fairies and stuff, but when I read your books, I do, but in a funny way. It's like, it doesn't matter if I can see them or not. Just the idea of them being out there is . . . I don't know. I want to say comforting, but some of the things you write about make me really uneasy. I guess I just appreciate how when I finish one of your stories I find myself looking at the world in a different way. Everything seems to hold possibilities."

"A writer couldn't ask for more," he told me. "Or at least this writer couldn't."

And then he inscribed my book. He wrote, *For Maxine, who appreciates the stories for all the right reasons. May the words flow from your pen when you decide to set them loose, and may your dreams always flourish.*

"I do some one-on-one mentoring through the Crowsea Public Library," he said as he handed me back my book. "And also at the Arts Court run by the Newford Children's Foundation. If you ever decide to get serious about your writing and want to talk about it some more, come see me."

"Thanks," I said. "I will."

Only I never did. Or at least I haven't yet. Though maybe I could write about this whole fairies business. Then I could take it to him at the library or the Arts Court and use it as a pretext to pick his brain about them, and dreams like Imogene is having, and dead boys who died because they couldn't fly the way that fairies do.

I fall asleep wondering about that: where I'd begin, how I'd put it all together, and if I'd even have the nerve to take it to Christy—just saying I managed to actually write something that wasn't completely stupid.

NOW: *Imogene*

It's long past midnight, but I'm still sitting up, not so much scared to sleep as unwilling to give myself over to the dreams that are coming every night now. You might think, "They're only dreams; big deal." But it's that whole control thing again. I don't like it that something—my mind, some outside influence, I don't know what—is deciding how my dreams will go.

It's not even that I mind seeing Pelly again, though I could do without the creepy gang of fairies and creatures that accompany him. I don't remember them being like that in my old storybooks. And that weird, off-key toy orchestra can go, too.

But it doesn't. Nothing does. They keep marching through my dreams, banging their tin and plastic drums, without so much as a hey, do you mind if we? . . . and I don't get to say yes or no.

Of course, if I *don't* fall asleep, then they can't come, which is why I'm still up.

I sit in a straight-backed wooden chair—the lack of comfort important because it won't let me nod off too easily—and stare out the window at the narrow view of the alley below. There's nothing moving down there, just like there's nothing moving in my room. At least not yet.

I keep coming back to how Pelly's changed. He's gone all cryptic on me where he used to be straightforward. But the weird thing is, I get the feeling that there's something he wants—maybe even *needs*—to tell me, only he can't seem to come right out and say it.

I hate when conversation becomes a game instead of communication. It's like that in school. It's like that everywhere you turn. TV, movies, books. I first ran across it in the fantasy books I used to read as a kid on the commune. It was already old for me by the tenth time I ran across some riddling wizard and his vague warnings. Now it's ho-hum ancient. If you've got something to say, just come out and *say* it. Though in those old stories, that'd kill half the plot, I guess, because instead of the characters having to try to figure out what they're supposed to do, they could just go and do it.

Like I could if Pelly'd just come clean.

I sigh and turn from the window to look around my room. I can't stay up forever. I have school tomorrow. I suppose I could blow it off, but getting good marks—really *earning* them—last year gave me a little buzz. It was like I could actually be good at something normal and law-abiding instead of just living fast and shoplifting.

So eventually I leave the chair by the window where I've been sitting and lie down on my bed.

But relaxed I'm not. I lie there all stiff and on edge, ears straining for the first whisper of that toy orchestra starting up. When it does, I have this dislocated moment of not knowing if I'm awake or asleep, but then I see Pelly sitting on the foot of my bed, and I know which is which.

Awake, the only anomaly in the world is the ghost of a dead kid who killed himself.

In a dream, any damn thing can happen.

I sit up and lean back against the headboard.

"So how's it going tonight?" I ask my old imaginary friend.

He gives his head a mournful shake.

"Yeah, yeah," I say before he can speak. "Beware the Ides of Who Cares and don't look sideways into the darkness or whatever. But do you remember when we used to just hang out and talk, and there wasn't all this weird crap in between us?"

"I'm not real," he says.

"Well, duh. Of course not. I'm dreaming."

"You should stop dreaming."

"I'd like to, but . . . to tell you the truth, I don't really mind seeing you again. I could lose your little friends and that creepy music, plus it'd be nice to have you talk to me like a friend instead of someone who can only go all mysterious whenever you open your mouth. But it *is* still good to see you."

He gives me a sad look with those eyes that know too much. Then he reaches for my foot and pinches my toe.

"Wake up," he says.

And I do.

* * *

I relate the dream to Maxine the next day while we're having lunch, just the two of us, as usual.

I had high hopes for this school year, but Barbie and Ken are still on our case. We're still the homo girls and only have each other because no one else wants to hang with us and get on the bad side of the Doll People, as I've taken to calling Valerie and Brent and their crowd. That's not so bad because we like each other and would hang together anyway, but it's the last year of school, and I really want Maxine to have a good one. I want her to shine with her newfound beach bunny confidence and win everybody over. But the first day we get back, Valerie has some scathing remark for her, and Maxine just retreats right back into her shell.

I almost take a swing at Valerie right then and there, but I grit my teeth and hold back, because that one punch would just lead to so many complications that would not only end in Maxine being disappointed in me, but in me being disappointed in me, too. I think I'm finally really unlearning the lessons I learned from Frankie Lee back in Tyson.

His philosophy was pretty simple: you take what you want and you solve problems with a fist, or better yet, a tire iron. And you always get even.

I guess I have to admit I'd still like to get even with the Doll People, but not in a violent way. Something subtle, though of course then it'd go right over their heads.

So anyway, Maxine and I are sitting together out by the baseball diamond where we first met, and I tell her my theory that Pelly's holding back not because he's playing games with me but because not being cryptic will only lead to something worse, though what that worse could be, neither of us can guess. Then she tells me her idea of going to talk to this writer who came to the school before I got here, some guy who specializes in collecting anecdotal evidence on fairies and stuff like that and treats the material like it's for real.

She's looking nervous as she's telling me this, and that makes my heart break. What does she think I'm going to do, call her an idiot? Not likely.

"Sure, we can talk to him," I tell her.

How he can help, I haven't a clue. But it's not going to hurt to go see him.

"Really?" she says.

"Well, yeah. Just because I don't believe in that kind of stuff doesn't mean I think that people who do are dumb or something. I reserve that for Barbie and her Doll People."

Maxine smiles. "God, they are so full of themselves this year."

"Well, they're full of something, all right." But I'm sick of talking about my dreams and the Doll People and decide to change the subject. "So Jared tells me he got tickets to Mr. Airplane Man."

"He asked me this morning if I wanted to go."

"And you said yes, of course."

Maxine grins. "Of course. Are you coming?"

"Definitely not. You guys need an actual date without me tagging along."

"But . . ."

"Don't worry, I'll be fine. Maybe I'll go see my own boy tonight."

She thinks I mean Thomas, and maybe I do when I say it, but Thomas is closing the shop tonight, so he won't be free until ten. I could hang out with him, which can be fun because it's dead on a weekday evening, and we could lounge on the old sofa they've got by the front window, listen to anything we feel like, and make out a little with that extra buzz of maybe getting caught if someone comes wandering in the door.

Instead, once it gets dark, I come back to the school.

* * *

"So what exactly are your superpowers?" I ask Adrian.

We're sitting in the stands by the baseball diamond, dangling our feet. It's a beautiful night, the kind of clear sky where the city's light pollution doesn't seem to make much difference because the stars feel so close and bright.

He gives me this confused look.

"You know. What is it that ghosts can do?" I start ticking items off on my fingers. "There's the invisibility, the walking through walls, the not needing to eat or sleep . . . "

"I guess."

" . . . the sending of weird dreams to innocent bystanders . . . "

"What do you mean?"

I shake my head at the guilty look on his face.

"Don't ever try to play poker," I tell him, "because your face'll telegraph your every hand."

"I'm not sending anyone dreams," he says.

"Yeah, right."

"I wouldn't even know how."

"But you know someone who does."

"I . . . I've got to go."

And then he does the fadeaway, and there's just me sitting there in the stands. Unless he's still sitting beside me, only he's invisible.

"If I ever figure out a way to smack around a disembodied spirit," I say on the off chance he's still around, "you'll be toast."

* * *

I don't even try to avoid the dreams tonight, but start to get ready for bed right after I finish my homework. I laugh as I put away my schoolbooks and wash up, thinking of what Frankie'd say if he could see me now. Studying. In bed before midnight. But who knows? Maybe he'd be happy for me.

Sure. And maybe he's given up his wicked ways and entered the police academy as a recruit.

This is pointless, I tell myself. Worrying about what Frankie'd think, or what he's doing now—that belongs to someone else's life now.

I get into bed and lay my head on my pillow.

Besides, I've got a whole new set of problems—problems that Frankie's kind of solution couldn't begin to solve.

Pelly seems to show up the moment I close my eyes. I pretend I don't know he's there. I keep my breathing even and peer through my lashes, waiting to see what he'll do. He comes over to the bed, and I really have to work at not tensing up as he reaches a hand to my face. But all he does is brush some hair from my brow.

He turns away then and makes for the window. When he gets it open, all those weird little twig-and-stick fairy creatures stream out of it onto the fire escape, taking the music with them, though I didn't see one of them even carrying an instrument, never mind playing one. Pelly's the last to go.

I give it a count of ten before I throw back the covers and look out the window. I'm just in time to see them disappear around the corner of the alley.

I look down at myself, surprised that I'm still just

wearing my T-shirt nightie. This being a dream, I was sure that I'd be fully clothed since I've decided to follow them. It doesn't matter. It just takes me a few moments to throw on some jeans, sneakers, and a jacket, then I'm out the window myself, creeping down the fire escape.

When I step out of the alley, there's no one on the street and no traffic. But I remember seeing Pelly turn to the right, so I run down the pavement in that direction, stopping at each cross street to listen for the little invisible toy orchestra.

Nothing.

I'm about ten blocks from home when I give up and start to head back. Turning, I bump right into Pelly.

We're alone on the street. No gangs of fairy creatures, no toy-instrument soundtrack. Just the two of us.

"So what happened to your friends?" I ask.

"They've gone to a revel."

"A revel."

"It's like a rave, only for fairy folk."

Of course. If you're going to dream about fairies, they might as well be the party-hearty types.

"You should go home," Pelly says.

"I am home. I'm just dreaming this."

"You should stop dreaming this."

"We've been through this already," I tell him. "It's not like I have any control over it."

"You should try harder."

"Oh, for god's sake. What's with you? I know I've changed since I was a kid, but do you have to treat me like this? You used to be my friend."

"I'm still your friend. That's why I'm telling you."

"What happens if I don't stop dreaming about you?"

He hesitates before he says, "Then they win."

"They? There's a 'they' now? Who are they?"

"Go home. Wake up. Forget about all of this. Teach yourself not to dream what others would have you dream. Please, Imogene."

I shake my head. "Not until you tell me who they are."

He tries to wait me out, but I stand my ground. I stare into his big eyes, refusing to blink. We used to have staring contests all the time, and I always won. Just like I do now.

He sighs and looks away.

"Fairies are doing this to you," he says.

"What? That little gang of critters that hangs out with you in my closet?"

He shakes his head. "The fairies in the school where your dead friend lives."

"I *knew* he had something to do with all of this. So what's his game?"

"He doesn't have one. He just wanted you to believe him, and the fairies offered to make that happen."

"So dreaming about you is supposed to make me believe in fairies? Hello, big difference between dreams and real life."

"Are you so sure of that?"

"Well, yeah," I say, except something in his eyes tells me different.

Oh, relax already, I tell myself. You're dreaming. Anything can seem real in a dream.

I tell him as much.

"Hold fast to that thought," Pelly says. "Don't give in to them."

"Who? The imaginary fairies living in the school?"

He shakes his head. "Just go home, Imogene."

"Not until I understand what's going on," I tell him.

He gives me a look that's—oh, I don't know. Tender and loving, which is really weird because he still has these seriously scary eyes. Then his gaze lifts from me, looks past me, and the warmth goes cold.

I turn to see what he's looking at, but there's nothing there. Just the street, the buildings fronting it, the shadows of the buildings that are pooled in the stoops, and the alleys running between them. Then I get one of those what's-wrong-with-this-picture feelings and I realize that the shadows are encroaching *into* the light cast from the street-lamps, and that's impossible.

"We'll talk more another time," Pelly says from behind me.

He pinches me on the back of my arm and I wake up, except here's the really weird part. I'm *still* standing on the street, just like I was in the dream. The only difference is there's no Pelly, and the shadows across the street are doing just what they're supposed to, which is retreat from the light cast on them.

Okay, I tell myself, as I can feel the panic rising in me. This is still just part of the dream. You haven't woken up completely.

So I try to wake up, but that's a no-go, and I'm totally

on the edge of wigging out now. I close my eyes and force myself to breathe evenly. I wait, and when my heartbeat finally starts to calm a little, I start for home.

It's not a fun ten blocks.

I keep expecting I-don't-know-what to come out of the shadows and jump me—fairies, monsters, maybe just your ordinary everyday mugger or rapist—and that's not normal for me because I'm usually fearless. It's what got me into all the trouble back in Tyson and why Frankie and his gang took me in. They couldn't believe this little hippie chick wasn't scared of anything. Well, except for people not liking me, and I never told them that and I'm pretty much over it now anyway.

But I make it home okay to find Jared sitting out on the front steps of our building, smoking a cigarette. We have the street to ourselves except for an old stray tabby that's watching us from a couple of stoops over.

"I thought you'd quit," I say as I sit down beside him.

"I have. I just wanted one tonight."

Jared's one of those obnoxious people who can smoke when he wants to but never *has* to have a cigarette.

"I thought you'd given up prowling around at night," he adds.

"I have. This is just a dream."

He gives me a funny look. "Well, at least you're still weird. It's been getting so I don't even recognize my own sister anymore. Used to be, I just had to look for the closest hullabaloo, and there you'd be, right in the middle of it."

"I like that word."

He smiles. "I know you do."

"Do you miss that other sister?" I ask.

"Nah. I'm happy to have you no matter what you want to be. Now go to bed."

"I'm not tired."

"I know. You're just dreaming. But you'll be sorry in the morning if you don't."

He puts out his cigarette and gets up.

"Coming?" he asks.

"Sure."

* * *

When I get up in the morning, Jared remembers our conversation from last night.

I hadn't been dreaming.

NOW: *Adrian*

After I leave Imogene at the baseball diamond, it takes me a while to track down Tommery. I feel bad for just fading away on her the way I did, but what was I supposed to do? It was obvious that she was mad at me, but she'd be even madder if she knew what I'd done. I didn't even know *what* I'd done, exactly, but these dreams of hers had to have something to do with my asking Tommery to let her see him and the others. And all because I wanted her to know that I hadn't been lying to her about them.

Tommery and Oshtin are racing beetles in an elf bolt off the computer lab when I finally find them. They've written numbers on the backs of the beetles with different colored Magic Markers and sit beside them, nudging the unwilling participants back onto the track drawn on the floor whenever the little insects go wandering out of bounds.

"Hey, Addy," Tommery says when I sit down beside them.

"What are you doing to Imogene?" I ask.

Tommery gives me an innocent look.

"Nothing," he says. "Nothing at all."

Oshtin giggles, but since he doesn't look up, I don't know if it's because of what Tommery's said or something that the beetles are doing. Tommery shoots him a dirty look, which says it all, I guess.

"You've got to be doing something," I say.

"Only what you asked us to do. Preparing her to see into the Otherworld."

"She says she's being sent dreams."

"That's how we do it, Addy. We send her dreams until they become more and more real to her, and then finally she *sees* when she's awake, just like she does in her dreams."

"She doesn't like it."

Tommery shrugs. "I suppose it's a little disconcerting, but they can't hurt her. They're only dreams."

"I suppose . . ."

"Don't worry so much," he says. "We would never hurt a friend of yours."

I can't argue that, but only because I've never had a friend before.

"You swear she won't be hurt?"

Tommery puts a hand on his chest and gives me a hurt look.

"You know I don't swear," he says. "I'm far too polite for that sort of thing."

"You know what I mean."

"I do."

"So do you swear?"

He nods. "I swear that we won't hurt her. But it's a big bad world out there, so I can't pretend she'll never be hurt. She might step in front of a bus. She might fall down some stairs. She might have her heart broken by the boy in the record store that she's dating."

He means Thomas, whom I hate for being able to do all the things I can't. He can hold Imogene and kiss her. All I can do is watch.

"Just so long as *you* don't hurt her," I say.

"On the root of my uncle's oak, on the trunk of my sister's ash, on the leaves of my own thorn tree, I so swear."

I don't know what all of that means, but it sounds pretty solemn, so I let it go.

"Thanks," I tell him.

"Not at all. Care to race beetles with us?"

I shake my head. "I think I'll go for a walk."

"Careful of the gatherers."

He means what I call the angels, these do-gooders who are always trying to convince dead people like me to stop hanging around in this world and move on to the next.

"I always am," I assure him.

Actually, I don't mind talking to them. It's not much different from talking to some evangelical activist. I never had patience for that kind of thing back when I was alive, but now I sort of like listening to someone other than a fairy from time to time. A few of them can get so persuasive it's scary, but most of them are okay and hardly preach at all after the first few times we've run into each other.

But I've never told Tommery any of that. He professes a complete lack of patience for anybody who gets involved in other people's business—conveniently forgetting how much he and his friends do it all the time.

I leave them to their beetle racing and wander out of the school onto the streets. It's late now, well past midnight, and I love the quiet. The whole city's muted, though there's still some traffic. Further downtown, the clubs are open and there are people everywhere. But around here, there's hardly anybody on the streets, and the light you see coming from people's windows is mostly the flicker of TV sets.

When I was alive, I'd sneak out of my parents' place and just go wandering and look in through the windows of houses. I don't mean I went right up to the glass; I just looked through them from the street. Doing that gives you all these little visual cues about what a person's like: the kind of decor or lack thereof, paintings on the wall, bookcases, light fixtures, that sort of thing. I'd always duck into the bushes when I heard a car, or saw somebody else out on the street. I guess I was afraid of being arrested as a peeper, though mostly, I think, it was wanting to keep this secret. Kids don't get to have a lot of secrets, not with the way their parents pry into their lives. Or at least the way mine did.

But one night, when I ducked into the hedge to avoid a passing car, I saw all these newspapers piled up on the porch of the house behind me. Right away, I knew what it meant: whoever lived there hadn't been home for a while.

I waited until the car was gone, then crept closer to the house, curious. There wasn't much to it—just an old clapboard house with a covered front porch. The stairs creaked as I went up onto the porch, and I froze. But nothing happened. I looked around, then tried the door. It was locked.

I don't know why I had this urge to get inside. I didn't want to take anything, and the fact that maybe whoever wasn't bringing in his papers was lying on the floor somewhere inside, dead from a heart attack, certainly occurred to me. But I couldn't seem to help myself. Or rather, I could have, but I didn't want to.

So I went around the back. There was a summer kitchen, but the door to it was locked as well. Then I had a look at the basement windows. There were two in the back. The first I tried wouldn't budge, but the second gave a little. When I pushed harder, it popped open. I hesitated a moment longer. Up until now I hadn't done anything really wrong, but as soon as I went inside, I knew I'd be liable to all sorts of criminal charges, starting with breaking and entering.

I went in anyway.

What did I do? Nothing. I just walked around, pulse

drumming, and looked at things. It wasn't much different from when you go over to visit someone by invitation. My eyes adjusted to the poor light coming in from the streetlamps outside, and I wandered around, looking at the photographs and art on the walls, the titles of the books on the shelves. I didn't touch anything. Finally I sat down on the couch and kind of dozed for a while.

I know; it doesn't make a whole lot of sense to me either. But I came back the next night, and the night after that. I would have gone in a fourth time, but when I walked by the front walk of the house that night, I saw that the newspapers and flyers had all been taken away and there was a light on in an upstairs room, so I just kept on walking.

After that I started looked for places like that old clapboard house, homes where the mail and papers were piled up and nobody was home. Every time I went in, I half expected to find that dead body that my imagination told me was going to be there, but all I ever discovered were empty houses full of stuff.

I'm thinking of all of this as I walk the quiet streets tonight. Being dead, I don't have to look for an empty place. I can go in anywhere, and no one's going to see me if I don't want them to. But old habits die hard, and I don't try a single place until I come to a dark house at the end of McClure Street and see those telltale newspapers scattered across its porch.

I don't have to test for an unlocked door or window. I just drift in through the front door and go slowly through the house, taking my time, trying to replace my anxiousness for Imogene and what Tommery might have planned for her with the clutter of somebody else's life. I'm upstairs, studying the faces in a scattering of family pictures on a dresser top in the master bedroom, when I hear the fiddle music rise up to me from down below.

The sound surprises me—not because someone's in the house playing music, but because of who it has to be and what he's doing here.

I step away from the dresser and go downstairs, and there he is. John Narraway sits on the sofa in the living room, head cocked to keep his instrument under his chin, some old-timey piece of music shivering its way into the air as he draws his bow across the strings. He stops playing when I come into the living room and lays his fiddle on his knees.

"Hello, Adrian," he says.

I nod back and sit down on the edge of the coffee table.

John's one of those angels, the people who go around helping the dead get on with their unlives and move on to whatever comes after. I wish he wasn't always playing that fiddle of his. I didn't like fiddle music when I was alive, and nothing's come along to change that since. But John himself is okay. For one thing, he's not at all pushy about his mission. So the reason I'm surprised right now is that he's come here looking for me. I mean, he *has* to be looking for me, because the only time I normally see him is when we run across each other by accident on the street.

Here's a funny thing about these angels: when you're around them, everything seems to lose its immediacy. Sounds get thinner, and your surroundings start to lose their color. The angels say that their presence lets the dead see how the world really is for them now, but Tommery says it's just something they carry around with them, like a little cloud of doom, and not to listen to them. I don't know which is true, but I don't much like the feeling.

"I haven't changed my mind," I tell him.

"I didn't think you had," he says.

"Then why are you here?"

"I'm not here for you."

I look around. It's obvious we're alone, and I already checked out the house. Sure there's a week's worth of newspapers on the porch, but there are no dead bodies inside. No ghosts for John to move along.

"Okay, I'll bite," I say. "Who *are* you here for?"

John gets that sad look that the angels do so well. It's supposed to let the dead know that they really *feel* for us, I suppose.

"I'm here for people like your friend Imogene," he says. "It's too late to help her, but not too late to help the next one."

Of all the things he could have said, that's the last I expect. It plays right into the fears I've been carrying around since I left Imogene in the schoolyard.

"What do you mean, it's too late to help her?" I say. "Help her with what?"

"Dealing with the *anamithim*."

"I don't know what that means."

"Roughly translated, it means the ghost- or soul-eaters. Your fairy friends call them the darkness."

If I had a pulse, it'd be quickening by now.

"What . . . what will they do to her?"

John shrugs. "I don't know. Swallow her light, I suppose."

"Swallow . . . "

I can picture it all too clearly, that wonderful glow of life she carries, just snuffed out.

"And you know what that means," John says. "She won't be able to go on. There'll be no light *to* go on."

"I don't understand."

"She will just end."

"You mean she dies."

I can barely stand to say the words, because saying them feels too much like making them come true.

John shakes his head. "No, *you* died. You cast off your body and instead of moving on, you wander around in the world pretending you're still alive. When the *anamithim* take her, she will simply end."

"I still don't understand. How did this happen? What is it I'm supposed to have done?"

But I do know. It has something to do with Tommery and the dreams he's sending her.

John doesn't reply, but he doesn't have to. I'm sure it's written all over my face.

"What can I do to help her?" I ask.

He gives me a slow shake of his head. "Nothing. It's too late for her. But it's not too late for the next one."

"The next one what?"

"Whose life you screw up because you won't move on."

Okay, this is a new one, not just for John, but for any of the angels.

"I don't like to have to be this blunt," he says, "but it's no longer just your life you're messing around with here."

"I don't have a life. I'm dead—remember?"

"You know what I mean."

"No, I don't know what you mean. Yes, I've talked to Imogene. And the fairies are sending her dreams to convince her that they're real. But that's *it*. Where's the nasty intent in all of this?"

"I don't know that there has to be intent. I just know that whatever you and your friends have been doing has brought her to the attention of the soul-eaters."

"There must be a way to change that."

John sighs, then asks, "Have you ever been in a room or somewhere, and the person with you asks if you can hear an annoying hum? It could be something electrical, or static, whatever. But until it was brought to your attention, you didn't even notice it."

"I guess . . ."

"And once it's been brought to your attention, you can't not hear it, right?"

I nod. "Until I get distracted . . ." Then I see where he's going. "I have to figure out a way to distract them so that they don't notice her anymore."

John shakes his head again. "That's not what I was saying."

"No, but it would work, wouldn't it?"

John stands up, plainly unhappy with this turn in our conversation.

"So who are you willing to sacrifice in her place?" he asks.

He walks through the door before I can answer.

I stand there as the color slowly returns to the room, my head whirling.

"Anybody," I say finally, my voice soft. "Anybody rather than her."

I know exactly what I'm saying, what it will mean to whoever gets taken by the darkness in Imogene's place. They'll just . . . end. No afterlife, no moving on to wherever, whatever.

But better someone else than her.

NOW: *Maxine*

It's hard to consider Imogene as being anything but cool, I think as I sit on the stoop of my building and watch her come down the street so that we can walk to school. Sure, the kids at Redding pick on her, but that's because she's different, not because she's a loser. I wonder what she was really like at her old school, because I don't think she's telling me the whole story. Sometimes I'm tempted to see if I can find out—like I could ask Jared—but that would be something Mom would do. What Mom's already done. No. I'll let Imogene tell me in her own time, or not at all.

After all, friends can have secrets from each other. I mean, we're not supposed to be exactly the same person or anything. But I can't help being curious, because she knows all this stuff that you don't expect a kid to know—or at least, it's stuff that I never learned about until I met her. Like curb crawling, or how to pick a lock—things like that.

"So how was your date?" she asks me with a grin.

All my curiosity about her past goes out the window. My head fills with memories of last night, dancing with Jared to Mr. Airplane Man.

And see, this is another way Imogene's cool. She lets me rattle on about my night, how I feel about Jared, how I think he feels about me, how I hope he feels about me, where this relationship can go. Jared graduated last year and he's going to a community college now, while I still have another year of school. So far he hasn't said anything, but is he *really* going to want to keep going out with some high school kid when he could have his choice of all those cool college girls?

Imogene doesn't say one thing about what happened to her until my joy and confusion have run their course and I finally get around to asking if she got together with Thomas last night.

She shakes her head. "No, I went to see Adrian instead. I confronted him with the idea that he's putting these dreams in my head."

"And?"

"And nothing. But he knows something. Trouble is, he pulled a disappearing act before I could get him to tell me what."

It's a sunny October morning, but when she says, "Adrian pulled a disappearing act," I know she means it literally, and I can't suppress a shiver. The spooky chill just gets worse when she tells me what happened in last night's dream.

"That's it," I tell her. "We're going to see Christy after school today."

She shrugs.

"No, really," I say. "This is getting too weird."

"I wasn't arguing."

"Okay, that's weird, too."

"But cute."

"Very cute," I assure her.

And just like that, with a wink and a grin, she takes the chill out of my bones. The spookiness-factor monitor in my brain gets turned all the way back down to normal. Now I know I can face a day of classes and possible confrontations with Valerie and her crowd without the extra stress of feeling the world shift under my feet.

* * *

At four o'clock that afternoon, we're sitting on a sofa outside a small office on the second floor of the Crowsea

Public Library, waiting for Mr. Riddell to be finished with the client he's got in there with him. I start to get all nervous again, though this time it's because I don't know what I'm going to say, or at least how I'm going to say it. Not because I think fairies are going to come popping out of the walls or anything.

I've already decided that I won't pretend I've got anything written down for him to look at, though I didn't tell that to the nice lady with the vaguely British accent who sent us up here from the main desk. No, we're just going to have to find the right words to tell him this weird problem Imogene has and hope that he's really as open-minded as he says he is.

The big surprise when the door opens is that the client who comes out is Jared's jock friend Ben Sweetland.

"Moonlighting from the big wide world of sports?" Imogene asks after we all exchange hellos.

"Well, you know," he says. "I like to keep my options open."

"Well, writing's certainly an option for you," Mr. Riddell says. "You're a terrific writer."

Ben beams like he just scored a winning touchdown. Giving us a wave, he heads off through the library, and it's our turn to be ushered into the office.

It's cozy inside. One wall's taken up with a built-in, floor-to-ceiling oak unit that has filing cabinets on the bottom and shelves above, stuffed with books, of course. The other walls have various posters from local theater productions and gallery openings, and one small oil painting of a red-haired wild girl standing in a field of tall grass and apple trees. His desk is oak, too, as are the two chairs—one for him, and one in front for guests. There's also a small two-seater sofa, where Imogene and I sit while he takes the guest chair and turns it around so that he can lean his elbows on its back.

He remembers my name—which surprises me—and insists we call him by his first name when I introduce him to Imogene.

"So are the two of you working on a collaboration?" he asks.

Imogene and I look at each other.

"Not exactly," I tell him when I realize that she's leaving the explanations up to me.

My first thought is that she's being pouty because I made her come here, except then it occurs to me that she's feeling shy, which would be really strange, because I've *never* thought of Imogene as shy.

Christy smiles. "So am I supposed to guess why you're here?"

Oh, god. Where do I start? *How* do I start without sounding like a complete idiot?

"Well," I say, "it's not so much about writing as it is about fairies."

"Ah."

He rests his chin on his hands and waits for me to go on. I give Imogene another glance before I plunge into our story.

Christy's attentive, and I don't get the sense he's just

humoring us, but I still feel like I'm having an oral exam, and I never do well on that kind of thing. You have to just kind of stumble through your presentation the way I'm doing now.

There's a long moment of silence when I finally run out of words. I expect Christy to be nice about it, but I'm sure he's going to see us out of the office. Something along the lines of, Ha ha, cute story, now run along, girls. But he doesn't.

"Dreams are funny things," he says instead. "From the way you've described it, it sounds like Imogene is having lucid dreams—that's when you dream but you know you're dreaming."

We both nod.

"And hers also seem to be serial, which isn't so common. I only know of one other person who has serial dreams on a regular basis, and that's an artist friend of mine named Sophie. She basically lives a whole other life at night in her dreamworld while she's asleep here in this one."

"I don't think I'm going off to any dreamworld," Imogene says. "Everything's pretty much the same as the world is when I'm awake, except that Pelly and these little creatures are in it."

"And this last time," Christy asks. "You say when you woke up, you were ten blocks from home, which was basically the distance you'd traveled in your dream?"

Imogene nods. "I guess I must have been sleepwalking . . . "

"Or in a trance," Christy says.

"I guess. Would that make me feel like I was dreaming?"

"Possibly."

"And is that what's happening to me in the school with the dead kid—with Adrian?"

"Except I've met Adrian, too," I put in.

Christy shrugs, which doesn't tell us anything.

"Can you at least tell me why I'm having these trances?" Imogene asks.

"Do you believe in ghosts?" Christy asks instead of answering her question.

"I guess I do now," Imogene says. "Do you?"

"I believe in spirits of all kinds."

"Even fairies?"

He nods. "Oh, yes."

"So this story Adrian's telling me, it could be true?"

"Considering what else has been happening to you, I'd say yes."

"Wow." Imogene smiles at him. "So are you supposed to be telling us stuff like this?"

Christy smiles back. "Probably not. But that doesn't change the fact that such things exist."

"So what about Pelly?" I ask. "Her invisible friend from when she was a kid. Is he real, too?"

"Pelly could be any number of things," Christy says. His gaze strays to the painting of the red-haired girl in the field, then comes back to Imogene. "He could be your shadow, the parts of you that you cast off as a child. Sometimes they come back to us as these invisible friends—invisible to others, mostly, but not always. He could be one of the Eader who live in the half-world between our world and that of the spirits. They're beings that are created out of imagination, who exist only so long as someone believes in them. Or he could be a spirit—a fairy—who has come to you in that particular shape."

"I don't get why he keeps insisting that I shouldn't dream about him," Imogene says. "I mean, so what if I do or don't believe in fairies? Why should that be so important?"

"That's something only he can answer."

"Great."

"I wish I could be of more help."

"Actually," Imogene says, "just the fact that you didn't have me taken away in a straitjacket is kind of comforting. You know, that you'd actually listen to what we're telling you."

"Listening is easy; it's what I do."

Christy looks from me to Imogene, waiting to see if we have anything else we want to say.

"I have a suggestion for a little experiment," he says when it's obvious that neither of us has anything to add. "If you're up for it."

Imogene shrugs. "I guess."

"Do you have trouble falling asleep?"

"That's the one thing I've never had trouble with."

"Even if there are other people around?"

Imogene shrugs. "It's not a problem."

"Then I think that tonight Maxine should stay up and watch you while you sleep."

"What for?"

"To observe what happens when you're dreaming."

"You mean like if I get up and go walkabout?"

"Something like that."

"That's a pretty good idea." She turns to look at me. "How come we never thought of it?"

"You're not a trained specialist like me," Christy says.

Imogene and I grin. He stands up and offers us each a handshake.

"Let me know how it turns out," he tells us.

"I don't know that I want to be in one of your books," Imogene says.

"It can be an anonymous entry."

"We'll see. But thanks for listening to us."

"My pleasure." As we're going out the door, he adds, "And Maxine, bring some of your writing next time."

I wish I could come up with some easy response, but all I manage is to nod and blush.

"You write?" Imogene asks after the door closes behind us.

I shake my head. "But I think I'd like to. I've been keeping a journal."

"Cool."

"So what was all that business about how he shouldn't be telling us what he did?" I ask as we start down the big staircase to the library's main floor.

Imogene shrugs. "Think about it. He's telling us that ghosts and fairies are real when what he's probably supposed to do is contact our parents and recommend psychiatric evaluations. Or at least warn them that our grip on reality seems to slipping. Could be drugs. Could be we're just crazy."

"No, *that's* crazy."

Imogene sighs. "I wish it was, but there are a lot of people in this world who freak at the idea of looking outside of the box. Just take your mother, for example. Or even me."

"You don't even know where the box is."

"Not true. I have to know where it is to avoid it. But you know what I mean. How eager was I to embrace this whole fairics theory?"

"Not very."

"And I'm not sure I do embrace it completely."

"But—"

She stops me before I can start in on my argument.

"But now I'm willing to consider it."

"Oh."

We smile and wave to the lady behind the main desk as we walk by and then go outside.

"So what did you think of Christy?" I ask. "I think he's so cool."

Imogene smiles. "I'm telling Jared."

"Oh, for god's sake. He's this old guy. It's not the same thing at all."

"Then I'm telling Christy."

"You're just pushing my buttons, aren't you?"

The smile broadens into a grin, and she pokes me in the shoulder.

"Is it working yet?" she asks.

"Just wait until you're asleep tonight," I tell her. "I have a black marker—with permanent ink, I should add—and I'm not afraid to use it."

"Just make sure you draw pretty designs," she says, and bounces down the steps to the sidewalk.

The only revenge I get is making her wait while I take my sweet time with my own descent.

NOW: *Imogene*

Maxine phones her mom when we get back to my place. Usually we have this way organized in advance with all the specifics of a study session, or a project for school, or *something* Ms. Tattrie will find impossible to counter, ready to offer up as an excuse for a sleepover. But we're so excited about what might happen tonight that neither of us thinks of it until Maxine is actually on the line with her mother. I watch her face drop and get depressed, because I know what that means. Ms. Tattrie never has a problem letting you know that no means no, decision final. She might have lightened up some when it comes to what Maxine and I wear, but there's still this whole uptight fierce thing going on with her.

So I'm expecting the worst and figure I'll have to let

Jared in on it so that he can watch over me tonight. But then Maxine surprises me.

"Well, then I guess I'll just have to stay with Dad," she says into the phone.

There's this long moment of silence, then I can hear her mom say something, though I can't hear what it is. Before I can even start to guess, I'm mesmerized by the rest of Maxine's side of the conversation.

"No, we're not planning anything," she says. "We're just going to have a pizza and watch some videos we rented, that's all. We'll be in bed before midnight. No, Mrs. Yeck is still at school but she should be back around nine thirty, ten. We will, Mom. Really. You sleep well, too."

She grins at me as she puts down the phone.

"Wow," I say. "Backbone City or what?"

"I can't believe she caved."

"I can't believe you stood up like that. I mean, I've always known you had it in you. I've just never seen you use it."

"It felt pretty good."

"You should hold that thought the next time Barbie Doll mouths off to you."

Maxine shakes her head. "It's not the same."

I could argue that, but I don't want to bring her down from the glow of having successfully stood up to her mom, so I let it slide. To get her thinking about something else, I ask, "So you and Jared aren't going to hole up in his room and ignore me all night, are you?"

Works like a charm.

"When have we ever done that?" she asks.

"Oh, about a million times."

"Not true!"

"What are you guys *doing* in there anyway?" I ask, and laugh when she blushes.

But while she can't control her blushing, she'll give as good as she gets—at least with me.

"Only what we learned from you and Thomas," she tells me.

But it just makes her go redder still.

* * *

We weren't lying to Maxine's mom. We do order a pizza and then watch *Ghost World,* which we've all been meaning to see, but none of us have. Conveniently, Jared brought it home when he got back from band practice. It's so cute watching the two of them sitting there through the movie, holding hands. If I hadn't been there, I guess they'd have been all over each other.

"That's so cool," I say when the bus pulls away at the end of the film.

"We can't let that happen to us," Maxine says.

"What? Taking a bus?"

"No, drifting apart."

"We won't. But I think we should start following people around—you know, insinuate ourselves into their lives and all."

Jared laughs. "So you can end up with a fifty-year-old nerd with a jones for vinyl?"

"Careful," I tell him. "You'll be fifty someday and you already have the vinyl."

* * *

It's kind of weird having Maxine sit in a chair instead of lying beside me on the bed where she'd normally be. She and Jared spent a while saying good night to each other in his room until Mom finally made a bunch of noise in the hall and started talking loudly about how tired she was and how happy she was to finally be able to go to bed. The lovebirds got the message, so now here's me stretched out on the bed, Maxine sitting in a shadowed corner, and I guess Pelly and his little dream fairies waiting in the closet to start up their orchestra.

I'm so not scared of the dark—even as a kid I never was—but tonight the shadows seem all wrong. They're like they were last night in my dream. My walkabout. My whatever. They seem to move in ways they shouldn't, just ever so slightly: a flicker here, caught from the corner of my eye; inching forward there, where they pool under Maxine's chair.

I feel so stupid. Shadows don't move on their own. But then I remember snippets of my first conversation with Adrian:

There's also the darkness . . .

And there was something in that darkness, something that he was scared of.

I don't know what they look like, but I've felt them . . .

. . . Tommery says they eat souls . . .

. . . the souls of people who walk at the edges of how the world's supposed to be . . .

Because those people are supposed to carry some kind of shine that attracts the darkness. And I guess I'm sort of walking on the edge of how the world's supposed to be right now, because tonight I believe way more than I don't. I can't stop thinking about it—you know, the way you can obsess on something. Even when you know it's not for real, it just keeps running through your head. You look at it this way, then that way, turn it upside down, right side up, and you never figure it out, so you start all over again.

Bottom line, I try to convince myself, is that Pelly's only a dream. And I'm pretty sure that all I'm really doing is spooking myself, but it doesn't feel like that. Because if Pelly and the little gang of whatnots that come out of my closet are real, then maybe the fairies in the school are real, too. And then maybe I *am* putting out some kind of shine and the darkness really *is* looking for me.

I sigh and turn my head away from the closed door of my closet.

As if.

I can see Maxine from where I lie, and she can see me. I want to ask her if this all feels weird to her, too, but talking's not going to bring a new night's dreams, so instead I close my eyes. I think I won't fall asleep—never mind what I told Christy—but I drift off almost immediately. Or at least I must have, because suddenly I hear the fairy orchestra start up, that now familiar sound, tinny and distant, and then the closet door creaks open.

The open door hides Maxine from my view, but maybe that's a good thing because it also hides her from the fairies. I peek through cracked eyelids and watch the little host go streaming over to the window onto the fire escape. Heading off for their evening's rave. What had Pelly called it? Oh yeah, a revel.

And then there's Pelly, following on their heels. He hesitates at the end of the bed to give me a considering look.

"Heading off again?" I ask as he starts to turn.

He jumps, like I caught him off guard, which strikes me as odd. You'd think fairies would be way too cool to be startled.

"So you're awake," he says.

I laugh. "No, I'm dreaming, just like I always am."

"Ah, yes."

"So you were telling me about these fairies in the school—how they're making me dream about you and how that's a bad thing."

He nods.

"And that would be because?"

He doesn't say anything for a long moment, and I figure he's going to blow me off with some more cryptic babble. But he doesn't.

"If you accept my being here as real," he says, "you'll start to believe in me again and then you'll be able to see me anytime. That, in turn, will open the closed door in your mind, allowing the Otherworld to become part of your world once more, just as it was when you were a child."

"What do you mean 'the Otherworld'?" I ask. "I never saw your little orchestra before, or anything else for that matter. I only ever saw you."

"That's only because you never looked for the others."

"Ho-kay. But you still haven't said why this is a bad thing."

He hesitates, the moment dragging out.

"I'm guessing," I finally say, "that it's got something to do with this thing called the darkness."

"Who told you about that?"

"Adrian—the dead kid who lives in my school."

"And what did he tell you about it?"

"That whatever lives inside this darkness feeds on souls. But not just any souls. Only those of ghosts and, um, people that walk on the edges of the way the world appears to be . . . or something like that."

Pelly nods. "Humans acquire a fairy shine when they interact with us."

"And this—what? Automatically sics the darkness on it?"

I'm talking brave, like it doesn't mean anything to me, but my creep-out factor is escalating way big-time. Because I can't forget how seriously wigged I got last night when I realized the shadows were all wrong and Pelly took off.

"Not usually," he says.

"Well, that's a relief."

"Except this time . . . "

His voice trails off, and he won't meet my gaze. It's funny, there's still this look of knowing too much in his eyes, but it doesn't bother me like it did when I first started dreaming about him. Now it's his *not* looking at me that's making me feel nervous.

"This time, what?" I ask. "And don't you dare go all cryptic on me."

His gaze turns back to me.

"This time," he says, "I think those fairy friends of your ghost are deliberately bringing you to the attention of what lives in the shadows."

"Oh, right. Like that's going to happen."

"I felt their attention last night, and it wasn't directed toward me."

I'd felt it, too, *something* in those shadows, something that didn't like me. That didn't like anything. I don't feel comfortable talking about it. It's like talking about it will draw them to me. But I realize I can't just ignore it.

"This is so stupid," I say. "Why would they bother to go through all that trouble? What have they got against me?"

"Nothing, so far as I know. It would just amuse them."

"I didn't know fairies could be so . . . so evil."

"They're not, generally speaking. Most of us just *are*. And the ones you might consider evil aren't so much that as amoral. They don't see right or wrong the way we do. I don't know if they see a difference at all."

"So aren't there any good ones we can turn to for help?"

"There are good fairies, certainly, but the trick is to find them."

"I still don't get why these bad ones chose me."

"Because you came to their attention."

I give a slow nod. "By going to see Adrian. So what do

you think? Did they kill him, or was he a suicide?"

Pelly shook his head. "I wasn't there to see it happen. It could have been an accident. The fairies in your school might not have been so nasty then."

"But you said they were amoral anyway."

"No, I didn't explain it properly. They *become* amoral. Those fairies were probably once house spirits, brownies of some sort. Maybe bodachs, or hobs. Their job, their reason for being, is to keep a place tidy. But they need direction, from an older brownie or hob, like a Billy Blind, or from the mistress of the building. Without that, they can go . . . wrong." He pauses, cocking his head to think. "It's like making homemade bread," he finally explains. "Baked just right, from goodly ingredients, it can be the best loaf you've ever tasted. But leave that same loaf alone long enough, and it becomes moldy and it will make you sick if you eat it."

"So these fairies went moldy?"

Pelly laughs. "Something like that."

"When I woke up last night," I say, "I was still on the street where we were talking. I wasn't dreaming, was I?"

"I'm sorry," he says.

"For what?"

"For not doing a good enough job of making you disbelieve what you once knew was true."

"So this stuff . . . you, the little orchestra . . . it's all real?"

He lays a hand on my comforter, and those strangely jointed fingers give my foot a squeeze.

"I missed you, too," he says. "Maybe that's why I didn't

try hard enough. So now all of this is my fault."

Before I can say anything, he turns and steps to the window. He's gone while I'm still trying to figure out what I want to say.

NOW: *Maxine*

I'm starting to nod off when the closet door opens. There's a long, squeaky creak, then the door swings silently toward me, cutting off my view of Imogene and the bed.

My first thought is that Jared hid in there while we were in the bathroom getting ready for bed, and I plan to tell him just how not funny I think this is, because my pulse doubled in tempo at that first creak and it's not slowing down yet. But then I hear the music Imogene told me about, and everything inside me goes weirdly still, like I'm a held-in breath. The music's just like she described it—the sound of a toy orchestra, muted and quiet, like it's coming from another room—but it's indescribable, too. Eerie and impossible, unless ...

I start wondering about a little tape recorder with a cheap speaker when the fairies come into sight.

Real fairies. Diminutive creatures, half of which seem to

be made of twigs and vines and bundled grasses. Wild-haired, wild-eyed. Some with animal features, some just plain ugly, some heart-stoppingly beautiful, but with something not *right*. Something not human.

I shrink back into the chair, trying to hide with nothing to hide behind, but they ignore me. I stare wide-eyed as three of them jump up onto the sill and muscle the window open, then they all stream out onto the fire escape and into the night.

I feel at that moment like I did when I first got my period—flushed and weak and sick. And scared. I mean, I knew there'd be blood, but there seemed to be way too much of it, and I just kind of freaked.

This is like that, too. I've wanted to believe in fairies forever. I've half convinced myself that I do. But when I see them actually show up in Imogene's bedroom, it's not the same. All of a sudden the world is bigger and stranger, and I realize I don't know anything about it. Not really. No one does. If all these experts can claim to know so much about all the things they go on about, but fairies aren't in their equation, then what else are they missing?

But that's not what I'm thinking right at that moment, or at least not clearly. I feel like I'm going to faint. The chair seems all spongy. Any minute I could be swallowed by the floor.

I hear voices talking, but I can't concentrate on what they're saying. It's taking all my concentration to just stay *here*. I close my eyes tight and grip either side of the chair's seat and hold on.

I don't know how long I'm like this, but it feels like a long time. A *really* long time.

"Maxine . . . Maxine . . . "

I hear my name, but it seems to be coming from far away. Someone seems to be touching me. I open my eyes and a hundred Imogenes do a slow spin in front of me. I start to feel sick again, my eyes rolling back in my head.

"I . . . I . . . "

Can't speak, I want to say. Can't hardly breathe, but the words won't come out.

"Put your head between your legs," those hundreds of faces tell me in one voice, and that just makes me feel dizzier. "Here, let me help you."

Someone—Imogene?—helps me lower my head.

The next thing I know, I'm stretched out on Imogene's bed and she's sitting beside me, holding a cool washcloth against my brow. She's got this worried expression on her face that lightens when she realizes I'm awake and looking at her.

"Way to go, Chancy," she says. "Give me a heart attack, why don't you?"

I start to sit up but I don't seem to have any strength. Imogene tries to keep me lying down, but then gives up and helps me rest against the headboard with a couple of pillows behind me.

"What . . . what happened?" I ask.

"I thought you could tell me."

And then I remember.

"There . . . there were . . . "

Just remembering makes me feel all weird again, but I force myself to deal with it.

"Fairies," I manage to say. "I think—no, I for sure saw your fairies."

Imogene doesn't even look surprised. Instead, she looks kind of mad.

"What did they do to you?" she asks.

"I . . . they didn't do anything. I kind of did this to myself. I saw them and I just wigged out."

"So they didn't hurt you."

"I don't think they even saw me. But I sure saw them."

I can see her relax. It's funny, I keep forgetting how she can slip into this Mother Bear mode. It usually only happens when someone's being mean to me at school, and even then I think I'm the only one that sees it. She's so determined not to make waves.

"I don't understand," she says. "You're the one who's been telling me to keep an open mind about them."

Just talking is making me feel more like myself, even talking about all of this. I guess it's true: people can get used to anything.

"Yeah, it's weird, isn't it?" I say. "You're all calm, and I'm totally freaked." I give her a closer look. "*Why* are you all calm?"

She shrugs. "I don't know. It's just . . . Pelly, I guess. He used to be real to me, and now I guess he really is real." She grins. "And isn't that being articulate?"

"Which one was Pelly?"

"How could you miss him? He was the tall one that was talking to me by the bed."

"I never saw him. I lost it when that whole gang of fairies went out the window."

So she tells me what he had to say, and that brings my nervousness back again, only this time I'm trying to see past her into the shadows. Because I totally buy into the danger. After all, I've seen the fairies.

"So what do we do?" I ask, hoping she doesn't have some mad plan to go confront the danger head-on.

But she only gives me another shrug.

"I don't know," she says. "I have to think about it. Do some research."

"What kind of research?"

"Well, now that we know they're real, it's time to find out what can hurt them." I guess she sees something in my face because she quickly adds, "Just to get them off our case."

And that makes me feel weird all over again. Because she's right. Now I'm a part of this, too. What happened to me tonight has put me with her right out here on the edge of how the world's supposed to be.

I just wish I felt as brave as she seems to be.

NOW: *Imogene*

Maxine's too nervous to go to sleep until I finally convince her that we're safe enough for now because Pelly's drawn off whatever nasty beasties might have been lurking in the shadows. I know it's not exactly true, but I don't *feel* a presence in the dark corners of my room—malevolent or otherwise—and she can't argue with me because she never really heard the conversation I had with him. Anyway, there's nothing we can do about it right now, and she needs her sleep because she's getting way too worked up.

We talk a little more, her voice getting sleepier and sleepier, until she drifts off, and then it's only me who's still awake, and I'm only up because my brain's too busy, not because I'm worried about the shadows.

I sit with my back against the headboard, Maxine stretched out beside me, and try to think of where to start. I know I have to go into serious research mode, but how do you seriously research something that everybody else thinks is make-believe?

I fall asleep like that, still sitting up, and have the worst crick in my neck when I wake up the next morning.

* * *

I decided that it was pointless to ask any adults for help,

mostly because the few in my life aren't exactly poster people for this kind of problem. I mean, my teachers are right out—I can just imagine the looks I'd get—and ditto with Maxine's mother. My dad would probably have all kinds of advice, but the trouble with him is it'd be coming to me through a veil of whatever he's smoking today, and while that can be funny, it's not particularly useful. Mom would be better, but she has no interest in mythology or fairy tales beyond how she can co-opt them into some anti-corporate, the-patriarchy-sucks rant that has nothing to do with my problem.

There's always Christy Riddell, of course. Maxine said he was the first person we should talk to about this, but I find myself wanting to use him as a last resort, if at all. I don't know why. He seems smart and kind and level-headed and . . . well, if I'm going to be honest, more interested in the anthropological listings of strange creatures and their habits than in helping anyone get them *out* of their life. And I feel that I'm more likely to end up as a case study in a book than actually have my problem solved.

But last night I murmured a halfhearted agreement with Maxine about contacting him, and repeat it this morning, though first, I tell her, I want to do a little research on my own.

"But he can probably tell us everything we need to know," she says, "right off the top of his head."

"I know. I just need to figure some stuff out . . . you know, with Pelly and Adrian and everything. This is pretty complicated."

"I guess."

"And if I haven't got what I need by the end of the day, we'll try to get in to see him."

"I just don't understand why we wouldn't go see him first."

"I'm not so comfortable with that," I have to tell her.

"But why not? He's the expert."

"He's the expert on writing this kind of thing up and then sticking it in a book. I can't believe we already told him as much as we did."

"He said he'd change our names."

"That's not the point," I say. "It's still our story, not his. Maybe we don't want it in a book, even with the names changed. At least I don't."

"We could ask him to not use it."

I nod, though I didn't get the sense that Christy was the sort of person who'd let a good story go.

"I just want to try a couple of other things first," I say. I stand up from the bed to go downstairs, then turn to look at her from the doorway. "You know, I can't count the weird shit on one hand anymore. Ghosts, fairies, imaginary childhood companions, these things in the shadows. . . . Do you see where all of this is going?"

Maxine shakes her head.

"Neither do I," I say. "I just know it's out of control."

Then I go downstairs.

* * *

Before Maxine and I leave for school, I ask Mom to write a note for me excusing me from classes for the morning. We're alone in the kitchen at the time. Jared's still catching the last possible moments of sleep before he has to get up, while Maxine's taking a shower.

"A note," Mom says with this odd look on her face.

I nod. "I need to do some research in the school library and maybe at the Crowsea Public Library."

But then I realize what the look on her face is all about. She's thinking, When has this wild child of hers ever asked for permission to skip school?

"You know, Imogene," she says, "I couldn't be happier about last year's grades and your new dedication to learning and school and fitting in, but I have to ask: are you doing this for yourself—because it's what *you* want—or to please me or somebody else? Because you know I'll support you in whatever you choose to do with your life."

I can't imagine anyone else's parents coming out with that kind of thing—for sure not Maxine's mother—but Mom's always been big on treating Jared and me as individuals. She insists that we talk stuff through—and let me tell you, we had a lot of talks back in Tyson—but the weird thing is, she really doesn't judge. She'll point out what's against the law, what's morally wrong, where she thinks we're making mistakes with our life choices and why, but she also supports us one hundred percent, even when we're doing things that other parents might frown at. Like when Jared and I started our junk business. Or my skipping school the way I used to—"I'm learning more on the street," I used to tell her. Yeah, like how to be a complete loser. But it didn't seem like that at the time.

Still, I understand her question. I guess she thinks I'm doing this for Maxine, which maybe in part I am, but only because Maxine's shown me that it's not such a bad thing to do well. Truth is, my going feral in Tyson had more to do with me trying to please Frankie and his gang than it had to do with me. I don't know that this new improved me is the real me either, but at least she's not in trouble all the time. It's kind of a relief to not have to deal with the constant fallout of my life. Though now I've got a whole new set of problems to deal with.

I don't get into any of that with Mom.

"I think I'm doing it for me," I say instead. "At least it feels like it."

She smiles. "Well, just remember. Do what you have to do, only—"

"Don't hurt anybody else while you're doing it," I finish for her.

"While you're doing what?" Maxine asks, coming into the kitchen on the tail end of our conversation.

She has a towel wrapped around her head, which makes her look wonderfully exotic.

"Whatever it is that you do," I tell her.

"Who wants breakfast?" Mom asks.

* * *

At school, armed with my mother's note, I leave Maxine and head for the library. There's really not much there, so I grab my jacket from my locker and walk over to the Crowsea Public Library, where I have the opposite problem. Here there are shelves upon shelves of books on fairy tales, myths, and folklore. I stand in front of them for a long moment, reading the titles on the spines, not knowing where to start. And of course I'm painfully aware of Christy in his office, although hopefully he's not aware of me.

After a while I go to the main desk and see that the nice woman is there again today. She has the look of actresses you see in movies made from books by old dead English writers—auburn hair pulled back in a loose bun, a peaches-and-cream complexion, a lightness in her body that makes her seem frail and strong at the same time. She's my mom's age, like in her thirties, but, also like my mom, she doesn't seem as old as, well, you know, old people usually are.

"Excuse me, Ms.," I say.

She looks up and smiles. "I remember you. Are you here to see Christy again?"

I shake my head. "I'm doing some research and I'm kind of at a loss as to where to begin."

"What's your project about?"

"You know how in the old days people used to believe in fairies and stuff like that? I'm looking into how they'd protect themselves from the fairies, but I don't really know what book to start with. There's just so many fairy-tale books on your shelves."

"It's not just in the old days," she says.

"What do you mean?"

"There are still people who believe in fairies."

Oh, great, I think. And you're going to be one of them. Though maybe that won't be so bad. Maybe that means she'll know exactly where to steer me.

"Um, right," I say.

"But between you and me," she says, "though it's sweet, it doesn't really make much sense if you stop and think about it."

"Why not?" I find myself saying, even though up to a day or so ago I would have been in total agreement with her.

"Well, think about it. If there were such things as fairies, don't you think we'd *know* for sure by now? News travels instantly, from all over the world. If there was proof anywhere, wouldn't the news services be all over it in an instant?"

"I guess."

"But that doesn't stop people from believing."

I nod. "And so for the people who do believe, what do they use to protect themselves. Or what did they use?"

"I'm not sure. But you won't find the answer in fairy-tale books. You have to look past the fiction into fairy folklore, and we have any number of books on the subject."

She does something on her computer, fingers tapping the keyboard with enviable speed.

The printer hums from somewhere below the desk. When she bends down to get at it, head turned slightly, I catch a glimpse of a tattoo on the back of her neck. It's a small fish, in blue and black ink. It's funny, but I just never thought of librarians as having tattoos.

"Here we go," she says, straightening up. She hands me a sheet of paper filled with book titles. "This should give you a start. They're up on the second floor in the reference section."

"Thanks."

"Do you want me to show you?"

"No, that's okay."

"My name's Hilary," she says. "If you need a hand with anything else, don't hesitate to ask me."

"I won't. Thanks again."

So back upstairs I go, this time armed with a reference sheet. I track down the first few books on the list Hilary printed up for me and take them over to a chair and start to read.

NOW: *Adrian*

I spend the day haunting the halls of Redding High, trying to decide whom I'm going to offer up to the soul-eaters in place of Imogene. It ought to be easy, but there are so many people I don't like in this place, so many who think they're better than everybody else, or who rag on people who aren't cool or popular. Or both. And even the ones who aren't strong enough to be bullies . . . I don't doubt that, given the chance, they wouldn't be any different from the jerks who are making their lives miserable right now.

I know I would have. I wouldn't have picked on the kids

weaker than me, but the bullies . . . they're a whole other matter. I'd still like to give them a taste of what they did.

It kind of makes me glad that I'm not alive, because I find that, in general, I don't much like people anymore. The faces are mostly different from when I went here, but they might as well be the same kids and teachers. Truth is, except for the fact that I'm dead, nothing's really changed. Because now I'm avoiding the fairies, and with Imogene mad at me, I'm still just wandering these halls totally on my own.

Always being the guy no one likes really sucks.

But at least I can't be hurt anymore. Or at least not physically hurt, since I don't have a body. But I do have a big ache in my heart because of how things are going with Imogene. Not that they were actually going anywhere before this. Let's face it, I'm dead and she's not, and that doesn't leave a whole lot of room for a relationship. But at least she used to come talk to me. Or she'd wink at me when she passed me in the halls. Today she left school right after homeroom, and I knew it had to be because of me.

I guess I don't blame her. She's obviously upset by these dreams that Tommery's sending her. She'd totally lose it if she knew about the soul-eaters. Not that getting mad at me is going to do her any good.

I wish I'd kept my mouth shut instead of getting Tommery to work on making her see that he and the rest of the fairies are real.

What difference does it make if she doesn't believe me? At least before this she was still talking to me.

I find myself drifting into the cafeteria. A noisy table by

the windows catches my attention. It's Brent Calder and his buddies, laughing at some kid Jerry Fielder tripped. The kid's on the floor and trying not to cry, his lunch spilled all over his pants and the tiles around him.

I guess I knew all along whom I'd choose—I mean, it's so obvious. Who better than the jerk who gave Imogene such a hard time when I first saw her?

Calder's not so different from Eric Woodrow, who'd made it his own personal crusade to ensure that my life was as miserable as it could be back when I was at Redding. Guys like that deserve to have their souls eaten.

I leave the cafeteria so that I don't have to watch the kid on the floor and his misery.

All I have to do now is figure out how to divert the soul-eaters' attention from Imogene to Calder.

NOW: *Imogene*

I check for fairies when I get back to the school—remembering what Pelly told me last night about how I was supposed to be able to see them now—but everything's the same: the usual gangs of kids in the halls, the odd solitary teacher looking harried or grumpy. It's got to be a tough and thankless gig, and I wonder, not for the first time, why they take it on.

But no fairies. No ghost either, for that matter.

Then I try what I'd read in one of the library's books, about how you can see magical creatures more easily from the corner of your eye. When I give that a shot, sure enough, there they are. It's not like I can suddenly see packs of them, running around the halls; just occasional glimpses of strange little men with Rasta hair and raggedy clothes. It's not much, but it's enough to let me know that they're really here.

I pretend not to have seen anything, and I don't mention it to Maxine either. I simply go to my last couple of classes, then take Maxine to one of the cafés on Williamson Street. I figure we need to have our war council in a public place, somewhere busy enough that the fairies won't be around. I check from the corners of my eyes as we place our orders, then carry our drinks to the table, but we seem to be in a fairy-free zone.

"Okay," I say once we're sitting down, "the first thing is we're not supposed to call them 'fairies.' Apparently it ticks them off, so we need to refer to them as 'the Little People' or 'the Good Neighbors' from now on."

Maxine nods. "I've read that."

"And when you do talk about them, you're supposed to start off saying 'Today is'—and you stick in whatever the day of the week is—'and the fairies won't hear us,' which frankly I find confusing, because what does it matter what day of the week it is? And you're using the no-no word at the same time."

"That's a new one for me. Where'd you get that?"

I look at my notes, but I didn't mark down what books I got what from, and there's nothing else there to clue me in.

"I don't remember," I say. "Actually, a lot of this is confusing. Supposedly iron wards them off, but the ones that have taken up living in urban centers have developed an immunity to it. Which begs the question, why haven't they developed immunity to any of the other stuff that's been around for as long or longer?"

"Like what?"

I consult my notes. "Wearing your clothes inside out. Carrying bread when you go out—supposedly they'll take it instead of a person, or it can be used to bribe them or something. And it can scare them off if the bread's been blessed or looks like a host."

"You mean like the wafers they use in Mass?"

I shrug. "I guess. I'm not a Catholic."

"Me, neither. It just seems that a loaf of bread would be a lot bigger than a host."

"Whatever. Also, if it's got salt in it, that can also ward them off because apparently they don't like salt." I look back at my notes. "You can also carry coins to give them."

Maxine giggles. "What? They're also panhandlers?"

I smile with her. "Apparently. Oh, and to finish with the salt—when you've been in contact with fairies, drinking some salt water can help break their hold on you."

"Yuck."

"Well, yeah. Then there's throwing a stone when you think there are fairies around."

"You mean like at them?"

I shake my head. "No, you throw the stone and then ask the wind to drive them away."

"Weird."

"Everything about this is weird. Anyway, leaving food out for them gets you on their good side. Milk or cream and sweet stuff like honey or molasses or cakes cooked without salt in them, only don't scrimp on the sugar. You're supposed to avoid fairy paths—"

"What do they look like?"

"I don't know. None of the books said. I guess you're just supposed to know. You're also not supposed to whistle or hum, because music draws them. So does wearing the color red."

"That knotwork tattoo on the small of your back has a lot of red in it."

I nod. "But if I wear a shirt and tuck it in, they won't see it, right? I think you're just not supposed to be obvious about the red."

"I suppose. Is there a color that they don't like?"

"Blue."

"Maybe you should dye your hair again, like you did this summer."

I smile. "But it was a little unclear, in the book where I found that anti-blue reference, if it meant fairies or some other kind of spirit. And I couldn't find a mention of it anywhere else. A lot of the material is like that, actually—in one text, but not in another. And then there's all this religious stuff that I don't get, because haven't fairies been around since forever, while Christianity's just a couple of thousand years old?"

"Not if you believe that God created the world in the first place. He'd have always been around; it's just the religions that would have changed."

"I suppose."

"So what's the religious stuff?" she asks.

"Making the sign of the cross or putting a cross in your window. Also calling on God or Jesus or the saints. Some of the books say it drives them off; some say it just annoys them."

"You sure you didn't stray into vampire research?"

"Ha-ha. There's a bunch more. Carrying oatmeal in your pocket when you go out at night, preferably with some salt in it."

"Cooked or just the oat flakes?"

"Uncooked, I assume. Twigs of rowan are also good—do we even *have* rowan trees growing around here?"

"It's another name for the mountain ash."

"Oh, right." I look back at my notes again. "And there was something in one book about sprinkling stale 'urin' on your house's doors and windows to ward them off."

"You mean pee? Like dogs marking their territory?"

"I don't know. It was spelled U-R-I-N, and I couldn't find another reference to it."

"Gross."

"I know. Coals are also good, or throwing a handful of embers from a fire, though how you're supposed to pick up a handful, it didn't say."

Maxine smiles. "I'm sure they mean with a little shovel or something—like the kind people use to scoop up ashes."

"I knew that." I set my notes aside and look at her. "So how does this relate to the stuff you know from the stories you read?"

She shrugs. "A lot of what you've dug up is totally new to me."

"And complicated," I say. "Plus there was nothing much in anything I read about actually bringing the battle to them."

"It's not a war, Imogene."

"No? It seems like that to me. And if these creatures in the shadows can suck away our souls, I'd rather deal with them once and for all than wander around forever with my clothes inside out and my pockets full of oatmeal and bread or whatever."

"Did you talk to Christy while you were at the library?" she asks.

I shake my head. "I didn't need to. That woman with the British accent at the front desk—her name's Hilary—she helped me track down everything I needed."

"So what do we do with all this stuff we've learned?"

I smile. "I was hoping you'd tell me."

"So you have no plan."

"Oh, I have a plan. I just don't know how to implement it. I think the next thing we need to do is bring all of this"—I tap my notes—"to Pelly and get his input."

"I don't know that I can sleep over again."

"That's okay. We'll come to you."

She just looks at me for a long moment, then says, "How are you going to do that?"

I grin back at her. "Magic."

* * *

We talk a little more, but all we're doing is going over the same ground. When we realize that neither of us has anything new to add, Maxine takes off to where Jared's band is rehearsing, and I go to the record store to see Thomas.

The after-school/after-work rush is over and he's alone in the store, sitting behind the counter reading the latest issue of *Mojo*, which is like his bible. I stand outside for a few moments and watch him through the window. He really is pretty much the coolest guy I've ever gone out with, and for sure the nicest. He's only a year older than me, which makes him Jared's age; not too tall, though he's still tallish beside me, with dreamy pale-green eyes, scruffy brown hair, and the sweetest smile.

When I come in, I see he's listening to the Streets, which is really just this one guy, not a band. Jared hates the album, but Thomas likes it. I do, too. I think it's the cadence of the singer's half-spoken vocals over these hypnotic rhythms.

Thomas grins when he looks up and sees me, then leans across the counter to give me a kiss.

"So how was school?" he asks.

"I skipped most of my classes and was at the library doing some research."

His eyebrows go up—this is how my Mr. Cool asks a question.

"You're Irish, right?" I say.

"Not really. I'm third generation, born and bred in Newford."

"But did your parents or anybody else in your family ever talk about life back in Ireland—you know, the customs and stuff?"

"You're doing a paper on Ireland?"

"Not really . . . It's just . . . what do you know about the Good Neighbors?"

He leans forward on the counter and gives me that smile of his, just a little crooked, dimple in one cheek, a twinkle in his eyes. Definitely meltworthy.

"Now what makes you call them that?" he asks.

I shrug. "I just heard that they don't like to be called by name."

"It's a funny thing, isn't it?" he says. "Everybody talks about fairies now. You've got your T-shirts and jewelry and tats and lord knows how many books on everything from their supposed living habits to how you can call them into your life to help you with your problems."

"I never thought about it like that."

"Oh, sure. It's fairy this and fairy that. We've even got CDs that are 'inspired' by the fairies, for god's sake. But it wasn't always like that. The way my grandparents told it, the one thing you didn't ever want was to get their attention. If you did, you made sure you treated them with great respect. And you never show your fear."

"Like with a dog," I say.

He smiles. "That's one way of looking at it. Only fairies are far more dangerous than any dog."

"Do you believe that?"

"What? In fairies, or that they're dangerous?"

"Both, I guess."

"So you're researching fairies?"

I give a nervous look around the store, checking things out from the corners of my eyes.

"You keep saying the word," I say. "I thought you weren't supposed to call them that."

He cocks his head and gets this teasing grin. "You know, I never took you for one of those girls who goes for fairies."

"I don't go for them," I tell him. "And the less I have to do with them, the better. But I don't really have much choice."

I stifle a groan. That just slipped out, and now he's going to think I'm a complete flake.

"But you're writing a paper on them," he says.

Well, I'm in this far, there's no point in holding back now. Besides, I really *like* Thomas. I might omit certain details about my life when I'm talking to him—just as I do with Maxine—but I try not to lie to him. I try not to lie to Maxine either. So far it's only been a couple of times. One day I'm going to have to tell her everything, but I'm dreading it because I'm pretty sure once she really knows what I was like, the stuff I've done, she won't like me anymore.

"It's not for a term paper," I say. "I'm trying to get them out of my life."

"Fairies."

"Mm-hmm."

"Real fairies."

"*Yes,* already."

"And you want to get them out of your life."

"Go ahead. Have a laugh."

But he doesn't laugh.

"Fairy trouble isn't any laughing matter," he says.

What, has *everybody* in the world always been a true believer except for me?

"Do you really know about this stuff?" I find myself asking.

"Only the stories I heard growing up."

He motions for me to come around the counter and sit on the tall wooden stool he's not using. He leans with his back against the counter, propped on his elbows.

"So what's going on?" he asks.

When he puts it as directly as that, I have to tell him. I start with Ghost and take it all the way through to last night. He shakes his head as I finish up, but not, I discover, because he doesn't believe me.

"Let me get this straight," he says. "On one side you've got the ghost of a dead kid, some bad-ass fairies, and some *really* bad-ass spirits that feed on people's souls. On the other there's you and Maxine and your imaginary childhood friend."

"Pelly. Who turns out to be not so imaginary."

"I don't like the odds."

"*You* don't like them? Try being in my shoes."

He gives me that smile he uses when he thinks I need to be cheered up.

"I couldn't," he says. "They're way too tiny for these big feet of mine."

"Ha-ha."

He reaches out and brushes his fingers along my cheek. "It's just . . . I'm worried, Imogene."

I know he is. What I can't figure out is . . .

"How come you believe me?" I ask.

"Why would you lie to me?"

"I wouldn't. But really, this is like totally stretching credulity, isn't it?"

"I suppose. Except I've had my own experience with the fairy world."

"You *have*?"

He nods. "I was just a kid, maybe ten or eleven; I can't really remember. It was the night my uncle died. I was lying in bed and I heard this wailing outside the house, so I got up out of my bed to see what it was. I thought it was, you know, a car alarm or something, but when I opened my curtains, there was this . . . " He shakes his head. "I don't even know how to describe it. This *thing* was hanging in the air outside my window, two stories up, with its face pressed up against the windowpanes. It looked like a corpse, skin as white as bone, with hair like snakes, and a mouth that almost seemed to split its face in two. And seriously deranged eyes."

"What . . . what did you do?"

"Screamed and fell to the floor, which is where my

parents found me when they came bursting in a moment later. Turns out what I saw was a banshee. It comes to a house and does its wailing thing when a relative is going to die."

"You parents told you that?"

He shakes his head. "My granny did. She saw it, too, at her house, the same night. The next day we found out that my uncle—her son—had died."

"So how come just the two of you saw it?"

"Granny says it's because we both have the Sight."

"You can see fairies?" I ask.

"I guess, but I've only seen the one, and that was plenty. Granny's seen others."

Neither of us say anything for a long moment. The CD's ended and it's quiet in the store. No customers. Outside I can see people walking by, cars and buses on the street, but it's like we're in this little pocket of silence, this totally quiet place that's somewhere *outside* the world.

"How come you never told me about that before?" I ask.

"How come you never told me about Pelly and the rest of it?"

"Because it'd make me seem like a total idiot."

"Same deal for me," he says.

"Oh."

"Though the truth is, I haven't even really thought about that night in a long time. It's not the kind of thing you dwell on, you know?"

"So you never saw it again?"

He shakes his head. "I don't ever *want* to see it again.

Uncle Sean's the only close relative I've lost. I'm hoping everybody else sticks around for as long as possible."

He has this sad look, and I feel bad for ever having brought any of this up and making him remember. I reach out and take his hand, give it a squeeze. He smiles back—not a big smile, but it's real.

"I'm going to talk to Granny after I finish up here tonight," he says. "See what she can tell me. Do you want to come?"

I nod. "But I should get home. I need to see Pelly."

"I don't like you being on your own with those *things* out there."

"I'll be okay. I'll call you on your cell if things get weird."

"Promise?"

"I promise."

Then I give him a big kiss and reluctantly head off for home.

NOW: *Adrian*

John Narraway told me how to get in touch with him if I ever changed my mind and was ready to move on. I still haven't changed my mind, but I hope he won't realize that until he's already come to me. And that when he comes, he'll at least hear me out.

I leave the school, duck into one of those old carriage lanes that run behind the tenements in this part of town, and call for him. "Stay in one place and call my name three times," he told me, "and I will find you no matter where you are."

So I call his name now. Once. Twice. Three times.

I know he's getting close when the sounds around me start to mute and all the color drains out of everything. Red brick goes to gray. Yellow and green garbage bins gray as well. When I look to where the lane begins, there's no longer any traffic on the cross street, vehicular or pedestrian. The silence becomes absolute until I hear the footsteps approaching from behind me. I turn to see John, fiddle case in hand. He slowly shakes his head as he gets near.

"Why do I know you're simply taking advantage of my good nature?" he says.

"I just need to ask you something," I tell him. "It's not a big deal." And then I throw him a bone. "If I can get this thing done, I think I might be ready to move on."

We both know that's not going to happen, but people like John live on the hope that everyone will come to their senses, eventually. That anyone can change.

"What do you need to know?" he asks.

"These soul-eaters you were telling me about . . . "

He nods. "The *anamithim*. What about them?"

"I need to know how I can switch their attention from one person to another."

He gives me a look that it takes me a moment to recognize. Then I realize it's respect.

"You'd be willing to sacrifice yourself for your friend?" he asks.

I feel small. I hadn't even considered that. I still can't consider it. I don't have much, but I died too young. I'm not ready to give up even this semblance of living that I have.

"Actually," I have to tell him, "I was thinking more of one of the bullies at my school."

I'm prepared for the way his face goes, this mix of sad and angry. He thinks I'm a coward. I *am* a coward, always have been. Death didn't change that.

"I've already told you," he says, his voice cool. "Once someone's brought to their attention, they don't forget."

"But it's just the soul they're after, isn't it? Does it matter whose?"

"Of course it matters."

"None of this was Imogene's fault."

"We both know that," John says. "But it's too late to do anything about it now. And besides, who made you judge and jury?"

I have to laugh. "This coming from you?"

"I don't judge," John says. "I'm just here to help souls move on. Whether they do or don't is their choice."

"There are a lot of people who deserve to meet the soul-eaters. Like Brent Calder."

"Sorry, I don't know the name."

"He's the current big-shot bully at my school."

"See," John says, "there's part of your problem right there. You don't have a school anymore. You're dead."

"Whatever. It still doesn't change the fact that Brent deserves this way more than Imogene."

"Because he's such a terrible person?"

I nod.

"How do you know he can't be redeemed? How do you know that he won't change his ways and perhaps make some great contribution to the world?"

"How do you know Imogene wouldn't?"

"We don't," John says. "But it's already too late for her."

"Do you have to keep harping on that?"

"Apparently, since it doesn't seem to stick with you."

I bite back the sharp retort forming in my mind and change tack. Because something occurs to me.

"Okay," I say. "I get what you're saying. I can't swap Imogene for Brent, or probably anyone else, right?"

John nods. "I'm sorry, Adrian. This isn't something designed to frustrate you personally. It's just the way it is."

"But what if I want to give myself up in her place?" I ask. "Is that doable?"

I can see the answer in his eyes before he speaks.

"You know what that means, right?"

I nod. "I just . . . stop."

"Forever. Whatever comes next, you don't get to find out."

"I know. Just tell me, is it possible?"

What I remembered was the look of respect he had for me when he first thought this was what I wanted to do. Something about that look, and the way he's regarding me now, tells me it *is* possible. Not that I've actually got the guts to do it. But I figure, if there's a way to put myself in Imogene's place, then there might be a way to fix it that so that Brent gets taken instead.

"Yes," John says. "Supposedly it's possible."

It's obvious he's reluctant to tell me even that much.

"So how does it work?"

"Adrian, this isn't the way to—"

"How does it work?"

"Not easily. The problem is petitioning the *anamithim* before they simply eat your soul."

"And how do you do that?" I prompt when he doesn't go on.

"I've heard conflicting stories. The method that's supposed to work best has you offering them a loaf of unleavened bread that contains sugar but no salt. Like an Indian flatbread, I assume. You offer the loaf from within a circle that has been drawn with salt."

"Salt wards them off?"

"Among other things," John says. "But their patience is infinite. If you call them to you from that circle and don't give them what they want, they can wait for eternity for you to leave the circle. Or for the wind to blow a gap in it. Or rain to wash it away."

"Unless you did it indoors," I say, "except I guess it would get pretty boring sitting inside a circle for the rest of your days."

John nods.

"So that's it?" I ask. "You just offer them this loaf?"

"No," John says. "That's just to get their attention. I guess you'd call to them as well."

"And then when you have their attention . . . ?"

"You bargain with them."

"I don't get it," I say. "Why would that do anything?"

"They're big on respect," John says. "On receiving it and giving it. And the one thing they respect above all else is bravery and selflessness. For you to offer yourself to them in place of your friend would show both."

I nod slowly. "I guess . . . "

I'm trying to think how I can turn this around so that it's Brent they take instead of me. But then I realize something else.

"How do I get the loaf?" I say. "I can't touch anything. I couldn't even make the salt circle."

"I know," John says.

"But you can touch the physical world, right?"

"I won't be part of this," he tells me.

"But—"

He lifts his hand to stop me. "No. And don't call me again, Adrian. Not even if you change your mind about this and decide to go on like you should have done in the first place. Someone else can help you cross over."

He fades away before I can argue further. Color seeps back into my surroundings. I can hear the traffic on the street again, see people walking by on the sidewalk.

Imogene, I think.

I don't have any choice. I have to ask Imogene to get me

the bread and salt, to make the circle. Only how do I do that without having to explain everything else? How could it work without her totally hating me?

I think of the fairies then.

They owe me, but that won't make any difference to them. Maybe I can think of a way to trick them into helping me.

Yeah, I think as I start back to the school. Like that's something I could ever pull off.

NOW: *Imogene*

It's funny. Tonight's the first time in a long while that I'm not nervous about going to bed. I'm actually looking forward to that weird music and seeing Pelly. No, I'm *counting* on seeing him. But as soon as I start to drift off, the shadows pull loose from the corners of my room, and I jerk awake.

Being awake doesn't help.

The shadows are still too deep in the corners, their edges moving as though I've got a candle burning. But I don't have a candle and now I think I see things in the darkness. There's more than movement. I feel the weight of *something's* attention.

I remember what Thomas said about not showing fear.

Yeah, like *that's* going to happen.

My pulse is drumming a crazy tempo. I draw my legs up, arms wrapped around my legs, and back up against the headboard, comforter pulled to my chin like it's somehow going to protect me. I want to scream, but I'm not so panicked that I don't realize what that'll do. It'll bring Mom and Jared running in. I've already messed it up so that Maxine's part of this weird curse I've acquired, but I'll be damned if I drag anybody else into it.

Now I think I see eyes in the shadows. Slanted, kind of yellowish, with deep red-black centers. Like little fires. Like *hungry* fires. They flicker, marking me, then they're gone, only to reappear a moment later in another part of the shadows.

It's not fair. I'm *awake.*

But it doesn't matter anymore, does it? I'm on the edge now, straddling my world and Fairyland. I know . . . for real, for sure . . . that the fairies exist, and that knowledge makes me fair game for these things in the shadows.

I think of the space under my bed and wish I hadn't.

They must be under there, too. Creeping out from below my box spring.

"P-pelly," I manage. "This'd be a good time to show."

I've gone through the last few years of my life with a who-cares attitude, but right now I find I care very much.

That makes me think of Adrian, and I feel a surge of empathy for him, cut down so young. Another victim of these damn fairies.

I can see actual shapes in the shadows now, pulling free

from the darkness. Vague hairless heads with those burning eyes. Arms and torsos.

The scream I don't want to give in to is pushing up my throat. I almost let it go, but then I hear a faint sound of discordant music—my fairy orchestra starting up—and the closet door bangs open.

Pelly's there, holding a clenched fist high in the air. He bounds across the room and lands on the bed, then shakes his fist at me, opening his hand. Like in that slo-mo instant in a traffic accident, I see that he's throwing some kind of powder at me. It glistens and sparkles. I feel like I can see every granule. Then it lands on me and I breathe it in.

I cough, my eyes tearing.

I hear a low moan—from under the bed, from the deep recesses of the shadows.

A pressure I didn't realize I was feeling is suddenly gone.

They're gone.

I cough some more, clearing my throat. Relief flows in a wave over me, and I kind of collapse against the headboard. Pelly bends down closer to me.

"Imogene," he whispers. "Imogene?"

"I . . . I'm fine." The words are hard to get out. But after the first couple, it gets easier. "You got here just in the nick of time. Thanks."

"It was nothing."

"No, it was a big-time rescue. Another minute and they'd have had me for sure."

I can feel some strength returning to me and sit up straighter. Then I realize there's something wrong with my arm—with the skin of my arm, I mean. It doesn't seem the right color, but it's hard to tell with the faint light coming in through my window.

"Watch your eyes," I say, closing my own as I turn on my bedside light.

When I open them again, I see that my skin's blue. I hold up my other arm. It's blue, too.

I give Pelly a confused look, then get up on my knees and look at my reflection in the mirror on my dresser. Everything about me is blue—my skin, my hair . . .

"I'm sorry," Pelly says. "I didn't know it would have that effect."

"I'm blue." I turn from my reflection to look at him. "How can I be blue?"

"It must be from the pollen," he says.

"Pollen," I repeat.

He nods. "It comes from an herb called vervain. There's a special strain that grows in the Otherworld. It's a ward against the *anamithim*—that's what they're called, those creatures in the shadows. The soul-eaters."

"So we *can* fight them off."

He sits back on the comforter and gives me another nod. "But the warding effect is only temporary. It will wear off in a day or two."

"Wait a minute. Are you saying I'm going to be blue-skinned for the next couple of days?"

"I'm afraid so. Your hair, too."

"The hair I can live with. I dye it all the time. But how am I supposed to walk around with blue skin? What do I tell my mom? How can I go to school?"

Pelly starts to get such a miserable look that I shut up about it. After all, he did just save my life.

"I didn't know," he says. "They didn't say."

"Who's they?"

"I went to Hinterdale, deep in the Otherworld, to ask for advice. They have a huge library there with the answer to every question, supposedly, if you have the time to look. But those answers can take a lifetime to find."

"Luckily, it didn't take you a lifetime," I say.

"I never looked. There were some scholars there who told me about the vervain and where to find it, but it was deeper still away. They also told me of a shop in Mabon where I could trade for some, though they warned me it would be dear because it's very rare."

I'm trying to imagine libraries and shops in Fairyland—somehow I'd never considered the place to have either.

"What did you trade?" I ask.

"A week's worth of stories."

I give a low whistle, because that *is* a lot. Back in the day, when Pelly and I played together near the commune, he told me about how in some worlds, stories were more valuable than anything. Just imagine how many stories you would have to tell to fill up a whole week.

"Did you have that many?" I ask.

He shakes his head. "And I didn't have time to tell the ones I knew. But the woman in the shop was very nice and allowed me the credit after I gave her a sample. I told the one about the Clock Man who stole Jared's spare time."

I smile. "I told Maxine that one awhile ago."

"I didn't mean to use the pollen all at once the way I did," he says. "But when I saw so many of those shadowy creatures, closing in on you from all sides, I panicked."

"I was panicking, too. So I'm glad you did."

"Except now we have to start all over again. The woman gave me the last of the vervain pollen she had in her shop, and it's a very long and arduous journey to get any more."

"We'll think of something."

I look at my arm again, lift my gaze to the mirror. I feel like some cheesy extraterrestrial in a low-budget science fiction film where the best they could do was give the alien blue skin. And I *really* don't know how I'm going to show my face outside my room until the blue's all gone.

"It doesn't seem fair," I say, "that if magic is going to be real, it should be so malevolent."

"It's not," Pelly says. "Or not always. It's no different from your world—there's good and there's bad."

I shrugged. "I suppose. All I know is, I never heard about these shadow creatures before. In all the stories I read as a kid, there might be some evil magician or monster that the heroes had to put down, but just being aware of Fairyland didn't automatically make you a target for this kind of crap."

"It's not," Pelly tells me, beginning to sound like a broken record so far as I'm concerned. "You're in this situation because someone directed the attention of the *anamithim* onto you."

I know that, but it doesn't make it any easier.

"Well, we've been busy, too," I say. "We've got a whole

pile of info, but it has to wait until we go over to Maxine's. I told her we'd be over, and after what just happened here, I'm worried about her."

Pelly nods.

"Wait here a sec," I tell him.

I grab a handful of clothes and slip out of my room, down the hall to the bathroom. Pulling my T-shirt nightie over my head, I check myself in the mirror.

Yep. Blue all over.

I wonder why I'm not more freaked. Something like this should be wigging me right out, but all I can think of is the inconvenience of having blue skin. Truth is, if it wasn't for that, I'd kind of like it. It's sort of like having a full-body tat, with the extra bonus of it keeping me safe from the creepy crawlies waiting in the shadows. Maybe I could make like the blue skin was my new fashion statement, and wouldn't that get the Doll People going at school? Maybe I could take a bath in blue dye once this wore off.

I grin at my reflection. My teeth gleam superwhite against the blue of my skin. I turn to look at my knotwork tat, and the red in it's gone purple.

Whatever.

I get dressed and go back to my room.

"Are you ready?" I ask, stepping over to the window.

"I've a quicker way," Pelly says.

He motions to the closet. As soon as he does, I realize that of course there's got to be some kind of portal or gate in there, because I never see him or the fairy orchestra when I look in. They've got to go somewhere when they're not here.

"How very *The Lion, the Witch, and the Wardrobe* of you," I say.

"Oh, yes. Just call me Aslan."

"I was thinking more of Puddleglum."

He fakes a heavy sigh. "Always the sidekick. Except tonight, I lead the way. Coming?"

I follow him into the closet, which is totally familiar territory. I mean, I'm in here all the time, messing with my clothes, rummaging through my storage boxes. Except tonight when we push through my clothes and step over the boxes, there's another door that's normally not there. I'm wondering how this works, but he just opens the other door and we're looking at Maxine's perfectly organized dresses and skirts. No wonder little kids think there are monsters in their closets. These are obviously such handy routes, I'm guessing the fairy folk use them all the time.

"Can you show me how to do this?" I ask.

Pelly nods. "I can teach you to see the doors. It'll depend on the strength of your will whether or not they will open for you. And you have to be careful. Always keep your destination firmly in mind. If you don't, you could end up in some unpleasant place."

When we cross over, pushing through the clothes, I feel this weird tingle on every inch of my body, here for a flash, then gone. A moment later we're opening the outer door of the closet and stepping into Maxine's room. That's when I realize that this is a big mistake, that we should have warned her, because when Maxine looks up from where she's reading in bed, she lets out this god-awful shriek.

I don't blame her. She thinks she's alone in her room, but then the closet door opens and out comes her best friend in her new blue skin along with the fairy man who made her faint last night. Of course she'd panic.

"Don't freak," I say. "It's really just me."

But then we all hear her mother's footsteps running in the hall outside the bedroom.

Pelly and I fade back into the closet and close the door behind us just as the bedroom door opens and Maxine's mother bursts in.

"Maxine," she cries. "What happened?"

I can't see Maxine's face, but I'm sure it's gone red.

"I . . . I . . . " we hear her say. Then she gives a nervous laugh. "God, I feel so stupid. I caught my reflection in the mirror and for some reason I thought there was someone in the room with me."

Nice save, I think.

Better yet, her mother totally buys it.

There's some more conversation, with her mom asking her if she's really okay, and Maxine assuring her she is. Finally, Ms. Tattrie leaves, but Pelly and I stay in the closet. We hear Maxine get up from the bed, then the closet door opens, and we're both blinking in the bright light that comes in.

"Is . . . is that really you?" Maxine whispers.

I push the dresses aside again and step into the light. Maxine's eyes go big as she takes in my new look, but she doesn't scream. She doesn't faint, either, when Pelly comes out behind me.

"Yeah, it's really me," I tell her, keeping my own voice

low. "Sorry about that. I never thought how it'd be for you when we suddenly come waltzing out of your closet."

"What *happened* to you?"

"Vervain pollen," Pelly says. "I used too much. Though maybe the smallest amount would have had the same effect. No one told me."

Maxine looks at him, then back at me, her confusion still plain.

"We had a bit of an incident with the things in the shadows," I tell her. "This pollen Pelly's talking about drove them off and turned me blue. What do you think?" I did a little pirouette. "I kind of like it."

"Is it . . . permanent?"

I shake my head. "It'll only last a couple of days."

"You won't be able to go *anywhere.*"

"Not even clubbing?"

"Don't joke."

"All she does is joke," Pelly says.

He's sitting by her desk, staring with fascination at Maxine's screensaver, which makes it look like you've got a fish tank instead of a monitor.

"I can be serious," I say.

I pull Maxine down on the bed beside me, then run over my day's research for Pelly's benefit.

"So are you a fairy, too," I ask him when I'm done, "or something else?"

"Something else, though I don't know what. I just know that none of those things you mentioned are troublesome to me."

I sigh. "We're not looking for troublesome. We're looking for something to shut them down, period, end of story."

"Stories never end," Pelly says.

"I didn't mean it literally."

"But you *are* being very fierce about it," Maxine says.

She's been quiet for a while now. I don't know if it's because of my blue skin, Pelly's presence, or the fact that all of this is real and it's finally sinking in that we really aren't safe anymore.

"We have to be," I say.

"But we're just kids."

Now would be a time I could tell her a little bit more about my life in Tyson, about how being a kid didn't mean that you couldn't stand up for yourself. Nobody in Frankie's gang was much older than we are now. I'd been the baby of the group and even I could hold my own.

But I don't want to go there.

"You don't have to worry," Pelly says. "I've already told you, you're safe for now."

"Until the pollen magic wears off," I say. "And what about Maxine and you?"

Pelly glances at Maxine. "I don't think they've paid particular attention to Maxine yet. As for me, there are certain rules of honor that apply. They can't do anything to me unless I swear fealty to them and then break my oath."

"So they don't just automatically eat your soul?"

"I'm like a fairy in that sense—I don't have a soul."

Maxine nods. "I've read about that, how fairies don't have souls. I always thought it was weird."

"Of course it's weird," I say. "Everybody has a soul." I turn to Pelly. "And that means you, too."

"I'm not so sure of that," he says. "What does it feel like?"

"Having a soul?" I look at Maxine, but she only shrugs. "I don't know," I tell Pelly. "I don't have anything to compare it to—you know, what not having a soul would feel like."

We all fall into a kind of awkward silence. I don't know about the others, but I'm working on what a soul is and not coming up with a whole lot. I mean, I just always thought of it as me—what I feel like being me. But surely Pelly feels like he's himself, so that means he's got a soul, right? But if that's not your soul, then what is?

It's weird and not something you really think about, is it?

"So anyway," I finally say. "That's what we've got so far." I look at Pelly. "So is there really no way we can get some more of this vervain pollen?"

He shakes his head.

"Okay," I say. "So I guess we load up on all this other stuff—the oatmeal and salt and everything—and face them down."

Maxine and Pelly could be twins from the identical looks on their faces.

"No, it's too dangerous," Pelly says.

"Ditto," Maxine adds.

"I'm not hanging around until they come to me," I tell them.

"Who says we can't?" Maxine asks. "Until we get an actual plan, I vote to lay low."

"No offense," I say, "but that's the same kind of thinking that lets the Doll People rag on us every day."

"And we don't do anything to stop that, do we?"

I shake my head. "But not because we can't."

"What's that supposed to mean?"

I wait a beat, then realize this is the time I have to tell her. Not everything, but enough so that she understands.

"The only reason I don't give as good as we get," I say, "is because I'm trying to stay out of trouble these days. But it's not like it's anything I'm a stranger to."

"But—"

"Back at my old school . . . I didn't just get detentions because of skipping class or mouthing off. I got them for fighting. People only ragged on me once. After that, they were either hurting too bad, or they decided they should try picking on an easier mark."

"How . . . how did you do that?"

I know what she's thinking. I'm just this skinny little thing who looks like any good gust of wind could blow her over.

"I ran with a rough crowd," I tell her. "I carried a roll of pennies so that when I hit someone, they really felt it. I know the best ways to take somebody down, even if they're bigger than me. I had a knife that I wasn't afraid to use." I sigh at the shocked look on her face. "I wasn't a nice kid, Maxine. I wasn't anybody you'd ever like."

"Except I *do* like you."

"Yeah, because I'm trying to be normal."

For some reason that makes her laugh.

"What?" I ask.

She shakes her head. "You and *normal* don't really fit in the same sentence."

"Whatever. You know what I mean."

"No, I don't. I only know the you you've been since we've met, and I like her. And I know I'm a better person because of knowing you."

"Yeah, well, that goes big-time for me when it comes to you."

"Really?"

"Of course, really."

For a long moment she just looks at me, like she's seeing me for the first time. I realize that maybe I should have told her sooner. I just assumed she knew that she'd been as much of an influence on me as I might have been on her.

"That doesn't change anything," she says. "This is still too dangerous a situation."

"It's not going away."

"I know, but . . . what about Thomas? You said he was going to talk to his grandmother."

I glance at her bedside clock. "It's too late to call him now."

"So can't we at least wait until you *have* talked to him?"

I want to say, What's with the "we"? because I'm certainly not dragging her into this any more than she already is. When it comes time to confront the soul-eaters, I'm planning to go solo.

But she's right about waiting to talk to Thomas. All we have is bits and pieces. Maybe they fit together and we just can't see it, or maybe something Thomas finds out will help us put it all together.

"Okay," I tell her. "We wait until we've talked to Thomas."

I can see Pelly visibly relax.

"So what are you going to do about your blue skin?" Maxine asks.

NOW: *Maxine*

I wait for a long moment after Imogene and Pelly step back into my closet and close the door behind them before I get up from the bed and open the door again. My clothes hang there just like they always do, and when I push them aside, there's no door in the wall behind them. There *is* a new smell, a faint whiff of I'm not sure what, exactly. Something . . . *other*. And there's a feeling in the air that tingles on my skin. Like static, only not so pronounced.

And Imogene and Pelly are definitely gone.

I run my hands along the back wall of the closet, but there's no secret panel, or at least not that I can find. And even if there was, what would that prove? I know what's on the other side of that wall. It's our living room.

I slowly close the door and return to lie down on my bed because I'm starting to feel a little shaky.

Okay, I tell myself. You didn't do *that* bad. You sat here and talked to Imogene with her skin all blue and her weird little friend and you didn't feel faint or anything. That's progress.

Except now my arms and legs are trembling and they won't stop. My pulse is way too fast. I don't think I could sit up even if I wanted to.

I try to think of something else, but that only brings me around to what Imogene said about what she was like when she lived in Tyson, carrying a knife and beating people up and everything. I try to imagine her like that, and I can't. And she was a couple of years younger then, too. So I try to imagine a fourteen- or fifteen-year-old Imogene with her knife and her toughness, and I *really* don't have any luck with that.

It's not like I haven't seen kids like she says she was. We've got them in school, the toughs and the gang members, some of them only twelve or thirteen. No one messes with them, not even the jocks like Brent. They live in a world of their own, smoking cigarettes just off the school grounds during lunch, sneering at the idea of school spirit and dances and sports and pretty much anything the rest of us are interested in.

I try to fit Imogene in with their crowd, and it just doesn't work. Sure, she looks punky tough some days, but she never *acts* it.

I wonder if she misses that old life.

I wonder if she still carries her knife.

I wonder if she would ever hurt me.

That stops me cold, and I feel guilty for even thinking it.

Of course she wouldn't.

I sigh. This is no good, but at least my heart's not drumming so fast and I feel like I have control of my muscles again. I sit up and look around my room. All the lights are on and there's not an inch of shadow anywhere—not even under my bed because before Imogene and Pelly showed up, I put my desk lamp down there. Happily, Imogene made no comment about my room having the feel of a brightly lit supermarket, though Mom wasn't shy about commenting on it. But she didn't push it, for which I'm grateful.

The only place that's dark is inside my closet, but the door to it is firmly closed. And I know there's nothing in there because I just looked. But if there are these magical doors that Pelly can open, who says that soul-eaters can't do the same?

After a moment I get up and wedge my spare chair under the knob and hope that'll work as well as it seems to in the movies. If Imogene comes back, she can just knock.

Maybe we should have worked out a password or some kind of code so that I'll know it's her.

Except what if these shadow creatures can take the form of someone else, or mimic their voice?

I could go crazy thinking about all of this.

I stand there and continue to stare at the closet door until finally I make myself look away. I go back to my desk and flip through the stack of fairy-tale books that I've been studying, though there's nothing useful in them. It's kind of funny. I'm the one who was totally into fairy tales and the idea of fairies being real, but Imogene found out way more after one morning's research than I ever knew. I guess it was because I've always read stories—and often those that are only based on fairy tales with lots of made-up stuff in them—rather than the reference books Imogene went through, where everything's clinical and cataloged and all.

After a few moments, I turn my attention to my computer. Earlier this evening I found this site called SurLaLune and spent an hour or so going through the archives of their forum, seeing if I could find something that might help. The site's all about fairy tales, and a lot of the people that post to it appear to be fairy-tale writers and scholars.

Anybody can log in with a question, so a few hours ago I pretended I was researching a school paper, wondering if anybody had any info on the darker side of Faerie. I check for answers now, and there are almost a dozen, but when I read through them, they're not much help. Books that I don't have are cited. I make a note of their titles. Someone brings up movies, and there are a few posts about how this sort of thing is more horror story than fairy tale.

Tell me about it, I think.

I know real fairy tales aren't happy little Disneyesque

stories of frolicking dwarves and singing animals. Some of them are downright grim and gory. But there's always a point to them. These soul-eaters hunting us from the shadows are too much like a hundred overwrought horror movies where a bunch of teenagers get killed off one by one in ever more imaginative ways, and that's it. I know we're not supposed to take it seriously—it's just good fun. Except it seems more like pornography than fun to me, way more so than some couple going at it hot and heavy.

I close my Web browser and check my e-mail. I see, as I scroll down through my inbox, that it's mostly spam, as usual. Then an unfamiliar e-mail return address jumps out because I recognize the subject line. It's the one I used for my post to the SurLaLune forum. I click the e-mail open.

Date: Thurs, 30 Oct 2003 01:54:03 -0800
From: efoylan@sympatico.ca
Subject: Re: The dark side of Faerie
To: fairygrrl@yahoo.com

Hello fairygrrl,
I like your name—very punky.

I have to smile at that. I wanted a Yahoo identity that went with my interest in fairy tales and added the "grrl" to toughen it up. Then my smile disappears because I think of how the very first time I actually see fairies, what do I do? Faint away like a real grrl never would.

I read your post to the SurLaLune forum and while I applaud any school that will allow its students to do research on fairy lore for a class project, I find myself having to do the very thing I swore I'd never do, which is sound like my mother:

That earns my correspondent another smile. I've made the same promise myself because we can't all have moms as cool as Imogene's.

Please be careful. Fairies aren't all Disney or even Brian Froud (though he can be a little shadowy in some of his depictions, can't he?). The spirits that hide in the shadows are dangerous and not to be approached on a lark—or even necessarily for a school project.

They have a hunger for what we carry in us—our mortal, short-lived souls—and are quick to take advantage of any opening we might give them. Remember what Nietzsche said: "When you look long into an abyss, the abyss also looks into you."

But perhaps you already know all of this and are setting about your project with caution. And as I reread what I've written, I'm afraid I must sound like some doddery old drama queen, shaking her finger at you and muttering, "Beware, beware!"

But please be careful all the same.

Esmeralda

P.S. A last word of caution from your overly cautious correspondent: tomorrow being Halloween, when the veils between our world and that of the spirits are at their thinnest, I'd wait on starting anything until the weekend.

It's too late for careful, I think. Or to wait until the weekend.

I wonder who this Esmeralda is and go looking for her on the SurLaLune site. Turns out she's not a lurker like me. I read through a few of her posts and get the impression that she's smart and really knowledgeable about pretty much every aspect of fairy lore. Plus, considering how much posting she does, she seems to have way too much spare time.

I try Googling her, but the only things that come up are those posts on SurLaLune.

I look at her e-mail again. I want to ask her for help, but I hesitate, because what do I really know about her? This e-mail might not even be from the same Esmeralda Foylan who posts to SurLaLune. For all I know, she might not even be a her. She could be some old guy sitting at a library screen making stuff up. Or some kid who likes to mess around with people, freaking them out with scary stories. After all, Halloween *is* coming up. Some people might think that acting all dire and foreboding in an e-mail to a poster named "fairygrrl" would be a good Halloween prank. A couple of days early, maybe, but it could be they were just setting me up for some big laugh on Friday.

Which—I glance at the time in the bottom right-hand corner of my screen—is already tomorrow, because it's long past midnight now.

But I decide to trust my unknown correspondent. I like the way her voice sounds from her e-mail, and if she knows as much fairy lore as it seems she does, she really might be able to help. And we need knowledgeable help. I know Imogene doesn't want us to contact Christy, but I've been tempted to do it anyway. We can worry about what he can use in a book or not later. But first we need to survive for there to *be* a later. So this is a good compromise.

Still, I can't help but worry about what Imogene will say when she finds out. Sure, I promised not to go to Christy, but I'm pretty certain Imogene won't see my writing to Esmeralda as a better option. Except it's not like Esmeralda's going to put us in a book—I mean, I did Google her, and all that came up was the SurLaLune posts. It's not like she's some famous writer like Christy.

It's all making my head spin, so I make the executive decision and compose an e-mail to Esmeralda outlining everything that's happened over the last little while: the school's resident fairies and Adrian, the hapless ghost; Imogene's Pelly and the fairy orchestra; the creatures in the shadows . . . it takes me a moment to remember what Pelly called them. Then it comes to me: the *anamithim*. I describe Imogene's encounters with them so far and how the vervain pollen turned her skin blue but also drove the soul-eaters away.

I finish up with:

It's funny how it works, isn't it? All my life I've wanted a fairy-tale adventure, but now that it's here, what happens? I faint away and now I'm too scared to do anything except sit here in my room with all the lights on. But I'm not a hero. I guess Imogene could be since she's way braver than me, but we're only seventeen. We're just kids. That doesn't seem to bother Imogene, but it really makes me nervous. What can kids do about stuff like this?

I read it all over and correct some of the spelling and syntax, but then make myself stop fussing with it and simply send it off. I want to sit up and wait for a response, but I'm finally getting tired, and what are the chances that Esmeralda's still up, waiting for me to respond to her e-mail? Not big.

So I let my screensaver fill the screen and stare at the fish doing their aimless swimming thing until I realize I'm nodding off. I crawl into bed and fall right to sleep, even with all the lights on.

* * *

My hopes are so huge that there'll be a response from Esmeralda waiting for me when I get up that I'm sure there won't be. Because that's the way it usually seems to work when you *really* want something. Or at least that's the way it usually works for me. But when I log on, the third new e-mail has that now-familiar return address of efoylan@sympatico.ca. The message is brief:

We need to talk *right now*. I'll be by my computer all day. As soon as you get this, click on the following link. It will connect your computer to my direct messenger service.
Your worried correspondent,
Esmeralda

I'm so grateful, and actually feel a glimmer of hope. Maybe she really can help. Maybe there's a way Imogene and I can get out of this mess all in one piece. I leave my bedroom and check around the apartment to make sure Mom's gone to work, then go back to the computer. I hesitate a moment, the mouse's pointer hovering over Esmeralda's link, before I click on it. Nothing happens at first, then a new Web page opens.

It stays blank for long enough that I think it's not working. I check the address line, and the URL has something about "th_messenger_services" in it along with a whole bunch of random letters, numbers, percentage signs, and the like. Then a line appears on the screen:

ef: Good morning, fairygrrl.

I look at the words, not sure what I should do. A cursor is blinking under the line, the way it does in a word processing document after you've hit *enter.*

A new line appears.

ef: Are you there? Simply type in your response

when the cursor is on a new line and blinking, then use your enter key when you're finished "speaking."

Okay. I type "Hello," and when I hit *enter,* it appears under the last line looking like this:

fg: Hello?

I wonder at the "fg," then realize it stands for "fairygrrl." Esmeralda must have set the program to automatically indicate who's "talking"—I guess it's so that when you look at the screen, you can tell who's said what, because the other lines she wrote earlier are still on the screen.

ef: Oh, good. You *are* there. I hope you don't find this too awkward. But since you said you were a schoolgirl, I thought a long distance phone call might be too prohibitive, though of course I don't know where you live or what your financial situation might be.

fg: No this is good.

I want to put a comma in after "No," but force myself to keep typing and not worry about that kind of thing.

I live in Newford. My name's Maxine.

ef: Newford, of course. That shouldn't have surprised

me. It's always been one of the busier centers of Otherworld activity.

It has?

fg: Can you hlp us?

I've already hit *enter* when I see the typo. She's going to think I'm such a dork.

ef: I hope so. Your e-mail laid the situation out very clearly. The only thing I didn't understand is this business of the high school fairies and how they brought your friend Imogene to the attention of the anamithim. What caused their enmity in the first place?

fg: We don't know. Pelly says they just did it for the sake of meanness.

ef: There certainly are beings such as that in the Otherworld. So just to clarify: none of you did anything? You didn't insult them, or take something from them, or try to move into their territory?

fg: Not that we know. Well, unless Imogene befriending Adrian falls into one of those categories.

ef: Adrian being the ghost.

fg: Right. Who had a relationship with the fairies before Imogene came along. I think he's got a crush on her.

ef: You mentioned that. And that he asked the fairies to help make Imogene believe that they existed.

fg: Do you think they're jealous of her?

ef: Possibly, but it's unlikely. Fairie *will* establish proprietary relationships with humans, but they are based on physical parameters. A ghost, by its very non-physical existence, would be of no use to them.

fg: What do you mean by "of use"?

I'm thinking she means some kind of sex thing, so I'm also thinking *ew.* I haven't seen much in the way of fairies so far—just Pelly, and that stream of them going out of Imogene's window—but they're all kind of gross looking.

ef: The primary use they have for humans is as a tithe to more powerful creatures.

fg: Like the soul-eaters?

ef: Possibly.

fg: But Adrian told Imogene that the soul-eaters also feed on ghosts.

ef: Yes, *and* they feed on fairies, so I doubt the group troubling you would have formed an alliance with the anamithim. For one thing, it would have been difficult—not to mention foolhardy on their part—to approach the anamithim in the first place. Beings such as the anamithim tend to feed first and ask questions later.

fg: So we're not the fairies' tithe to them?

ef: No. For them to be able to use you as a tithe, you would have to be beholden to them in the first place. But since they can lay no legitimate claim to either you or Imogene, they couldn't use you for such a purpose. It would seem that your friend Pelly is correct. They have simply involved you for the sake of their own amusement.

fg: It's so not fair.

ef: I agree. But this is the sort of thing that happens when house fairies are abandoned and go bad.

fg: So what can we do?

ef: I need to do more research. But as I mentioned

before, tomorrow is Halloween, when all the barriers between the worlds come down. To try to deal with the anamithim in the next day or so would be suicide. What you need to do is lay low—at least until the weekend is over.

fg: But what if they come for us?

ef: Keep your room well-lit so that there are no large shadowed areas from which they can manifest, and you should be able to keep them at bay.

fg: Will you come and help us?

ef: I'm sorry, but I can't come to you. I'm the caretaker of a gateway into the fairy realms, and the potential for trouble is too great if I'm ever away from it for too long—especially at this time of the year. But I truly will do my best to help. I just need to do more research into this and consult with some experts I know.

fg: Thanks. I wish you could just wave your hands and solve everything, because if magic works, it'd be nice if it'd work for us, too. But we appreciate anything you can do.

At least I hope we do. I can't answer for Imogene, but surely she'll be okay with this.

ef: You know, I've been thinking as we sit here. There could be another reason for the anamithims' interest in Imogene. I'd have to actually meet her to be sure, but it's possible that she's one of those people who carry myths under their skin.

fg: You've totally lost me.

ef: <lol> I'm sorry. I read that description somewhere, and it's always stayed with me. It refers to how we all carry stories—the genetic memories of events and deeds and people whose DNA combined to make us who we are. But some of us carry traces of older and stranger genetic codes, bits and pieces of deep-rooted secrets and mythological beings who were once as real as you and I, but are mostly long gone now. Ghost traces of them remain in many of us, and in a very few, the traces run stronger—strong enough to attract the attention of beings such as the anamithim. They can remain hidden for . . . well, forever I suppose. But contact with elements of the Otherworld will often spark an awakening, and the next thing you know you have all these myths stirring under your skin. And that, in turn, will attract the interest of the anamithim.

fg: That's sort of what Pelly said. How if you know too much about Faerie—though I think he said it's more *believing* too much—it wakes up some kind of light in you.

ef: Yes, it's often referred to as a "shine." And commerce with fairy can certainly wake it. If this is the case, your friend's shine will be like a beacon. And that becomes more of a problem because the anamithim have an old enmity with the mythical beings that first walked our world. They're the ones who banished the anamithim into the shadows in the first place, so the soul-eaters like nothing better than to swallow up the spirits of their ancestors, no matter how faint the bloodline.

fg: So if they do attack us, what can we do?

ef: They won't attack you—not if you keep out of the shadows. Sleep with all your lights on and don't leave a lit room for a dark one.

fg: But if they do?

ef: Do you know the story of Tam Lin?

fg: Sure, he was the fairy knight whose girlfriend won him back from the fairy queen. What about it?

ef: If the anamithim should grab hold of your friend, you have to grab hold of her, too. And whatever they do to her, whatever they change her into, you can't let go.

fg: That doesn't sound too hard.

ef: Except they will change her into the shape of whatever you fear the most.

I remember more about the ballad, as I read what Esmeralda's just written. Tam Lin got turned into all kinds of animals and things, but finally the fairies let him go because his girlfriend was so brave and tenacious. I don't know if I could do that. Imogene could, but she's the one being grabbed.

fg: Why does that work?

ef: They respect exaggerated resolve and bravery—you know, the stuff of heroes. The heart that maintains its capacity for love and loyalty and joy—especially in the midst of a great trial—impresses them no end. But courage most of all.

Great. That's the last thing I have.

ef: I need to go. Please stay in and keep the lights on. I know it's boring, but it will only be for a couple of days. We'll figure this out.

fg: Staying alive isn't boring.

ef: I agree. Life is a glorious gift. Good-bye, Maxine.

fg: Good-bye, and thanks.

I highlight our whole conversation and copy it into a word processing file, where I save it. Then I go back to the Web page, wondering how to sign off, but the page closes as I watch, and I'm staring at my tropical fish screensaver again.

I realize that I never asked Esmeralda anything about herself. Who she is, where she lives, what being a gatekeeper means. Maybe there'll be the chance to do so another time, because she sounds really interesting.

Leaning back in my chair, I glance at the time and get a huge shock. It's already midmorning. I've missed homeroom, my first class, and most of my second. That's never happened. I've *never* been late before. Sick a couple of times, but I have an almost perfect attendance record.

I jump up and get washed and dressed in record time, expecting a call from the school office to come at any minute. What'll I say to them? What if they tell Mom?

The phone rings as I'm going out the door, and my whole body jerks with guilt and surprise. Then I realize it can't be the school calling because it's my cell phone that's ringing, and they'd never call me on it.

Do I wish I had caller ID now? You bet.

My phone rings again.

My heart sinks as I realize that it's probably Mom. The school must have called her, and now she's checking up on me.

It's on the last ring before it'll go to voice mail when I press the talk button.

NOW: *Imogene*

I leave a note on the kitchen table before Mom and Jared get up, explaining how I went to school early, then go and make a rough bed in my closet. I lie there, half dozing while I wait for both of them to leave. For a while I experiment with opening doors on the back wall the way Pelly showed me when we got back from Maxine's last night, but I just look through them at the closets they open up into. It's not that I'm scared to step through them so much as I don't trust that there'll be a way back if I do manage to cross over.

It's amazing what people shove into the back of a closet. Boxes of papers, piles of shoes, old toys, sports equipment, vinyl records—all the stuff they don't need easy access to anymore.

I don't know who the closets belong to because I'm not concentrating on specific ones, the way Pelly did. I'm just kind of browsing, because that doesn't seem as nosy as checking out the closets of people I know. But it grows old, and it makes me sleepy.

I've dozed off again when I hear a door slam.

That'll be Jared, I think, who can't go quietly through a door these days. So Mom will already be gone.

But I wait a little bit longer while I listen for sounds in

the apartment. When I'm sure I'm alone, I hurry to the bathroom to have the pee I've been holding for the past few hours. Still blue all over, my reflection in the mirror shows me. Which means I'm still safe from the soul-eaters.

I boil some water. I'm just pouring the last of it into the coffee filter and wondering if I should see if Pelly can show up in the daytime and if he wants to have some coffee with me, when I hear the front door open. It's too late to hide. Mom walks into the living room, talking to herself about some paper she forgot that she needs for a morning class.

I stand frozen while she rummages around her desk in the corner of the living room. Maybe she won't come into the kitchen. Maybe she'll find her paper and just go. Except she doesn't. I mean, she finds what she's looking for, but then she walks into the kitchen—drawn by the smell of the coffee, I guess.

"I thought you'd already gone to school . . . "

Her voice trails off as my blue skin registers. She stands there looking at me, not saying a word, trying to take it in.

"I kind of lied," I say.

"Because of . . . " She waves a hand helplessly in my direction. "Your new look?"

"Pretty much."

"So are you going to tell me what's going on?"

I look at her, phony explanations taking shape inside my head, but I realize I don't want to lie to her either. Frankie Lee wouldn't understand, but I'd rather Mom thought I was crazy.

"I've been cursed by fairies," I tell her.

"Fairies."

"You know . . . spirits of the woods and all that, except it turns out they live in the city, too."

She shakes her head. "It's been a long time since I heard you talk about fairies. Not since we used to live on the commune."

I shrug.

"So . . . these fairy spirits turned your skin blue."

"No, the blue's a protection against them, except it got out of hand."

"And now you're blue." She pauses a moment, then adds, "All over?"

I lift my T-shirt.

"I see," she says. She looks at where the coffee's almost finished dripping through the filter. "I think you need to pour us both a cup and tell me about this from the beginning."

I leave a lot out—like just how bad the soul-suckers are—but mostly I tell it like it happened. Mom doesn't bat an eye, but then she's always been like that. I can remember how back on the commune she just accepted that I had an invisible friend named Pelly and never went into this routine, the way other adults would, about how he wasn't real and couldn't possibly exist. For all I know, maybe she was seeing some kind of fairies, too.

"I always thought there were real spirits," she says when I'm done.

"And it turns out you were right."

She gives a slow nod. "So is this—" She reaches across

the table to touch my blue arm. "Is it permanent?"

"It should be gone in a day or two."

She nods again—still processing all of this, I guess.

"So what happens now?" she asks.

"I just have to get these other fairies to back off," I tell her.

"How dangerous are they?"

I realize I have to play the "little white lie" card so that she doesn't get too wigged out.

"So far they just stare at me from the shadows," I say, which is still walking on the edges of the truth.

"We're never going to have a normal life, are we?" she says.

"Would we want to?"

She gives a slow nod. "Sometimes, I think yes. Or at least that I want one for you and Jared. I worry what those years in the commune, and later in Tyson, have done to you."

"They made us open-minded and self-reliant."

"I suppose."

"Really, Mom. We're okay."

"Says the blue-skinned girl."

"It's only temporary."

"Unlike the piercings and the tattoos."

I give her a surprised look.

"I didn't think any of that bothered you," I say.

"It doesn't, really. I just have to keep reminding myself that whatever we create, whether it's a work of art or a child, they go on to live their own lives, to make their own connections to all the things we can't influence, or sometimes even warn them about. All we can do is stand back and watch and hope we did a good enough job with what we made."

"You did a great job, Mom."

She smiles. "Well, if that's the case, it was luck more than planning, though I always wanted the best for both of you."

"Jared's perfect," I assure her, "and I—well, I get along fine. Really."

When she stands up, I do, too.

"Is there anything I can do?" she asks.

I shake my head.

"Then I think I'll go to class. Promise me you'll be careful."

"I'm always careful."

"The funny thing is," she says, "for all the trouble you can get into, I actually believe that."

"Don't worry," I tell her, and give her a hug.

"I have to worry," she says into my blue hair. "That's a parent's job, and I don't think it ever stops."

She kisses me, gives my blueness another long look, then shakes her head and heads off to school. I get myself another coffee and have a piece of toast with it while I wait for 9:30 to arrive. As soon as it does, I call the record store. Thomas answers, and I can feel his relief when he recognizes my voice.

"I'm glad you called. I was getting worried."

"We're all fine," I say. "We chased off the bad guys and

bought ourselves a little time, but I ended up blue."

"Don't be. We'll work this out."

"No, I mean I'm literally blue—all over. Every inch of my skin."

"Oh." He waits a beat, then adds, "I'd like to see that."

"You would."

"Hey, I'm your boyfriend."

He really is, isn't he? And he doesn't think I'm nuts. How cool is that?

"Did you learn anything from your grandmother?" I ask.

"Getting rid of house fairies like your friend Pelly said are living in the school is easy. You just have to leave them a gift of new clothes and thank them for the great job they've been doing."

"That really works?"

"So Granny says."

I think of how grubby the school is, which is no surprise, considering it's got lazy fairies and an alcoholic custodian.

"What if they've been doing a lousy job?" I ask.

"You lie. It works either way."

"And the soul-eaters?"

"She says there are stories about all sorts of demon spirits—old hags that feed on children, fearsome black dogs with blazing eyes, *phoukas* who will try to drown you—but nothing like the ones you describe."

"So no help there."

"Well, she did say that such creatures feed on your fear, so if you come into contact with them, you should show them respect, but no fear."

I shiver, remembering how I felt from just those glimpses I had last night of what's in the shadows.

"Easy for her to say," I tell him.

"I suppose."

"Did she have any advice on how to bring the battle to them?"

Thomas laughs. "Well, I didn't quite put it like that, but apparently on Halloween—"

"Which is tomorrow."

"Which is tomorrow," Thomas agrees. "On Halloween the borders between the worlds are hazy. If you can find a fairy mound, or some other place known to be their haunt, and run around it nine times, you can gain entry into the fairy realms."

"I wonder—are they stronger or weaker there?"

"I don't know. But I do know that you're not supposed to eat or drink anything in Fairyland. I think you're safe unless you do."

We talk a little more. Before we hang up, I promise not to run off and do something crazy without calling him first. Then I dial Maxine's cell phone.

"Oh, you're picking up," I say. "I thought you'd be in class and I'd just leave a message."

"I'm not at school yet. I was just going out the door when you called."

I blink in surprise. She's just leaving *now*?

"Okay," I say. "Who are you, and what have you done with Maxine?"

She laughs. "I know. It's too weird, me being late. What's up?"

I tell her about how a gift of clothes can get rid of the fairies in the school and ask her to stop by the thrift shop and pick up some doll or toddler clothes that will do the trick. "Make sure they're nice," I add. Then I tell her about my mom coming back and catching the blue wonder that is her daughter, making coffee in all her blueness.

"She must have totally freaked," Maxine says.

"Not really."

"You're kidding."

"No, she was really pretty good about it."

"I don't get your family. My mom would have gone ballistic."

"You seem to get Jared pretty well."

"Don't start," she says, but I can hear the smile in her voice, and I know she likes it.

"So you were okay last night?" I ask. "You know, after we left."

"No spooks. But I've been following some leads—"

"You watch way too many cop shows," I tell her.

"—and," she continues, ignoring me as any sensible person would, "I'm hoping for some good news soon. One thing I have found out is that we need to lie low tomorrow because of Halloween."

"When the borders between the worlds are thin."

"Exactly. How do you know that?"

"From Thomas's grandmother," I say. "How do you?"

"From . . . "

She hesitates, and my heart sinks.

"You've been talking to Christy," I say, "and now we're chapter three in his next book."

"We might already be," she says, "but, no. I was messaging with this woman who responded to an e-mail I sent to a fairy-tale site."

"You told some stranger about all of this?"

"Yes. No. Not exactly. She doesn't know our full names or anything. But she's really up on all of this stuff, and I've learned a lot from her already. I printed out our chat to give to you."

"How do you know she's not some cyber-stalker?" I ask.

"I guess I don't. But I find myself trusting her all the same."

I have to think about this for a moment, but by doing so, I'm making Maxine anxious.

"Imogene?" she says. "Are you still there? You're not mad, are you?"

"No, it's cool. I guess we need help. It's just . . . I'm used to dealing with my problems on my own—you know, without dragging half the world into it."

"I'm sorry. I should have asked you first, but I thought you'd say no, and I think we really need some help, and since you nixed the idea of talking to Christy, I just had to—"

"It's okay," I say, breaking in. "Really." I hear a weird

kind of honking sound from her end of the line. "Where are you anyway?"

"Almost at school. I'm walking up to the front door right now, so I have to go."

"Okay. Say hi to nobody for me."

"Can I tell everyone you're all blue?"

I laugh. "No, only Barbie and Ken."

"So we're okay? About me contacting Esmeralda?"

"We're always okay, Maxine. That's the deal with being best friends."

"Yeah, it is, isn't it?"

"Have fun at school," I tell her.

"Don't get too blue," she says with a giggle, then cuts the connection.

I cradle the phone, smiling. Yeah, everything that's happening is weird and freaky, but I've got Maxine and Thomas on my side. Hell, I've even got my mom. And maybe I did used to have to deal with the crap in my life by myself, but it doesn't have to stay that way.

My coffee's gone cold, but I'm too lazy to zap it in the microwave, so I just take it back to my room to grab some clean clothes to put on after I have a shower.

And who's waiting for me but my friendly neighborhood ghost, standing on the fire escape outside my window. He's giving me a goggle-eyed look—picking up on the blue-skinned wonder that is now me, I guess—but I'm not feeling particularly charitable toward him at the moment.

I open the window and glare at him.

"So now you're a perv, too?" I say.

"What do you mean?"

"You're peeping at my window—that's what pervs do."

I can see I've struck a chord, and that really ticks me off. How often has he been skulking out there, watching me?

"That's pretty low," I tell him. "Have you been enjoying the shows?"

"This is the first time I've ever been here."

"Yeah, right."

"It's true."

He's acting so stiff and affronted that I find myself believing him.

"You're blue," he says.

"How observant."

"Why are you so mad at me?"

"Well, duh. Could it be because you sicced some heavy-duty soul-suckers on me?"

"I didn't," he says. "At least I didn't on purpose."

"And the difference is?"

"I just wanted you to believe me. The fairies said they could make it so that you could see them. I didn't know all of this would happen."

"So now it's my fault for not believing you?"

"You're impossible," he says.

"This from a ghost."

He sighs. "I only wanted to be friends. For you to like me and believe me, but I screwed everything up."

"No argument from me on that front," I tell him. "So why are you here? What do you want?"

"I've found out a way that we can deal with the darkness—the things that live in there are called *anamithim.*"

"Yeah, I know."

He gives me a puzzled look, but I don't fill him in.

"Anyway, there's a way we can call them to us," he says.

He goes on to explain about the ring of salt and the offering of unsalted, sugary bread.

"And then what?" I ask.

"Then we convince them to take someone else in your place."

"Did you hear what you just said?"

"Oh, I know. It sounds terrible. But I don't mean someone nice. I was thinking of Brent."

"I hate to admit it," I tell him, "but that's almost tempting."

"Look, the only reason I'm telling you is because I can't make the bread or the circle or any of that. But I'll be there with you."

I don't say anything, not because I agree or disagree with what he wants to do, but because it's got me thinking. This would be my chance to come face to face with the soul-eaters, but they wouldn't be able to touch me. Only then what?

"I wouldn't ask you," Adrian says, "but there's no one else except for the fairies, and I can't trust them."

"Well, duh."

"So will you?"

I shake my head. "Not to sic them on somebody else—

not even somebody like Brent, though it would serve him right. But I like the idea of being able to summon the soul-eaters and them not being able to touch me."

"Why? What would you do?"

"I don't know. But there's got to be some way they can be hurt."

"I don't think they can be. The only thing you can do is bargain with them, but you have to show them respect when you do it."

"Everything should be respected," I say, "unless they prove they don't deserve it."

"Like Brent."

"Brent doesn't deserve respect," I say. "But he doesn't deserve to have his soul swallowed up either. That's just a bit too harsh."

"Why is everybody so concerned about Brent's feelings and Brent's future?" Adrian asks. "You think he cares about anybody else's?"

"Who else is concerned?" I ask.

"The angel who told me how to summon the darkness."

"Well, maybe it's not so much what Brent does or doesn't deserve, so much as what it would mean for us. You know, our own karma for doing something like that to him."

"So he can just push everybody around and beat them up."

I shake my head. "He ever tries to lay a hand on me

outside of school, and I'll feed it back to him in pieces. Simple self-defense. But that's not the point."

"No," Adrian says. "The point is I've doomed you, and there's nothing I can do to make it up except . . . "

His voice trails off. I can tell by his face that he's said more than he wanted to.

"Except what?" I ask.

"Nothing," he says, and fades away on me before I can press him further.

"One day," I tell the air where he might still be, invisibly watching me, "I'll figure out a way to smack you in the head for doing the Invisible Man on me like this."

There's no response, but I'm not expecting one.

I turn from the window. I don't feel like taking a shower now, not with a possible audience to follow the proceedings. Adrian can go to one of the peep shows on Palm Street if he wants to get a cheap thrill.

In my head, I can see the long day stretching out in front of me for what feels like forever. I suppose I could do some homework, or make a plan or something. Instead, I go into the living room and switch on the TV. I flick through the channels and it's all crap.

Sighing, I return to my bedroom. I can't see Adrian, but that doesn't mean he isn't still hanging around. Walking over to the closet, I open the door and call Pelly's name.

NOW: *Adrian*

I think as I beat a hasty retreat from Imogene's window, all I ever seem able to do is annoy her more. But what was I going to say? There's nothing I can do to make it up except sacrifice myself in your place? Considering the way Imogene feels about me, she'd probably say, "Please do. And could you get a move on while you're at it?"

I look up and see her closing her window.

Even with her skin all blue, she's gorgeous.

I turn away and start down the alley, wondering how it happened. For all I know, she did it on purpose. Tomorrow is Halloween, after all. She could be planning to go as Mystique from *X-Men*. . . .

I stop dead in my tracks.

Halloween.

How could I have forgotten?

It's the one night when the dead can walk freely in the world, and supposedly sometimes even make physical contact. I don't know the details—it's nothing that ever interested me before—but I know where I can find out.

So instead of heading back to the school, I go the other way, through a few blocks of old run-down tenements until I get to the crumbling stone walls of All Souls Cemetery. If

I was alive, I'd have to use the old rusted gates of the entrance, or climb up the thick vines that almost cover the walls, but being a ghost, I can just walk through those old stone walls. And I do.

It's a funny place—a scary place, if you want to know the truth, even in the daylight. Or at least it is to me. I'd never have gone there when I was alive and I don't like going even now, when I'm dead and I know nothing can hurt me. It's not like a normal graveyard—more like something out of a Southern Gothic novel, full of dead and dying trees, old-fashioned mausoleums and crypts, with paths of uneven cobblestones winding narrowly between them. There are regular gravestones, too, but mostly the place is one of those architectural follies, out of place in this time and age.

It's probably been fifty years since anybody was buried here, and the only reason it still exists the way it does is that the Crowsea Heritage Society has stymied any potential developers with a wall of paperwork up at City Hall.

I'm here because this is where Bobby Novak was buried—the first ghost I met after I died. Bobby's what they used to call a juvenile delinquent. These days a twelve-year-old gangbanger would make Bobby look like a pacifist, but that doesn't stop him from channeling this James Dean attitude with his greased-back hair, white T-shirt and jeans, the pointy-toed black boots, and the ever-present cigarette dangling from his lips.

When we first met, I asked him why he still smoked, because he couldn't get anything out of it. He just laughed.

"I died with this pack of smokes," he said, pulling them out to show me. "I had seven left the day I wrapped my Mustang around that tree, and there's still seven here; doesn't matter how many I smoke."

"But what's the point?"

"Well, I'm not going to get lung cancer."

"But you can't taste them."

"Sure, I can," he said. "They were with me when I died, so they're part of what I am now. And besides, they give me something to do."

And I guess it's true. Whenever I see him, he'll be leaning against some building, or sitting at a bus stop, smoking his cigarettes and watching people, this small, knowing smile lifting one corner of his mouth. Everything's got a funny side in his view of the world.

I guess he was considered a hard case, and maybe he would be still, but it doesn't matter. Alive, he's not the kind of guy who'd ever have been my friend, and that isn't changed by the fact that we're both dead. But he tolerates me when we happen to run into each other.

There aren't a lot of us hanging on to whatever echoes of life we can, because most people who die don't stick around.

He doesn't have a crypt or a building, just a stone in a far corner of the graveyard where this old rose bush has gone wild and turned into a thorny thicket that gives up a few flowers every so often—reluctantly, I always think. His stone has his name—Robert Novak—and his dates of birth and death. Lower on the stone, someone's scratched "My Angel" inside a heart.

"Ellen Sue did that," he told me. "She was my steady, and I suppose my dying broke her heart."

Bobby's sitting on the steps of a nearby mausoleum when I reach his gravestone.

"Hey, four eyes," he says.

Yeah, we definitely would never have been friends.

"I was wondering if you could help me with something," I ask.

He shrugs. "You never know, so try me."

So I ask him if it's true that we can actually interact physically with the world of the living on Halloween, and if it is, how do you do it.

"You're just checking into this *now*?" he says. "Christ, kid. It's the only day of the year we can go out to get drunk and laid." Then he laughs. "But I guess those aren't exactly going concerns for you, are they?"

"Funny."

"I thought so."

He lights a cigarette from the one he was smoking and flicks the butt into the dry grass, but it disappears before it touches the ground.

"So it is true," I say.

"Oh, yeah. Just make sure you're at the exact place you died when the moon comes over the horizon tomorrow. That'll be at two fifteen in the afternoon this year."

"How do you know that?"

He shrugs. "How do you not?"

"What if there's no moon?"

I'm thinking of nights when the sky's dark except for stars.

He laughs again. "There's always a moon, kid. You just can't see it some of the time."

"So when it sets, we go back to being ghosts?" I ask.

"Nope. We're good until the dawn. Moonrise to sunrise."

"Which this year . . . ?"

"Is seven fifteen, sharp. Nice tidy numbers. Though I'd show up early anyway, just to be on the safe side. Something like this you don't want to miss because your watch is running late. Do that and you're screwed. You'll have to wait for another whole year."

"Right."

"So what are you planning on?" he asks.

"Maybe I'm going to get laid."

He breaks out laughing. "Yeah, right."

I want to tell him off, but even though I know he can't hurt me, I'm still too chicken. Instead I just thank him for his help and try to leave before he thinks up some new witty put-down. But with Bobby, that's never going to happen.

"Don't forget a rubber!" he calls after me.

I pretend I didn't hear.

NOW: *Maxine*

I wait until lunch hour before I go to the thrift store to look for doll and children's clothes like Imogene asked me to. I don't have much luck with doll clothes—mostly what they have is much too frilly and girly, more suitable for Mom's doll collection that she pretends she bought for me—but there are lots of choices in the baby and toddler clothes section. I'm not sure how many fairies we're outfitting, so I get enough for ten of them: T-shirts, regular shirts, vests, jeans, and two of the cutest little pairs of overalls.

Back at the school, I stuff my buys into my locker and look at my watch. I have just enough time to check my e-mail. The good thing about never being tardy, never really missing any school—when I get sick it's almost always on a holiday or the weekend, which is totally unfair—is that I didn't get in trouble for coming in late this morning. And I'd probably be okay if I was late getting to my first afternoon class, too, but why push it?

There's a machine free when I go into the computer lab, so I quickly log on.

Yes, there's a message from Esmeralda:

Date: Thurs, 30 Oct 2003 12:23:16 -0800
From: efoylan@sympatico.ca
Subject: Re: The dark side of Faerie
To: fairygrrl@yahoo.com

Hello Maxine,

I've had some luck tracking down more information on the anamithim for you. It appears that they aren't fairies—or at least not exactly fairies. Apparently they can appear in many forms and have been here since the dawn of time—though I think I already mentioned that this morning, when I explained the enmity between them and the first people and their descendants.

The most recent information I uncovered is that they're also known as the Adversary—and not simply the way Christians refer to Lucifer. They were the snake in Eden, the Titans banished by Zeus and the other young gods, the unseen terrors that waited just beyond primitive man's campfires. . . . Well, you get the idea.

The only useful thing I've found so far is that the shine or light that attracts them to people such as your friend Imogene can also be used to repel them, although how that's accomplished I've yet to discover.

I shall continue my research and hopefully, if we can chat tonight, I'll have more concrete information to share with you.

Yours,
Esmeralda

I hear a bell and realize I'm going to be late for my next class, so I respond with a quick "Thanks, I'll talk to you tonight," and sign off, gather my books, and hurry down the hall.

Jerry Fielder appears out of nowhere near my math class—flying solo, without his ever-present hero Brent at his side. He tries to trip me, but I do a deft sidestep that surprises both of us and make it to my class in time and in one piece.

I don't catch my breath until we're five minutes in—boring math, though only boring because I'm about ten chapters ahead of the rest of the class. I haven't run into any of the problems that some of the other students obviously have, because most of our time is taken up with Ms. Rice explaining stuff that I figured out a couple of weeks ago.

So I tune them out and sit there with my textbook open on my desk. I think about Imogene with her blue skin and the weird creatures that live in her closet. I think about the *anamithim* and how the shine might be used to repel them. I also think about Jerry Fielder and wish I was big enough and strong enough, not to mention brave enough, to give him a taste of his own medicine.

NOW: *Imogene*

Pelly and I spend the afternoon working on the stories he owes the shopkeeper for the vervain pollen. I thought making them up wouldn't be nearly as interesting as having them told to me, but I was surprised. And really, 90 percent of what we did was Pelly telling me the stories, anyway. I'd read him bits out of the newspaper, or show him pictures from magazines, and he'd figure out the narrative, or expand on what was already there. Whenever he got stuck, I'd offer up a suggestion, and off he'd go again.

We're still at it when Mom comes home.

I'm so used to having Pelly around again that I think Mom's wide eyes are because she forgot about my blue skin. But then I get it.

"Oh, my," she says, and feels her way along the back of a chair until she can lower herself into it. "I think I need to catch my breath."

I turn to look at Pelly, trying to see him for the first time the way she is, and yeah, I can see her point. He's not even *remotely* normal, remember? Weird, skinny cross between a hedgehog and a boy, the floppy rabbit ears, the monkey's prehensile tail. Kind of furry and spiny at the same time, dressed in a baggy pair of brown pants and a sleeveless shirt of brightly colored cotton. Fingers are too long and have that extra joint. And then there are those eyes of his. I've gotten used to them by now, but they're so dark and they really look like they know too damn much, with a lot of what they know not being good.

"So this is . . . ?"

"Pelly," I say. "Pell-mell, actually, but I've always called him Pelly."

"Pleased to meet you," Pelly says.

Mom gives him a weak smile. "I thought he'd . . . " She looks embarrassed, then changes that to, "I mean, I thought you'd be . . . jollier somehow."

"Because he was some kid's imaginary friend?" I ask.

She nods.

"It's the eyes," I explain. "They've gotten too knowing."

Pelly gives me a puzzled look and gets up to look at himself in the hall mirror.

"I see," he says, his voice soft. He returns to sit beside me on the couch. "It's a look we get when we've . . . "

He seems reluctant to go on.

"When you've what?" I ask.

"Been abandoned."

"Oh."

That makes me feel small, and an uncomfortable silence falls over us until, after a few moments, Mom clears her throat.

"So," she says, "you're a fairy, then?"

"I'm not sure what I am," he tells her. "I'm just Pelly."

Mom nods the way you do when you're not really sure

you understand what you've just been told, but you're pretty sure you don't need to know more.

"So, will you be staying for dinner?" she asks.

* * *

We're at the dining room table, getting ready to eat when Jared bursts in through the front door.

"Sorry I'm late," he says, dumping his knapsack in the hall. "But I stopped off at Henry's to get the money he owes us for that chest of drawers we found in the Beaches the other night, and we got to talking . . . "

His voice trails off when my blue skin registers. Then he sees Pelly. I understand the look he's giving us—I mean, it *is* weird—but it's also starting to get old for me now.

"So, did I miss the memo?" he asks.

I blink at him. "What memo?"

"That Halloween's been moved up a day. Who are you going to be? Disney's Genie of the Lamp or a Smurf?"

"Ha-ha."

He gives Pelly a closer look.

"Man, that is a seriously good costume," he says.

"Don't be rude," Mom tells him. "This is how Pelly always looks."

She's totally adjusted now.

"Pelly?" Jared says.

Like he doesn't know, but then I see him make the connection, and he gets it. He remembers me back at the commune, going on and on about my invisible friend.

"Seriously?" he asks.

We all nod.

"Wow."

He takes the empty chair across the table from Pelly.

"So, how come you're not invisible anymore?" he asks.

I don't know why, but that breaks us all up.

* * *

I fill Jared in over dinner and decide that Maxine's right, my family *is* weird, because Jared just eats his stir-fry and nods as he listens, asks a question here and there, and nowhere does he get all wigged out about any of this.

"So how long will you be blue?" is all he asks me.

I shrug. "It should wear off in a day or so."

"Are you sure?" Mom asks. "Because your skin looks darker than it did this morning."

I lift my arm and look at it. She's right. My blue skin's a shade darker than it was the last time I thought to look at it. I turn to Pelly.

"I don't know, I don't know," he says worriedly.

"Maybe we should take you to the doctor's," Mom starts.

"And tell her what?" I ask. "That some vervain pollen turned me blue? This type of vervain probably doesn't even exist in our world." I look at Pelly. "It doesn't, does it?"

He shakes his head.

"So you can't even look it up in some obscure medical book to find out how to treat it."

"I know," Mom says, "but . . . "

"I can deal, Mom. Really."

"Turning blue's a good start," Jared says.

I shoot him a dirty look. "Thanks for the support."

"Sorry. But maybe Mom's right. Maybe you should have someone look at it—especially if you're getting bluer."

I sigh. "This is magic stuff. Do we have a family magician we can go see?"

"No, but—"

"So let's just leave it for now," I say. "It's all going to be dealt with in the next couple of days. Trust me."

Pelly gives me a surprised look, which thankfully only I catch. I think "shut up" at him and I guess I've become telepathic, too, since he doesn't say anything.

"We're just worried," Mom says.

"I know. I understand. But this is kind of like all those books you used to give to me when I was a kid—the ones you read when you were ten or so and just knew I'd love. Remember how you'd say that?"

"What books?"

"You know. Like those *Swallows and Amazons* ones by Arthur Ransome where the parents trust their kids to do the right thing."

"What about them?" Mom asks.

"Trust me to do the right thing, too."

I don't know where this might have gone because just then the doorbell rings. Jared answers to find Maxine there, so the rest of us turn away to let them have a big smooch and hug. When they finally let each other go—which I'm sure has everything to do with Mom coughing loudly into her hand—they join us at the table. Maxine gives Pelly a surprised look, and I can see she's still adjusting to my blue skin, but she's cool about it all.

"Are you coming to band practice?" Jared asks Maxine.

His band's got a Halloween gig at the Crib, this great club down the street from Your Second Home in Foxville. It's an all-ages show, so we were totally looking forward to it, but with all that's been going on this week, I'd completely forgotten about it.

"No, I came over to see Imogene," she says. "We've got some, um, research we need to make sense of."

"So, you'd rather study than rock'n'roll?"

"It's not so much a matter of rather . . . "

"I'm kidding," Jared tells her. "I'll miss you at rehearsal, but I like the idea of dating a smart girl."

That's the cue for Maxine to blush, and she does.

Mom starts to gather plates.

"It's okay," she says when I get up to help. "You two—" She glances at Pelly. "Or is it three? Whatever. I can get these. You go do your studying."

"Thanks, Mom."

Jared and Maxine take forever by the front door to say good-bye, but finally she, Pelly, and I are in my room.

"Have you gone bluer?" Maxine asks when I close the door.

I sigh. "Yes, and I wish everybody would stop focusing on it."

"Sorry."

She looks a little hurt, and that makes me feel bad.

"No, I am," I say. "I shouldn't be so snippy, but I've been cooped up in this apartment all day and I'm starting to go nuts. And to tell you the truth, the blue going darker's got me a little worried, too. But there's nothing we can do about it, right? So, I think we should concentrate on stuff we can do something about."

"Maybe I could ask Kerry about the blueness," Pelly says.

We both look at him.

"Who's Kerry?" I ask.

"Kerry Wickland. She's the owner of Kerry's Cauldron, where I got the vervain pollen."

"In Fairyland."

"In Mabon, yes."

"Is that the fairy word for Fairyland?"

He shakes his head. "It's just the name of a city in the Otherworld."

"They have cities over there?" Maxine asks.

"Apparently," I say. "You can ask her later," I tell Pelly. "Right now let's go over what we have."

I relate my conversations with Thomas and Adrian, then Maxine tells us how she's got the clothes for the fairies in her locker and pulls out her transcript of the chat she had with this Esmeralda woman. As Pelly and I read through the pages, I revise my skepticism toward the woman. I can see why Maxine thought she could be trusted.

"Is this it?" I ask when I get to the last page, which I pass to Pelly. "What did she say tonight?"

"I tried using that link she gave me," Maxine says, "but either it's dead, or she's not at her computer."

"This is interesting," Pelly says, "if unclear."

We look at him.

"The part about the light that attracts the *anamithim,*" he says. "She writes that it can also be used to repel them. What does she mean by that?"

"I don't know," I say. "But I do have an idea as to how we can put all this stuff together that we *do* understand."

I lay it out for them. We get rid of the fairies in the school, then we set up in the gym: the circle of salt to keep us safe, the bread to get the soul-eaters to come, lights from the drama department.

"Are you sure this is going to work?" Maxine asks.

"Not one hundred percent, but I've got nothing to lose. They can't touch me with my blue skin. And they can't survive in the direct light; that's what everyone says, right?"

Pelly gives an uncertain nod.

"Except I'm going to be there, too," Maxine says.

"You can't. You don't have the protection of blue skin."

"But I'll be in the circle of salt with you."

I shake my head. "I need someone to work the lights—someone they don't see, so they won't know you're there."

"Pelly can do that."

"I can try . . . " he says, but the doubt is plain in his voice. "Except I've never been very good with things that are mechanical."

"It's just turning a switch on," Maxine says.

"I understand. But anything not natural has a tendency to break down around me—it's like a curse."

"What could be more natural than electricity?" Maxine says. "It's what lightning's made of."

"Give him a break," I say. "He can't do it."

"Then we'll get Jared."

"He's got his gig. The band worked really hard to get it, and I won't ask him to give it up."

"No," Maxine says when she realizes what that means. "We're not doing it tomorrow night. Didn't you read what Esmeralda wrote? Tomorrow night's way, way too dangerous."

"If we wait any longer," I tell her, "I might not have the protection of the blue skin anymore."

I can see she wants to argue that, but instead she takes another tack.

"Then we'll ask Thomas," she says.

I sigh and shake my head. "It's not like that, Maxine. I don't want to involve *anyone* else. Not Jared, not Thomas, not my mom. I don't want the soul-eaters to become *aware* of anyone else. I already feel bad enough that I got you into this."

"But we're getting rid of them. They won't be a threat anymore."

"Unless we screw it up."

And there's nothing she can say to that. Because now she understands the logic of my argument and she doesn't want the ones she loves hurt any more than I do.

"So we're agreed?" I ask. "I'm in the circle. You work the lights, Maxine. Pelly's with you for moral support and whatever might come up that he *can* handle."

Maxine gives me a slow, reluctant nod.

"What else might come up?" she asks.

I shrug. "It'll be Halloween. Now that we know that

ghosts and goblins and witches are real, who knows?"

"Okay." She waits a beat, then adds, "Maybe Esmeralda will have more for us."

"It's worth checking," I say. "You can even tell her our plan, if you like. Get her opinion on it. Just don't tell her when we're doing it."

She gives me another nod, then changes the subject.

"What do you think it was that Adrian didn't tell you?" she asks.

"It's Adrian," I say. "Who knows what he was thinking?"

NOW: *Adrian*

At five past two on Friday afternoon, I'm standing in front of the school at the exact spot where I died. Everyone's in class, so there'll be no one to see me materialize unless they happen to look out the window. And even if they do, they won't believe I just appeared here. People are like that. Nobody believes in what doesn't make sense, or what they don't want to. It's like everybody knows that at some point they're going to die, but they still just go on like they'll live forever.

The time drags as I wait for 2:15 to come around.

I find myself worrying that maybe Bobby was just

having me on. It won't be the first time someone tried to play me for a fool. It won't be the first time I fall for it, either.

I've already scoped out the home ec classrooms, and everything I need is there. Flour, sugar, milk. Boxes of salt for the circle. I don't have a particular skill at making any kind of bread, but I don't think it really matters. I'm sure the offering is meant to be symbolic.

What I haven't decided on is *where* I'm going to do it, once I have the bread made. Anywhere in the school, and the fairies will find out and probably screw it up. But I don't want to do it outside where the wind or whatever might mess up my protective circle of salt.

I'm just settling on the house where I last ran into John Narraway when it happens.

At first I don't get it. It's been so long since I physically felt anything that this weird numbing cold doesn't make any sense at all. I get lightheaded. I smell something weird, then realize that it's simply my olfactory senses working again. I've never quite figured out why ghosts can see and hear but not smell. Same reason they can't feel physical sensations, I suppose, but sight and sound are also conveyed to the brain by physical organs, so that doesn't really answer the question.

Right now I don't care. I stamp my foot on the pavement and I can actually *feel* the impact.

I start to laugh.

No wonder Bobby looks forward to this one day a year

the way he does. It's like being alive again. I *am* alive again.

I'm giddy with the realization until I start to do my usual worrying. If I'm physically present, then I can be hurt again. What happens if some kids beat me up? Do I carry the pain and bruises all the way through to next Halloween? What if I have an accident? Get hit by a bus?

I laugh again. What does it matter? I'm already dead.

I look at the school. I still have hours before I can sneak into the home ec rooms. I decide to go exploring the city the way I never did when I was alive. Not skulking around in the night like the peeper Imogene accused me of being yesterday, but the way everybody does, in the broad daylight.

I'm going to live a little. I'm going to cram as much of the years I missed from being dead into the time I have today.

I walk away from the school, from the place of my death, and I don't look back.

NOW: *Maxine*

I'm uncomfortably sure that something's going to go wrong.

I know, I know. You're not supposed to put that kind of thing out into the universe because then you just make it happen. But I can't stop thinking that Imogene's plan is *too* simple.

"That's the beauty of it," she told me when I tried to talk her out of it one last time. "Things have more of a chance of messing up when you make everything complicated."

Which is true, I suppose, but only up to a point. Sometimes a plan can be so simple that it's just stupid, and the more I think about this one, the more I worry. I can't talk to anyone about it, and I certainly can't talk to Imogene, and she's the one I talk to about *everything.*

Esmeralda's no help either. There was another e-mail from her waiting for me when I got home last night:

Date: Thurs, 30 Oct 2003 22:07:38 -0800
From: efoylan@sympatico.ca
Subject: Busy busy busy
To: fairygrrl@yahoo.com

Maxine,

I saw from my server log that you tried to contact me earlier and I'm sorry I wasn't available to chat, but this time of year is always very busy for me—a hundred small crises. The borders are so thin, so naturally things keep leaking though that need to be dealt with.

Since you didn't send a follow-up e-mail, I'm assuming it was nothing urgent.

We'll definitely deal with your problem once Samhain is behind us. I'll write back on Saturday, or better still,

Sunday, when I've had a chance to rest up a little.

Oh, but before I forget, I did mention your situation to a colleague of mine who's better versed in shadow lore than I am. She said that if the anamithim take definitive forms when they manifest, then traditional fairy protocols can be invoked and the anamithim will respect them.

I know. It seems odd that such Unseelie creatures would obey what are really nothing more than social mores—albeit from a different social structure than our own—but Kate—my friend—assures me this is the case.

And now I really *must* run. Stay inside and keep the lights on!

E.

None of which was a real help, except it did start me wondering again about just who this Esmeralda was. Exactly what sort of problems did Halloween bring anyway? It had to have something to do with that gate she mentioned earlier, but that didn't help me understand.

And who was Kate? Maybe I should ask Esmeralda for her contact info so I could try talking to her directly.

Except I had school all day, after which I had to lay out the clothes for the fairies, and then it was showtime. There wasn't going to be the opportunity to get more advice.

There was always Christy, but I couldn't go to him without asking Imogene first, and I already knew there was no way she was going to agree to that.

So here I am at Redding, trying to get through the day, which is really hard for me, because for the first time I can remember, I don't want to be at school. I don't mean between classes or at lunchtime, when I'm never very comfortable, but during the classes, too. I'm in this total daze and think I should have stayed home the way Imogene has. Except I'm the one who has to lay out the clothes for the fairies, and it'd be hard to show up at the end of the day when I've missed all my classes. How would I explain *that* if one of my teachers spotted me?

I can tell how out of it I am when Valerie says something to me at lunch that has all her friends laughing and I don't even know what it is she said. I wasn't paying attention, just as I've been too dazed to do my usual scan-and-avoid-the-bullies routine before coming into the cafeteria.

"What?" I say, forgetting Imogene's first rule of bully avoidance: "Don't engage them in conversation, because then they *know* you're paying attention to them and that's all they really want. Someone to pay attention to them."

"Jesus, Chancy," Valerie says. "You are *such* a total lezzie loser."

One of her friends gives me a shove. I lose my grip on my books and my lunch. They all start to laugh again when the books fall to the floor. My binder pops open, and my notes go all over the place. My lunch bag tears, and the apple I'd put in it this morning goes rolling away under a table.

I want to say something like, You're the loser. And what's wrong with lesbians, anyway?

Or better yet, just smash a book in her face.

But all I do is flush and bend down to try to retrieve my notes.

Someone slides their foot against mine and pushes so that I lose my balance. I fall down on top of my books. My knee hits my lunch bag, and I feel my sandwich squash under it. Everyone laughs yet one more time—not just Valerie and her friends, but the kids at the nearby lunch tables, too.

That kind of thing always disappoints me.

You'd think they'd know better, because what's happening to me could be happening to one of them instead. But they don't think of that—or maybe they're just glad that it's happening to someone else and not them. I never laugh—that's something Imogene didn't have to teach me. Laughing at the victim's misfortune is like showing your approval for what the bully's done.

When Imogene's around people getting bullied, she gets this dark look in her eyes and scowls. She doesn't do anything, but anybody who sees her usually stops laughing and looks away. Embarrassed. I remember what Imogene told me about her old school and realize that maybe they're a little scared, too. Maybe they see something in her that I haven't: the potential for retribution. I don't know. What I do know is that even Valerie never pushes Imogene too far and she always keeps her distance, even when she's being mean.

Obviously, I'm not so lucky.

I hunch my shoulders, waiting for the next attack, but

Valerie's finally moved on. I collect my books, proud that at least I didn't cry. When I finally get my stuff together, I stand up and give a quick look around. Valerie's on the other side of the cafeteria, with Brent and the rest of their crowd.

I make my escape and hurry down a hall, not stopping till I've found one of the side stairwells that isn't used as much as the main ones. I sit on the stairs there and try to reorganize my notes. I eat my squashed sandwich. I wish I had my apple.

I realize that I really miss Imogene. Not just her physical presence—let's face it, her *protective* presence—here at school, but the Imogene she was before all this got so serious. The lighthearted and funny Imogene, who always seemed to say the last thing that you'd expect.

I wonder if I'm ever going to get her back.

* * *

I get through the rest of the day without incident—mostly because I've got my bully radar turned up to high and avoid the possibility of any further contact with them. I go to the library after my last class and pretend to study until Ms. Giles comes over to tell me that they're closing.

I have the halls pretty much to myself. There's not much in the way of after-school activity inside the building on a Friday unless there's a dance, but then I realize that today's one of the last big football games of the year. It's the city finals, and we're playing against Mawson High. That means there's going to be stragglers in the gym for hours afterward, using the locker rooms and showers, goofing and fooling around. They'll be full of relentless good cheer if we win, totally bummed if Mawson does.

I make my way to my locker, wondering how I could have forgotten that there was a game. I take out the bag of clothes I bought at the thrift store, then sit down by my locker and turn on my cell phone. Imogene answers on the first ring and I explain about the game.

"So the gym's out."

"Maybe we should call it off," I say, trying not to sound hopeful.

She laughs. "I don't think so. I'll still meet you outside the drama rooms around seven thirty. We'll figure it out then."

I want to ask her, Doesn't anything faze you? Not bullies, not monsters in the shadows, nothing?

But all I say is, "Okay."

I leave my jacket and books and everything in my locker, only keeping my cell phone, which I stick in the pocket of my cargo pants, and a flashlight, which I stick in a pocket on the other leg to balance the weight. Closing my locker, I pick up the bag of clothes and head for the basement.

I keep expecting to see Adrian or one of the fairies—I mean, if I can see the ones in Imogene's room, then I should be able to see them all, right? But there's only me and the custodian in the labyrinth that's the school's basement. Though maybe he's watching the game. If he's not, I'm hoping he's in that room where he drinks and sleeps off his drunks.

I walk in the opposite direction from where Imogene told me he hangs out and make my way to the furnace room. It's huge and really spooky, with all these weird boilers and heaters and pipes and everything. It's not actually pumping hot water through the pipes at the moment, but the hulking machines mutter and gurgle to themselves like drowsing dinosaurs.

It makes sense to lay the clothes out there. It's a place no one's going to come, probably not even the custodian.

I feel a little stupid taking off my shirt and putting it back on inside out, just like I do about the oatmeal and rowan twigs I've got in my back pockets, but I promised Imogene, so I do it. Then I lay the clothes out in little groupings in the middle of the room: shirt, pants, socks, hats, jackets. Ten sets in all, mismatched, some missing a hat, or a jacket, but they're mostly pretty complete. I didn't bother with shoes because I couldn't begin to guess the fairies' sizes. The clothes weren't so hard because Imogene told me the fairies are only a foot or so tall.

When I'm done, I stand back and clear my throat.

"Thank you, spirits," I say aloud, hoping my voice won't draw the custodian, "for your hard and selfless work to keep this building clean and safe the way you have over the years. We know you can never be fully repaid for all you've done, but we hope these small tokens of our gratitude will bring you even a fraction of the pleasure that your presence in this building has brought to us."

I half expect them to pop out of thin air, but nothing

happens. Maybe they've already peeked and hate what I brought. Or maybe they're just too shy with me standing here.

I smile to myself. Maybe they're off watching the game.

I look at my watch. I still have loads of time before I'm supposed to meet Imogene, so I find myself a hiding place behind some big metal vat that I suppose is part of the heating system and settle down to see if I can catch a glimpse of the fairies before they have to go away.

NOW: *Imogene*

The first thing I do when I wake up Friday morning is check the color of my skin. Still blue, but I was expecting that. The question is, am I any bluer than when I went to bed?

I can't tell. Maybe. Or maybe it just looks different from last night because of the sunlight coming in through the window.

I suppose I could ask Mom or Jared, but I don't want to remind them. It already turned into a point of contention last night, and I know if I'm not a noticeably lighter blue by tomorrow, Mom's going to insist we see the doctor. She's too worried to think it through properly, but all I can see is myself stuck in some laboratory for the rest of my life while they run tests on the stupid blue girl.

I understand Mom's anxiety, just like I understand what Thomas is feeling. He called last night and wanted to come see me, but I had to put my blue foot down and say no, and then of course he thought I was mad at him. He told me not to be embarrassed, that he liked me for me, not for what color my skin is, but that wasn't the point. The point is I don't want him any more involved in this than he is already. Whatever Maxine, Pelly, and I manage to do tonight, the less the people I care about are in danger, the better I'll be able to concentrate.

It's bad enough that Maxine's so insistent on seeing it through to the end, right by my side.

But I couldn't tell Thomas any of that. In the end I told him I'd see him at the Crib where Jared's band is playing. It's not a complete lie. If I survive the early part of the evening, dealing with the *anamithim,* I am *definitely* going to want to party.

That seemed to appease him, and when he calls me this morning we have a normal conversation—well, normal except for the big hole of trust that I'm digging in our relationship by *not* telling him what I have planned for tonight. But he doesn't come straight out and ask me, so I don't have to lie in response. I just don't volunteer the information.

* * *

"Do you believe in God?" I ask Pelly later in the day.

We're hanging in the living room again, working up

more stories for him, while the bread we made is baking. It's made the apartment smell really good.

"I don't have a soul," he says, "so it's not really relevant to me, is it?"

I wonder if that's the difference between humans and fairies and whatever Pelly is. We grow up being told we have a soul, so we believe it. Or at least we consider the idea as possible, perhaps even plausible, instead of outright dismissing it. Souls and God and heaven and hell. And even if we do end up abandoning the concept of God, we often come back to it in our old age. Or at least Mom says so. It happened to her parents. They were complete atheists for years, then suddenly became fervent churchgoers around the same time that they got a senior citizen's discount.

"But I believe in fate," Pelly adds.

"You mean like where the future's laid out before us, everything planned?"

He shakes his head. "That we make our own fate."

"I think that's called free will."

"I suppose."

We fall quiet again. I wish it was warm enough that we could go up on the roof, but Indian summer's been and gone, and it's so cold outside that you can see your breath. And while the roof is fine—I've hung out up there lots—when it's the only place you can go, it feels just as close as the apartment does.

I turn to look at Pelly, and when his gaze meets mine, I'm reminded of something he said last night.

"I'm sorry I abandoned you," I say. "I don't even know

how or why it happened. It . . . you just didn't seem real anymore. Like you couldn't be."

"You grew up."

"No," I say. I've been thinking about this. "I grew *down*. I let my mind get smaller instead of open and big the way it was when we were always together."

"I know you didn't do it on purpose," he says.

I give a slow nod. He's right about that much. I can't remember there ever being a time when I just decided I wasn't going to believe in him anymore. It just happened so gradually that I never saw it coming. Didn't know I'd changed until I was already standing on the other side of belief.

"It's going to happen again," I say.

"What is?"

"I'm going to abandon you again. I'm going to abandon everyone. I don't want to, but I messed up, Pelly."

He gets this look that tells me he understands, but "What do you mean?" is all he says.

"This plan isn't going to work. The *anamithim* are big and strong and old and smart. The most I can hope for is that they'll take me, but leave everyone else alone."

"You don't know that," he says. I feel he's trying to convince himself as much as me. "It seems like a good plan to me."

"Promise me you'll get Maxine away and safe."

"I can't promise that. She's as stubborn as you are."

"Promise you'll try."

He looks away and doesn't answer.

"Pelly, please."

"I'll try. But if they get wind of her . . ."

"I know."

I think about Maxine, my wonderful best friend, who's always been so honest and open with me.

"Does she shine?" I ask Pelly. "I mean, she shines to me, but does she shine to fairies?"

"Not like you do," he says. "You're like a beacon—it's why you can draw a ghost like Adrian to yourself so easily and why you could draw me to you when you were a child. Maxine has a luminescence, but it's not the shine of the Otherworld—the knowing and *seeing* that you have."

"Even though she's met you and believes you exist?"

He nods. "I don't know the whys and wherefores of what attracts the *anamithim*. But not every soul that sees into the Otherworld becomes their prey."

"And my mom and Jared?"

"No shine," he says. "They just give off the light that everybody does."

That's good, I think.

"But if you want my advice," he adds, "you shouldn't go into tonight's endeavor already thinking that you've lost."

"I'll work on that," I tell him.

* * *

It's five o'clock when I leave the house. Normally I hate how it gets dark so early at this time of year—especially since we put the clocks back an hour last weekend—but I'm grateful for it today. It means I can go out, because my skin's not so noticeably weird in the dark, and it being

Halloween, anyone who does notice is just going to think I'm on my way to a costume party.

It doesn't take two hours to get to school, but I want to walk around a bit. I've been cooped up for two days now and I am so not an indoors kind of person. I loved tramping around in the woods when I was a kid, and since we moved to Tyson, and later here, I get as much pleasure from the concrete forest. There's sure more wildlife—if you count all the weird people.

Pelly's gone back into wherever and is going to hook up with us at the school. He was worried about me being on my own, but I couldn't very well have him tagging along—the way he looks is *really* pushing the idea of a Halloween costume. Anybody who got too close a look would totally wig out.

And when he brought up the argument about the *anamithim* being out there in the dark, I just held up my arm.

"Blue skin," I told him. "Protected and all that, remember?"

We packed up a bunch of stuff in a knapsack: the bread we'd made this afternoon, boxes of salt, a bag of oatmeal, and a whole bunch of other stuff from my research yesterday: blue clothes, coins and a jar of honey as additional bribery in case the bread doesn't cut it, bottles of salted water to drink in case they try to enspell us, stones to throw, even a Bible and a crucifix. The last two I found on my curb-crawling rounds. I'm not a believer, but it didn't seem right to leave them on the curb, waiting for the garbage truck.

We didn't know what would work best, so I was going to try it all. First thing I'd do when I got to the school would be to turn my jacket inside out.

I'd also put in a lighter and some candles, a flashlight, and a bunch of firecrackers, then got my old switchblade out of the bottom of my sock drawer. That went in the pocket of my blue jeans.

I hefted the knapsack, and it weighed a ton.

"I'll take it to the school for you," Pelly said, lifting it like it had nothing much in it. "Be careful," he added before going into the closet.

"It's my new middle name," I assured him.

And I *am* careful as I walk through the streets, breathing in the crisp air. It's *so* good to finally be outside again. The streetlights are on now, and the shadows have stopped lengthening; now they're just pools of darkness in the mouths of alleyways and outside the reach of the streetlights. With my blue skin and all, I'm not so nervous about the shadows, but it turns out they're the least of my worries.

I wander around, but find myself at the school earlier than I expected. The lights are turned off on the football field, and not many people seem to be around, although there are a few cars in both the students' and teachers' parking lots, and small clusters of kids hanging at the front of the school. Talking. Waiting for rides, I guess.

Maybe we can use the gym after all. I've also been thinking of the auditorium, which might even be better because it's already got all kinds of lights in there, so we won't have to haul as many stage lights to it.

I stay in the shadows near the cedar hedge, then cross over to the side of the school once I'm out of sight of anybody who might happen to look over. I start for the side door, keeping my gaze on the hallway on the other side of the glass, ready to keep walking on past if I see anyone. But the hall's empty. The door, when I try it, is locked, but that's no problem. I get out my tools to start to work on the lock.

"What'd I say about getting in my space, bug?"

The doorway's wide, and I was so focused on who might be inside looking out that I didn't realize Brent Calder was nearby until he steps from the shadows at the side of the door and opens his big stupid mouth. I didn't realize, and I still don't care. I've got real worries on my mind.

I look him straight in the eye.

"Blow it out your ass," I tell him.

I turn back to the lock—I know, I know, what am I thinking? But for all his bullying and threats, I've just never taken him seriously. I've known dangerous people, and he's not one of them. Except, he *is* bigger than me and he *does* have a chip on his shoulder, and he *for sure* can't stand me.

Before I realize how stupid it is for me to ignore him, he gives me a shove that sends me sprawling.

"I don't like that mouth on you," he says as I bang into the wall on the far side of the doorway.

Now, here are the things I don't know right then:

Redding lost the game against Mawson. They should have won, they would have won, except the pass Brent threw to Kyle Hanley was too long. Kyle made a grab for the ball anyway, tipped it with his fingers, and bounced it right into the hands of Mawson's Andy Phipps, who took it back down the field for a first down that their team then parlayed into the winning touchdown.

Brent, of course, didn't take responsibility for the loss. Never mind that he overthrew—Kyle should still have caught it.

In the crowd, apparently, were a couple of college talent scouts.

I don't say this to excuse Brent's actions. It just explains why he was in a fouler mood than usual tonight.

The upshot was, he caught Kyle in the locker room and put him in the hospital with a broken nose, two cracked ribs, a possible concussion, and an eye so swollen he can't see out of it.

But like I said, I don't know any of this yet.

What I do know is that he's knocked me to the ground. It's when I'm picking myself up I see that Valerie's here, too. She's crouched against the wall in the other corner of the doorway, crying, holding her stomach. Her bottom lip is cut and bleeding. Her left eye's swelling up.

How did I so totally miss the two of them being here?

Brent says something else, but I don't hear it. Adrenaline kicks in, and my brain just explodes with all the months I've had to put up with him and his crap; all the fear I have about these soul-eaters in the shadows; how I've tried to just be a normal kid, but nothing will let me.

I lift my gaze to see him coming right for me, so I bunch my legs up against my chest. Then just as he's reaching down, I straighten one leg, hard, fast, and the solid heel of my boot gets him in the shin with all my strength behind it. He's big and I'm small, but it makes him cry out and lose his balance all the same.

I get up as he's going down. I'm not even thinking of what I'm doing. My switchblade's in my hand. I flick the button and the blade springs out. He starts to rise, but I'm already moving, the knife arcing toward him.

I kept that blade sharp as a razor, and it hasn't had any use since I stuffed it away in the bottom of my sock drawer when we moved here.

It slices through the material of his jeans, through skin and flesh, through sinew and muscle. Right below the knee.

He falls again and this time he goes down hard. His eyes widen with shock. He grabs his leg and his hands go bloody. His gaze comes back to me, and I kick him in the side of the head. I don't think I broke his jaw, but I definitely loosened a few teeth.

He drops yet one more time, this time banging his head on the cement.

I step forward, ready, but he's just whimpering now.

I wipe my blade on the sleeve of his jacket. He tries to grab at me with a bloody hand, but I kick the hand away.

I go over to where Valerie is huddled, staring at me as wide-eyed as Brent did when I cut him.

"We need to get you to a hospital," I tell her as I help her to her feet. "Can you walk?"

She gives me a slow, numbed nod.

"I . . . I need help, too . . . " Brent says.

I give him a cold look. "Yeah, I guess you do. Good luck with that."

"You . . . goddamn bitch. I'll—"

I lean Valerie up against the wall and take a step toward him. I don't get any real satisfaction in seeing him flinch. Truth is, I'm starting to feel sick to my stomach at what I just did. It's Frankie Lee all over again. There had to have been a better way to handle this, but I hadn't bothered to try to think of it.

And now I'm not caring again because Brent won't let it go. He's cursing at me, and I guess anger makes the nausea go away.

"You're not going to do a damn thing," I tell him. "Think anybody's going to believe a little bitty thing like me could have hurt a big strapping thug like you?"

"You can—"

I give the bottom of his foot a little tap with my boot—the foot at the end of the leg that's bleeding all over his hands. He actually squeals from the pain.

"Here's the thing," I tell him. "You're going to be laid up and not moving fast. If I can take you when you're not hurt, just think how easy it'll be for me later."

"Just . . . just wait . . . "

"Until what? Your problem is you thought you were dangerous, but you don't know the first thing about what's dangerous. Back in Tyson, the kids I ran with would chew you up and spit you out without even breaking a sweat."

He's shaking his head. "I . . . I'll get you."

"Sure you will. Except you've got to sleep sometime.

What happens when I sneak into your house with my knife? Just think about all the ways I can hurt you, you sorry-assed loser, and let me assure you, I know at least a dozen more. And here's the kicker. I'm not afraid to do it. You think I've been scared of you? Sure. But that's not why I let you push me around. I just didn't want any trouble. But you know what? I don't give a crap anymore. So just give me an excuse—any excuse—to finish what I started here, and I guarantee you're going to really learn the meaning of pain."

I give the bottom of his foot another tap.

"We clear on this?" I ask.

The fear in his eyes is stronger than the hate.

"Now I've got to get your girlfriend to the hospital and see if I can't convince her to press charges against you. You just lie there and behave until we're gone."

"Help . . . help me . . . "

I can see it took a lot for him to get that out.

"Yeah," I say. "Like that's ever going to happen."

Then I go back and collect Valerie and walk her toward the front of the school. Behind us, I can hear Brent start to sniffle.

"There's still some cars out front," I tell Valerie. "We'll get somebody to drive you to emergency."

"Please, no . . . "

I give her a confused look, but then I get it. She doesn't want anybody to see her like this, beat up by her own sorry-assed boyfriend. I check my watch. The hospital's not far. I can get her there and still get back in time to hook up with Maxine and Pelly.

"Okay," I say. "We'll find our own way."

I take her back along the edge of the cedar hedge, the way I came, and turn away from the school. I manage to flag down a cab at the next cross street.

"I need to get my friend to the hospital," I tell the cabbie, "but I don't have any money."

I never thought to bring any.

He takes one look at Valerie, then leans over his seat and opens the door.

"Get in," he says.

* * *

Once the nurse in emergency makes sure that none of Valerie's cuts and bruises are life-threatening, she has us take a seat in the waiting room.

Of course the bright lights in here make the blue of my skin—not to mention my hair and fingernails and eyebrows—really jump out, so I've been fielding questions ever since we got here from other people in the waiting room as well as the nurses and hospital staff. Valerie's only comment was, "What's with the blue skin? That's weird, even for you."

To her I just shrugged. My answers to the rest of them would start with "It's for Halloween," then I'd add something like, "I'm supposed to be Mystique—you know, from *X-Men*—only with clothes."

And when they wanted to know how I did it, I'd just tell them it was a trade secret.

It kind of surprised me how they'd just nod sagely and leave it at that.

Valerie's interest in how I look tonight is way down

on her importance scale, which is a big change for her, but I can't really blame her, considering what she's been through. And I'm just as happy not to have to talk about it with her.

I check the clock above the nurses' station. It's a little past seven. Time to go.

"You're going to be okay now," I tell Valerie. "Just tell them what happened and for god's sake, press charges against him."

I don't bother to ask her to leave me out of it. After tonight, after what happens when I get back to the school, it's probably not going to matter.

"I . . . I don't know if I can," Valerie says.

"This isn't the first time, is it?"

She shakes her head. "But it's . . . it's the worst. Usually, he just yells at me, or . . . you know. Pushes me around a little."

Yeah, I'll bet.

But, "You want it to happen again?" is all I ask.

She gives another shake of her head.

"So this is how you do it. You press charges."

"But—"

"Or next time, maybe he'll hurt you even worse."

She just looks at me. Every bit of the stuck-up high school princess is gone. But I don't have any illusions. She's not going to turn into some nice, considerate person overnight. That only happens in the movies.

"You hear me?" I say.

She nods. "I will," she says, her voice small.

"Good. So I've got to go now."

"No, please—"

"It can't be helped, Valerie. I really have to go. You're going to be okay. Brent won't touch you here. The doctors'll patch you all up, good as new. You don't need me here."

"Please . . . stay," Valerie says as I start to get up.

I shake my head, but she touches my arm and holds me a moment longer with a question.

"Why did you help me?" she asks.

This is worth an answer.

"Well, that's the thing," I tell her. "I believe we're all here to look out for each other, even when the other's a person like you. If I didn't help you, I wouldn't be able to respect myself."

"But—"

"You treat Maxine and me like shit, so why should I bother?"

She gives a slow, unhappy nod.

"Because if I didn't, then I'd be no better than you and your boyfriend."

"You . . . you could have done something to us anytime, couldn't you?" she asks. "All those times we were ragging on you."

"Your point being?"

"Why didn't you?"

"I told you last year: I don't want trouble at school. And remember what else I told you?"

You don't ever *want to see me out of school because I will so beat the crap out of you.*

I can see by her eyes that she remembers. And now she knows I wasn't just bullshitting her.

"Remind your boyfriend of that," I tell her.

"He's not my boyfriend. Not anymore."

"Whatever."

"He's going to kill you."

Stand in line, I think. By the time the soul-eaters are done with me, there won't be enough left to get hurt. But all I say is: "I wasn't joking. Tell him if he tries, I'm really going to hurt him."

"I hated you," Valerie says as I start to rise again. "Right from the first time I saw you."

She delivers the words in a matter-of-fact voice that doesn't have any passion in it at all.

"Yeah," I tell her. "That's been kind of obvious."

"But I don't know why."

She looks at me like I'm supposed to have an answer for that, like I can explain what goes through her head.

"That's something you've got to work out for yourself," I say.

I almost add, "princess," but something stops me. I guess I just want to let all of this go.

I glance at the clock again. Seven twenty.

"Don't be too hard on yourself," I tell her, not that it's going to make much of a difference.

And then I do get up and walk off, looking for a phone before I head back to the school. I've already put Valerie's problems out of my mind by the time I find one. Instead

I'm thinking of what's waiting for me at the school. I remember what I'd said to Pelly, earlier in the day.

Do you believe in God?

I wish I did. I wish I could pray to him for a miracle and at least pretend to myself that maybe he'd deliver.

NOW: *Maxine*

I actually fell asleep, hidden there behind this huge metal monstrosity. The soft gurgling sounds it made were soothing enough to let me drift off, even on a cement floor. I'm dreaming of little fairy men trying on thrift shop clothes when my cell phone wakes me. I jerk my head up, banging it against the wall behind me, and I don't have a clue where I am.

At the second ring, I remember and suddenly worry about the sound of the phone scaring off the fairies. I fumble the cell out of my pocket, flick it open, and push *talk*.

"Hello?" I whisper into it.

"You okay?" Imogene says. "I can hardly hear you."

"I'm in the basement," I tell her, "waiting to see if the fairies take the clothes we left for them."

"You didn't have to do that."

"I know. But it was hang here, or find some closet somewhere where no one would ask me what I'm still doing at school."

"So did they take them?"

"Let me look."

I peer around the tank of whatever it is I'm hiding behind and check where I laid out the clothes.

"They did!" I say, my voice at a more normal volume. "Some of them, anyway."

I get up and walk around the machine. I count the sets I laid out.

"Five sets are gone," I tell Imogene.

"Well, now we know *that* works."

"I guess. Unless they're still here, but running around dressed like weird little thrift shop kids."

Imogene laughs.

"So where are you?" I ask.

She tells me what happened, and my heart speeds up in my chest. My palms get all sweaty. She's so matter-of-fact about her encounter with Brent—she sounds completely normal—but I'm feeling this whole weird mix of emotions. Relieved she's okay, of course. Bad for her that she had to go through this. But scared, because it's true—she really *can* do this stuff.

"Are you sure you're okay?" I ask when she's done.

"I'm fine."

"You sound so calm."

There's a moment's silence on her end. It's quiet enough that I can hear some doctor being paged.

"I don't like that I had to do it," she says finally, "but I don't regret that I did it. Brent Calder is over twice my size, and there's no way I could have stopped him without his underestimating me and me having my blade. Did you hear what he did to Kyle Hanley, just because he didn't catch a pass?"

"No."

"Valerie told me he put Kyle in the hospital. Then he beat her up, and he was ready to do the same to me. He's not just a bully anymore. He's turned into some feral thing. He had to be stopped."

"I . . . I wasn't saying you shouldn't have done . . . what you did. It's just . . . I don't know how you *did* do it. How you could be that . . . I don't know, brave, I guess."

She sighs. "I don't know that it was bravery, Maxine. I was just mad. It's like he flicked a switch in my brain and he let out this other me, the one I've been trying to keep locked up in a little part of my brain since we moved to Newford."

"So you . . . you've done this before? Back in Tyson."

"No, I never cut anybody. But like I told you, I've been in fights before and I've pulled my knife on a couple of people. I just didn't have to use it."

She might not be fazed, but I feel like I'm in shock, and I wasn't even there.

"So," I say, "are we still . . . you know . . . "

"On for tonight? Absolutely. I just wanted to give you a heads-up before I left the hospital to let you know I might be a little late. I don't have any money on me. We got a free ride from a Good Samaritan cabbie, but I have to hike back."

"I have money."

"But we don't want you waiting in front of the school to pay off the cab, now do we?"

"I guess not."

"Don't worry," she says. "I won't be that long."

"Okay."

"Oh, has Pelly showed up yet?"

"I haven't seen him. I haven't seen anybody."

"Let's keep it that way," she says. "He's probably up in the drama rooms, waiting for us. Just sit tight and give me half an hour or so, okay?"

"Sure."

She says good-bye and cuts the connection. I pull my cell from my ear and look at it for a long moment before I press *end*, fold it closed, and stick it back in my pocket.

I'm feeling kind of numbed. What happened to Imogene tonight has nothing to do with the fairies or the *anamithim,* but it brings what we're about to attempt into way too sharp a focus. This isn't a fairy tale; it's actually happening. The danger is real. We might get hurt. Though when you think about it, fairy tales—real fairy tales, not the sanitized ones that end up in picture books and Disney cartoons—are all about danger and pain and terrible things happening. People get hurt in them all the time. And they don't always end "happily ever after" either.

We could get hurt.

We might not get the happy ending.

I guess this is the moment when I actually get brave myself, because I realize that, scared as I am, I'm not going to let that stop me from helping Imogene.

NOW: *Adrian*

The football field's lit up and there are kids everywhere when I get back to the school. So much for my plans to sneak into the home ec rooms.

I hesitate at the edge of the school grounds, trying to decide whether to wait inside, or do some more wandering. It's not really a choice I can make. I *want* to experience *everything*. But the way I'm feeling, I'd rather just find some place to curl up. I'm definitely overstimulated.

It was odd out on the streets this afternoon. In the beginning, having a physical presence was amazing. I walked around like some rustic hick on his first visit to the big city. Everything felt immense and so very *here,* especially myself. I went all the way down to the pier at the end of Williamson Street, wandered around inside the Williamson Street Mall, then followed the boardwalk and bike paths along the lakefront to Fitzhenry Park before making a zigzagging way through the various blocks of tenements and storefronts to get back here to the school.

By now I actually have sore feet, but that's not what makes me want to find some place to hole up. I might have been like a hick, but I was also like a little kid, gorging on hot dogs, ice cream, warm pretzels, chocolate bars, soda pop—all the things I want when I'm intangible. The only reason I stopped was because I pretty much ran out of the money I'd had when I died. All I have left is some change. But I would have had to stop anyway, because just as I was getting close to the school, that junk food caught up to me.

This is the part of having a corporeal form that's not so much fun.

I decide to sneak into the school before the doors get locked for the night. No one pays any attention to me—I'm just another kid—and I make my way up to the home ec rooms. I open a door at random. I lie down on the floor at the back of the dark classroom, and hope my stomach will settle down a bit.

I'm kind of surprised that Tommery or one of the other fairies hasn't shown up yet to see what's going on with me. You'd think they'd get a kick out of seeing me sick to my stomach, and be curious about how I was back in my body for the night.

But they don't.

So I lie there feeling miserable and sorry for myself.

And lonely.

It's funny. That's never happened to me as a ghost. I'll

drift through the cafeteria and wish I could have a soda or a bag of chips. I'll be in the library and want to be able to pick up a book, or go surfing the Internet in the computer lab. I'll definitely lust after the girls in the hall. But loneliness isn't a part of my afterlife.

I'm not sure why that is.

Maybe it's because most of the time I'm not even here, if that makes any sense. To be honest, until Imogene came around, I hadn't been doing much of anything. I just drift around. Sometimes days can go by while I'm—not exactly sleeping, but not really in the world either. I don't know where I go, or if I go anywhere. Maybe ghosts don't sleep. Maybe when we do the equivalent of sleeping, we just shut off and we're nowhere until something turns us back on again.

All I do know is that right now, nauseous as I'm feeling, I'm so lonely it hurts. It's been building up ever since I became tangible, but it's hitting me worse now—I guess because I'm already feeling so miserable. At one point, I thought of going by Imogene's place but then I realized that with me being tangible as I am now, she really could hit me, so naturally I chickened out.

Or maybe it's not my present misery. Maybe it's *because* I'm tangible. Maybe having a physical presence intensifies everything. Like I'm a virgin—no surprise there, right? I never even kissed a girl before I died. I wanted to, but I knew I didn't stand a chance. I don't stand a chance with Imogene either, but the thing of it is, if by some miracle she *was* interested, we could actually do something. Physical, I mean. Well, at least we could tonight. Like that would ever happen.

This is no good.

I sit up and the world does a slow spin.

Sick as I am, I know I'm wasting precious time. Time when I should be making up for the danger I put her in, that is. I want to forget my stupid little fantasies about her.

So I decide to find Tommery and see if he's got some kind of fairy cure for a sick stomach.

Moving's not as bad as I think—at least not once I stand up and hang on to the nearest counter for a minute, waiting for the world and my stomach to stop churning.

I find the fairies in their favorite elf bolt—the one at the top of the school's main stairs. They're cavorting around in kids' clothing, acting all excited, and it takes a moment before anyone notices me leaning against the wall, making a valiant, and so far successful, effort not to throw up on myself. I try to figure out what they're doing dressed like this. Tommery's in a pair of OshKosh overalls that are way too big for him, wearing a pink T-shirt that says "Florida." It probably says more, but the rest is hidden under the bib of the overalls. The others are wearing Care Bear shirts, Little Mermaid pajama bottoms, a Barney hoodie . . . that kind of thing.

I decide they're up to some Halloween prank when Quinty finally spies me.

"Addy!" he cries.

"Well, look who finally figured out Halloween," Tommery says.

It figures that they'd known all along and hadn't bothered to tell me. "Do you have something for a stomach ache?" I ask.

He shakes his head. "The one night you can walk around in corporeal form, and you get sick?"

"We already know I'm a loser," I say. "I'd just rather not have to throw up as well."

"Ginger's good," Krew says.

"Like ginger ale?" I ask.

I think I have enough change to get a can out of the vending machine in the cafeteria.

He nods. "It's best when it's flat. But I was thinking more of ginger root."

"Or tea," Sairs says.

Krew nods. "The tea's very good."

"You wouldn't happen to have any?" I ask.

They shake their heads. I see Tommery getting a considering look, like he has some new misery planned for me, but then he shrugs and gives me a smile.

"Help him out, Quinty," he says. "Give him a taste of your healing hands."

I give Tommery a suspicious look.

"Why are you being so helpful?" I ask.

"I'm in a generous mood tonight, Addy. And besides, you're our friend. Friends help each other, expecting nothing in return."

I flinch when Quinty steps up and puts his hands on my stomach, but whatever it is he does, it takes the nausea away, just like that.

I blink, feeling normal for the first time in what seems like hours. You ever notice how everybody takes their health for granted until they get sick? And how *good* it feels when you're better again?

"Wow," I say. "Thanks."

Quinty smiles at me, then does a little pirouette, holding out the bottom of his Olsen twins T-shirt to show it off.

"What do you think?" he asks.

"Well, it's . . . great." I look from him to the others. "So what are you guys up to?"

"We're going home," Oshtin tells me.

"Home?"

They all beam.

"We were thanked for our hard work," Tommery says, "and given the gift of clothing. That means we're finally free to go."

I'm still mulling over the idea of any of them doing hard work, when what he says sinks in.

"Somebody put these clothes out for you?" I ask.

Tommery nods. "And thanked us, too."

I'm remembering the story of the cobbler and the fairies who did his work for him until his wife laid out clothing for them.

"So who was it?" I ask.

"Don't know," Tommery says. "Don't care. We heard the thanks being said in the furnace room and when we went down there, we found our clothes waiting for us."

I can't imagine who would do this. I think of Imogene, but even if she knows the story, why would she bother?

"So you're going away," I say. "And you seem pretty happy about it."

"Why wouldn't we be?"

"I don't know. I thought you liked being here, playing tricks on everybody."

"We did, Addy," Tommery tells me. "We did. But now it's time to go home."

"To Fairyland."

"It's been a very long time since we've seen our home." Then he shrugs. "Besides, it's not like we have a choice. When we're thanked . . . it's like a *geas*."

"Like a what?"

"A thing we must do."

"Well . . . bon voyage, I guess."

"We'll miss you," Tommery tells me.

I nod. Like I believe that.

"So before you go," I say, "can you tell me how to stop the *anamithim* from taking a soul?"

"Now where did you learn a big word like that?"

"From one of the gatherers."

"You don't want to listen to them. They're as ready to send your soul on as the shadows are to take it."

"Right. But back to my question. How can the *anamithim* be stopped?"

"It's simple," Tommery says. "Don't be noticed by them. Stay off their radar and you'll be fine."

"But if someone *has* been noticed?"

They all actually look a little uncomfortable.

"Oh, you mean your girlfriend," Tommery says.

I don't bother to argue that there's as much chance of Imogene being my girlfriend as there is of me living a normal life now.

"They're after her," I say.

"We didn't do it," Tommery says. "At least, not on purpose."

He gives me that guileless look that he always does when he's lying.

"I just need to know how to stop them."

"You can't. Sorry about that."

"But—"

"If you want to save your girl," he says, cutting me off, "you know what you need to do."

And I do. All along I've been pretending that there was some other way, but I've always known there wasn't.

"Yeah," I say. "I guess I do."

This, I realize, is just one more joke for the fairies. I think maybe I hate them more for it than for any of the others.

"Hey," Tommery says, "perhaps if you tell her what you're about to do for her, she'll feel so grateful, she'll have sex with you."

I have to admit that's a pleasant fantasy, but it's never going to happen. Not with Imogene. Not in a million years.

But, "Yeah," I say. "She probably will."

They're starting to fade now, stealing my ghost shtick, except they're slipping away to . . . wherever. Fairyland, I guess. For a moment, I feel a breeze on my skin that holds a sweet smell of apples and roses and reminds me, for no good reason, of all the things I've never had, all the things I'll never have.

"You've been fun, Addy," I hear Tommery say, followed by a chorus of good-byes from the others.

Their voices seem to come from as far away as far can be.

And then they're really gone.

* * *

I'm going to take this night for myself, I decide. I'll take it and then I'll give myself over to the shadows. But I deserve this much.

I'm not sure what I'm going to do. What I'd like to do is talk to Imogene, but that doesn't seem like a particularly good idea. Instead I'll go out into the city. Maybe I can find Bobby. Maybe he'll pretend we're friends and let me tag along on whatever adventures he has planned.

But first I'm going to check out the furnace room to see if I can figure out who sent the fairies packing.

NOW: *Imogene*

It takes me half an hour to hike back to the school. When I get close, I sneak into the sunken parking lot of the apartment building next door. It's quiet down here. Sometimes the skateboarders use the ramp, but I have the place to myself tonight. I hoist myself up at a low part of the wall and push my way into the cedar hedge. Hidden, I check out the lay of the land.

There's no sign of Brent. No sign of anybody, actually. No police, teachers, students, or even Mr. Sanderson, who you'd think would be cleaning up Brent's blood. But Sanderson's probably passed out drunk somewhere, or well on his way. The teachers and students will all have left for home. As for the police, well, depending on how big a mouth Brent has, they might be knocking on Mom's door right now.

I feel bad about that. Mostly for the worry it'll cause her, but I also know that she always gets nervous around the police. It comes from having lived so many years with—and *as,* if we're going to be honest—a dopehead like my dad.

But the police will just be an inconvenience for her. When it comes to me, they could be big trouble. Assuming I make it through the night.

When I'm sure the coast is clear—and I mean *completely* clear this time, no abusive guys beating on their girlfriends in the shadows—I step out of the hedge and dart for the door.

It's still locked. I check the shadows on either side of me again—don't say I don't learn from my mistakes—then work on the lock. It doesn't take long to get its tumblers all aligned. I pull on the door, take a last look around, then open it wide enough to slip inside. Once through, I catch the door with my hand so that it doesn't bang shut. I wait another moment, listening while I take off my jacket and turn it inside out. When I'm sure I haven't attracted any unwanted attention, I start up the stairs, heading for the drama department.

I don't mind the empty halls, or the soft scuffle of my boots on the marble floors, but it's different inside the drama department's rooms. I can't chance a light at this point, so the strange shapes of the props they have stored here feel stranger. And kind of spooky.

I'm berating myself for suddenly going all wimpy, when something stirs in a corner where the shadows are deepest. I dig out my switchblade and wish I hadn't given Pelly all our protective stuff as I let the blade *snik* out. Sure, I have the blue skin, but who knows how long its defense lasts? Maybe the protection wears off before the color.

"Who's there?" I say.

I take a step in the direction of the corner, my knife held out before me, glad that at least my voice sounds firm.

"It's only me," a familiar voice says, and I feel like an idiot.

It's Pelly. Of *course* it's Pelly. This is where I'm supposed to meet him and Maxine.

"Where's Maxine?" I ask, and put away my knife.

"I haven't seen her. I haven't seen anybody."

My eyes are adjusting to the dim light in here. I can make out Pelly now, the knapsack slung from one shoulder.

"Did you look in any of the other rooms?" I ask.

Pelly nods. "There's no one."

"But she said she was meeting us here."

"Maybe she went home," Pelly says.

"Yeah, right."

Pelly shrugs, but I know he's worried, too. The only reason Maxine wouldn't be here is if she ran into trouble.

This is why I should have my own cell phone. If I had one, I could just call Maxine, and we'd know exactly where she is and how she's doing.

"I called her about a half hour ago," I tell Pelly. "She was in the basement then."

Pelly walks by me, heading for the door.

"Then that's where we should go," he says.

"Are they here?" I ask him as we leave the room and start down the hall. "Is there something watching us from the shadows? Because I can't tell."

"There are always things watching from the shadows," Pelly tells me.

And isn't that comforting.

"The *anamithim*, I mean," I say.

The halls are dimly lit. Instead of all the fluorescents glaring supermarket bright, like they are when classes are in session, there are only lights every twenty feet or so. Which leaves plenty of space for shadows to gather. I study the dark patches ahead of us, trying to sense what he does. But my senses aren't nearly as finely attuned.

He nods. "I know what you meant. I can't tell. Shadows are a kind of borderland, and there is always traffic in the borderlands."

"What kind of traffic?"

"Everything from the soul-eaters to the curious beings

and spirits that like to peer into the worlds on either side of the border, simply because they can."

I don't find any of this comforting. All I can think of is Maxine, alone in the basement. I quicken my pace, my boots clomping on the marble. I know the noise might attract Sanderson, but at this point, he's the least of my worries.

"What about the fierce lights?" Pelly asks, hurrying along at my side.

For a moment I don't know *what* he's talking about. Then I remember our plan.

"You mean the spotlights? We don't have time to set them up. It's not like we can just ask the *anamithim* to hold on a sec while we get ready."

"But without them—"

"I know. We've got nothing except for the junk you're lugging around in that pack."

Truth is, I wasn't all that confident that the lights would have worked anyway. The whole *real* idea behind my plan was to let me confront the *anamithim* without everybody trying to talk me out of it. I don't like plans. I know they work for some people, but I've always preferred to solve problems as I go, hoping that in the middle of the crisis, a solution will come. It's worked so far in my short little life.

Just as I'm thinking this, the room we've just trotted by registers, and I get an idea.

"Hold on," I say, and start backtracking.

"But Maxine . . ."

"I know. But I've got an idea."

I get back to the door of the art room and open it. There's no time for fumbling in the dark with the flashlights in Pelly's pack. I flick on the overheads, and we both blink stupidly for a moment in their sudden glare.

"Back there," I say, pointing to where the art supplies are stored.

I grin at Pelly's confused look.

"C'mon," I say, "and give me a hand."

NOW: *Maxine*

After I get off the phone with Imogene, I stand there for a while, staring down at the five little piles of clothes on the cement floor. Should I gather them up now—that's the compulsive neatness Mom's drilled into me kicking in—or leave them here in case some fairies haven't gotten their outfits yet?

I'm still trying to make up my mind when I hear footsteps. By the time it occurs to me that footsteps mean that someone's coming, and therefore I should find a place to hide, Adrian steps into view.

I let out a breath I hadn't been aware of holding.

"You," I say.

I'm angry, not so much at his startling me like this, but because of how he got us into this whole mess in the first place. So he's pretty much the last person I want to see at the moment, if you can call a ghost a person.

I stare daggers at him, except he doesn't even seem to notice.

"Maxine," he says. "What are you doing here?" His gaze goes to the piles of kids' clothing. "Are you the one who sent the fairies packing?"

"Maybe."

"Why would you do that?"

"Maybe we didn't like them. Just like we don't like you."

"You don't like me? What do you mean? And who's 'we?'"

He's looking around the room while he fires these questions at me, as though he expects someone to come popping out from behind one of the furnaces or tanks.

"Well, considering how you sicced these soul eaters on us," I say, "what did you expect?"

"Oh, that. But it wasn't really my fault."

I give him a look.

"Okay, so I'm partially responsible. But that's only because Tommery didn't explain what he was going to do. It's not like I meant for any of this to happen."

"That doesn't change the fact that our lives are in danger."

"What do you mean 'our'? Are they after you, too?"

His alarm appears genuine.

"We're not sure," I say. "But probably. Or they probably will be."

"You keep saying 'we.' Is Imogene here?"

"I don't really have time to talk," I tell him.

I go to walk around him—because I'm really not up for the weird chill of another ghostly encounter—but he grabs my arm. I jump back, pulling myself free.

Then I realize what just happened.

"You're real," I say, rubbing my arm.

It's not sore or anything. I'm just a little stunned from his actually being able to touch me.

"I mean, you're really here," I add.

"It's Halloween."

"So you just get to walk around on Halloween—I mean, with your body and everything?"

He nods. "Yeah, I know. It's weird, isn't it? I didn't know it could really work."

"You never noticed any other year?"

"It's not an automatic thing. You have to be at the place you died exactly at moonrise, or it doesn't happen. I didn't know that."

"Another one of those stupid rules," I say.

"What rules?"

"Haven't you noticed that everything to do with fairies and magic's all bound up in rules? Like the way we got rid of the fairies by leaving clothes out for them and thanking them for a job well done."

"What job did they ever do well besides getting me killed, putting you and Imogene in danger, and, oh yeah, pretty much tormenting anyone who happened to catch their interest?"

"It was just what you're supposed to do to get rid of them."

"Oh."

He looks down at the clothes that I still haven't decided what to do with yet, though I'm leaning more and more toward just leaving them here on the floor.

"So, it really worked?" I ask. "They're all gone?"

He nods. "But that's not going to stop the *anamithim*."

"We've got another plan for that."

"I want to help." He's peering into the shadows again. "Where is Imogene anyway?"

"I don't think your helping is such a good idea," I tell him. "Considering how you got us all into this."

"I told you, that was an accident."

"Well, we don't need another accident."

"Oh for—"

"And I'll tell you something else. If anything happens to Imogene, I'm going to find a way to get you for it."

This time the angry look I give him registers, and he takes a step back.

It's funny: I can't stand up for myself, but it turns out I can be totally fierce for Imogene.

"But I really want to help," Adrian says. "That's all I've been trying to figure out these past few days."

I want to stay mad at him, but he looks so miserable that I can't. Instead I tell him what we've found out so far, from Imogene's research—"Oh, I heard about the bread bit," he says—to Esmeralda's odd warnings about the ballad "Tam Lin" and how Imogene figures we can use spotlights from the drama club to trap the creatures in their glare.

"That's a better idea than I had," Adrian says.

"What were you planning to do?"

"First I was trying to figure out a way to give them somebody else in her place."

"Oh, *nice.*"

"Well, it was going to be a creep like Brent Calder."

"Too late for that," I say. "He's already in the hospital."

So then I have to tell him about it.

"Wow," he says. "She really *is* tough."

I give a slow, unhappy nod. I mean, I'm glad that Imogene's okay and everything, but it's weird, especially the way she can just carry on afterward like it's no big deal.

"So I assume you changed your mind about the sacrifice," I say.

"Well, yeah. It wouldn't be right. Even for someone like Brent."

"So what then?"

"Well, I was going to offer myself up in her place. You know, nothing fancy. I'd just . . . " He faces the darkest corner of the basement, spreads his arms wide, and declaims in a loud voice, "Okay, here I am and I'm telling you that you can't take Imogene. You want someone, I'm right here, waiting for you."

I'm trying to stop him as soon as he starts. I grab at his arm, but he shakes me off.

"What?" he says. "I'm just showing you . . . "

"I just don't think you should be . . . " I'm saying at the same time.

Our voices trail off as we hear it—no, we *feel* it. Something stirring in the shadows of that dark, dark corner.

I so don't want this to be what I know it is.

"Oh, *crap*," Adrian says.

I echo that sentiment, but the words can't seem to get past my lips. As the three figures step from the shadows, my mind's too numbed to be able to do anything so complex as make my muscles work.

The first thing I think when they come out into the light is that they're like angels. Or at least the way I always imagined angels to be: stern and tall and way too bright.

Except no way are they angels. Because angels have mercy, too, right? And these . . . these creatures . . . I'm sure they have none. They're gaunt and hairless, wearing thin, loose robes that reach to the floor and cling to their shapes so their musculature is hyperdefined. Their gazes are flat, I mean *completely* expressionless, like we mean nothing to them. I *know* we mean nothing to them.

And they seem to be made of light.

But it's not a light that shines out, so much as in, as if they swallow it into the slick sheen of their skin. It was gloomy enough down here in the basement before they showed up, but as soon as they stepped from the shadows, the overhead lights went dimmer. And right now I can feel *myself* going dimmer, as though just being in their presence is taking something from me.

Shadows writhe around the bottoms of their legs, as though dozens of half-realized things are shifting shape down there, unable to completely take form, or unwilling to settle on just one. I see, here, a small triangular head with a mouthful of sharp teeth; there, a bony limb ending in claws or talons. They're horrible, but not nearly as bad as the motionless figures towering over them.

It's funny. Before the *anamithim* showed up, I knew this was all real—that the soul-eaters were for real—but deep inside, I never quite believed it. I'd sit there making plans with a blue-skinned Imogene and a fairy-tale Pelly, but I never truly believed that these creatures actually existed.

I believe it now. How can I not believe in these tall white figures with their legs disappearing into that fog of shifting, squirming shadows?

The foremost one beckons for us to approach, but no way am I getting any closer. I can't move anyway, but if I could, I'd be running as fast and far from here as my legs could take me.

He—it?—says something in a language I don't understand; the words make my skin crawl, like there are cockroaches flowing all up my legs and torso and scurrying into my ears.

And then my body betrays me, because it takes a step forward of its own accord.

I fight the loss of my body's motor control, but I might as well be trying to bottle a spoken sentence.

My body takes another step.

I'm wailing in my head—this gibbering wordless panic that would put horror movie actors to shame if it could ever come tearing out of my mouth.

I know I'm going to walk right up to the *anamithim*.

I know I'm going to let them put their hands on me and I'm going to feel the touch of their horrible light-stealing flesh on mine.

And there's nothing I can do to stop it.

Right then—if I was never sure before—I know that we all do have souls that burn and glow like a light inside of us.

We carry beautiful, warm fires that the darkness covets.

And they're going to take ours from us.

They're going to drain the light right out of us, and then there'll be nothing left of us.

Nothing left at all.

At least Imogene's not here, I think.

Maybe they'll be satisfied with us. Maybe once they've taken us, they won't have the same hunger for Imogene.

Except then I hear the sound of running footsteps from behind us. I can't turn my head.

Go back, go back! I want to shout.

But nothing comes out of my mouth.

And then I hear Imogene say, "Get them open, Pelly."

NOW: *Imogene*

Now I had no idea if blue paint was going to do anything, but that's what Pelly and I picked up in the art room. Four big plastic pails of liquid poster paint. I thought we could pour the paint around ourselves to make a protective circle, because we know blue works, and who really knows about this salt business? Or maybe we could just pour it over Maxine and Pelly, so that they'd be protected, too.

But when we finally reach Maxine, I have a better idea.

"Get them open, Pelly," I say as I work the lid free from one of the pails I'm carrying. "Then follow my lead."

Oh, they're big and scary, all right, these *anamithim*, and don't look anything like I expected. I was thinking the Ringwraiths from the *Lord of the Rings* movies—just these horrible *shapes* in tattered black cloaks. And maybe they're super powerful and everything. But they're messing with my friend.

I've spotted Adrian, too. It figures he'd be here. He probably led the *anamithim* to Maxine. But I figure we can deal with him later. He's a ghost. What's the worst he can do? Call some more bad guys down on us?

I check to make sure Pelly's ready. There are three of the tall-white-and-uglies and a whole mess of squirmy shadows moving around by their feet. The big one in front starts saying something in a language I don't get. He seems surprised about something—maybe he was mouthing some spell?—but now I'm right in his face.

Up goes the pail, and blue paint goes flying all over the three of them.

"Pelly?" I say.

When I turn around, I see he's frozen in place, so I run back and get another pail.

The uglies are all yelling something now, but I don't pay any attention. I just pry off the lid of the second pail and start back toward them. The front guy sticks his arm out and points at me, still shouting something, when the second pailful of blue paint goes washing all over him and his buddies. The front ugly gets a mouthful and he stumbles back, choking.

The mess of wriggling shadows is gone now. And it seems brighter in the room. I couldn't figure out why it was so dim compared to the rest of the basement.

The creature in front's still trying hard to do some kind of magic thing to me. If the rage in his eyes was a physical threat, I'd be dead.

I throw the empty pail at him. I miss, but whack the guy standing behind him, who gets this startled, stunned look.

Well, what do you know?

I was thinking the paint would—oh, I don't know—damage them in some way, but this is turning out way better than I could have planned. Because I can tell from the looks on their faces that we're not supposed to be able to touch them. I guess it was part of their magic—the same enchantment that lets them travel through shadows and just take shape when they want to.

But they're locked in their physical shapes right now. And the shadows won't be taking them anywhere.

"Rules have changed, boys," I say.

I take out my switchblade and thumb the button. The blade *sniks* out.

Time to finish this.

As I step forward, Pelly's suddenly by my side. I guess the *amamithim*'s spell wore off, or they're too busy right now to maintain it. Pelly flings the contents of his pail over the creatures, covering them with yet another coating of blue paint.

"Sorry, sorry," he says to me. "I didn't lose my courage. It was magic that stopped me."

"I know," I say.

It was those words that the leader was saying, which is also why Maxine wasn't able to move. But those magic words didn't work on me.

I glance at Pelly. "Keep an eye on ghost boy while I put an end to this."

They're tall and they're repulsive, and not big on courage, either, it seems. I mean, any one of them is twice my size, and there's three of them. But I guess they can't touch the blue-skinned girl, and she's got the knife.

I move toward them, and they back away from me until they're right up against the wall. That tells me everything I need to know.

They can be hurt.

They can die.

I shake my head. "I can't believe we were supposed to be scared of you sorry losers."

I remember Frankie Lee's coaching. Sharp edge of the blade up. Put your whole shoulder into the thrust. Plunge it into the stomach, then rip it up.

I step up to the closest of the *anamithim*.

"Imogene, don't!"

I can't believe what I'm hearing.

"Maxine, they were going to *eat our souls*."

"I know. And I could actually feel it starting to happen."

"So your problem is?"

"If you kill them, that makes us no better than they are."

I shake my head. "I'm not too concerned with which of us is morally superior. Do you think they cared?"

"No, but we should."

"I understand what you're saying," I say. "I know all about how the bad things you do come back on you, believe me. But this is something that has to be done. So for the record, it's my doing, not yours, not Pelly's."

"The Imogene I care about wouldn't do it," she says.

"Maybe the Imogene you thought you knew never existed."

"I don't believe that. And neither do you."

I'm not entirely sure she's right. I dealt harshly with Brent. I never stopped to think about it. I just cut him and then left him to bleed.

I know if I survive this, I'll have to deal with the fallout.

With what I did to Brent, I'll have to deal with the police and the legal system, and probably Brent trying to get his own back, because he's just dumb enough to need to do that. But here . . . here I have no idea except that I know Maxine's right.

It's my own words to Adrian about karma, coming back to haunt me.

I'll have to carry the weight of what I've done, and the worst-case outcome of killing the *anamithim* will be that the Imogene I've been trying to be, the one that Maxine considers her friend, won't exist anymore. If she ever did. Maybe this past year has just been some pathetic joke fate's been playing on me, letting me pretend to be a good kid. To be normal.

"You know if we leave this now," I say, "we're just going to have to deal with it later."

She shakes her head. "No, we'll deal with it now."

She steps up beside me and faces the leader of the creatures. "Are you ready to hear the terms of your survival?" she asks.

He turns his head and spits out some blue paint. When he looks back at her, he says something in that unintelligible language of his.

"Speak English," Maxine says.

I'm impressed. There she is, with her back straight, her voice firm, standing up to him like she never did the bullies at school.

He glares at her, but says, "What are your terms?"

His voice is guttural and heavily accented, but we can understand the words now.

"If we let you go," Maxine says, "you leave us alone. You leave us and our families and our friends and anybody we know or might come to know alone. In other words, it'll be like you never were a part of our lives and you never will be."

"And . . . and in exchange?"

Oh, I can tell he had trouble getting that out.

"You get to live," she tells him.

He stands up straighter, towering over us. Even with that blue paint splashed all over his sickly white skin and robe, he manages to look pretty damn scary.

"Do you have any idea with whom you are dealing?" he says.

Not even the accent and guttural tone of his voice can hide the prideful disdain he holds for us. I can feel Pelly trembling beside me.

But Maxine just says, "Actually, I do. You're the creatures who picked a fight with the wrong people."

For a long moment the two of them lock gazes. Then the creature smiles—or at least I think that grimace pulling at his lips and showing his teeth is a smile.

"You have a bargain," he says.

I shake my head. "Maxine, how are we supposed to trust these things?"

He turns to look at me, and this time I can tell that he's really pissed.

"You question our word?" he demands.

Maxine didn't bat an eye when he was staring her down, and I'm not about to, either.

"Well, yeah," I say. "Maybe you're some big important guy where you come from, but here you're just an ugly monster that came gunning after us for no good reason that I can see. That doesn't make you particularly trustworthy in my book."

The leader turns his attention on Pelly. "Tell them," he says. "Tell them how our word is our bond."

"It . . . it's true," Pelly says when I look at him. He sounds apologetic, like I'm going to blame him. "Across the borders, one's word is one's only currency. It's not like here."

Maxine gives a slow nod. "Esmeralda said something about that in her last e-mail."

The soul-eater holds out his hand.

"Cut my palm," he says, "and I will give you my blood oath."

I glance at Maxine and she shrugs, so I let the edge of my blade kiss the palm of his hand. A greenish red blood seeps from the wound.

"Now you," the creature says to Maxine.

"Wait a minute," I say.

But he shakes his head. "Our bargain is with her."

The other two *anamithim* make rumbly noises that I take to be agreement. Reluctantly, I offer Maxine the switchblade, hilt first.

"Just hold it," she tells me.

"Careful," I say, turning the knife around again so that the blade faces her. "It's really sharp."

She lightly touches her own palm against it. When she pulls her hand back, blood wells from the cut. Red, normal blood. Which makes me wonder if mine would be blue and that's why the creature wants to seal the bargain with Maxine.

He offers her his hand and they shake, the creature repeating his promise to hold up their side of the bargain. I go to where the piles of clothing lie on the floor. I clean my blade on a pair of shorts, put it away in my jeans, then pick up a T-shirt and give it to Maxine. She wraps it around her hand. I hesitate a moment before picking up a second one.

"So do you have a name?" I ask.

He refuses the T-shirt and shows me his blue-spattered hand. The cut's already disappeared.

"We do not give out our names," he says.

We stand there for a moment, nobody moving or talking.

"Okay," I tell them. "You can go."

"We cannot. Not until we clean this abomination from our skin."

I realize that I'm enjoying this. "Oh, right. Well, there are washrooms upstairs . . . maybe a sink down here somewhere."

He just looks at me.

"You know," I say. "With water. To wash off the paint?"

"I will show them," Pelly says.

The soul-eater nods and lets Pelly lead them away.

"Remember," I call after them. "Pelly is definitely in the friend category."

He just gives me a look, and then they're gone. When I turn to Maxine, she grabs hold of me and hugs me like she's never going to let go. I can feel her shaking and realize then just how scared she was. In my book, that makes her way braver than me. I was too pissed off to be scared.

"I thought we were all going to die," she says with her face buried against my neck.

"Me, too," I tell her.

I look over my shoulder at Adrian. He hasn't moved or said a word since I came into the room.

"What are you still doing here?" I say.

Maxine pushes back from me.

"Oh, don't be mad at him," she says. "He was only trying to help."

"By siccing those uglies on us in the first place."

"He made a mistake," Maxine says. "Everybody makes mistakes."

"But not everybody's mistakes . . . "

Put people's lives at stake, I'm about to add, but I let it go. She's right. Everybody screws up. Just look at me: I'm the poster child for screwing up.

"I'm so, so sorry," Adrian finally says.

"He speaks," I say.

"Imogene," Maxine says.

I look at her. "I'm just razzing him. Can't I even do that?"

"He was going to give up his soul for you," she says.

"That's what his plan to make things right was."

I blink and slowly turn to Adrian.

"For true?" I ask.

He shrugs. "Not that it matters."

"Of course it matters."

"Plus he's real," Maxine adds. "I mean, he's corporeal."

I keep thinking that we should be way too freaked to be having an ordinary conversation like this, but I guess the very normalcy of it is what's helping us the most. I walk over to him and reach out with a finger to touch his chest. Sure enough, my finger presses against real flesh. He gives me an uncertain smile.

"How'd this happen?" I ask.

"It's got something to do with Halloween," Maxine says. "He never really tried to do it until this year."

"So how's it feel?" I ask.

"Like being alive."

I nod, then I make a fist and punch him in the shoulder. Hard.

"Ow! What was that for?"

I give him a sweet smile. "For all the times you disappeared on me in the middle of a conversation."

He's rubbing his arm when I turn away.

"What time is it?" I ask Maxine.

She checks her watch, then shakes her head.

"Almost nine thirty," she says. "I thought it'd be way later than that."

"No kidding."

We hear something at the door and we all turn to look.

I guess I'm the only one who's totally paranoid, because the first thing I do is reach for my switchblade. Then I realize it's only Pelly.

"Are they gone?" Maxine asks.

He nods. "And they will keep their word."

I shake my head. I'm not disagreeing; I just don't know what to think.

"I think it's pretty cool that your word means so much in the Otherworld," Maxine says. "Too bad it couldn't be like that here."

"So they never lie?" I ask Pelly.

He laughs. "Everybody lies. They lie and they cheat and they do all manner of wrongs. But once they give their word, they keep their side of the bargain."

"Whatever works," I say. I turn to Maxine. "Can I borrow your cell?"

She digs in the pocket of her cargo pants and hands the phone over to me.

"Who are you calling?" she asks.

"My mom."

Mom picks up on the first ring. "Imogene?"

"Hi, Mom. Everything okay with you?"

"I've been so worried."

"Worry no more," I tell her. "I still have a bit of a blue tint to my skin—"

"Liar," Maxine mouths at me with a grin.

"—but otherwise I'm okay."

"The police were here."

"Yeah, I kind of thought they might be. Did they say why?"

"They wouldn't tell me *anything*."

"Okay. The short story is, I caught some guy beating up his girlfriend and I gave him a taste of his own medicine."

"Oh my god, are you *sure* you're all right?"

"Totally, Mom."

"When will you be home?"

"Well, that's the thing," I say. "If I go home, I'll have to spend the night trying to explain myself to them and I *really* wanted to see Jared's band play tonight. I have had such a crappy week, I figure I deserve that much. And it is Halloween."

"Did this boy hurt you?" she asks.

"No way."

She sighs. "Are you going to be in a lot of trouble?"

"Probably. The guy I hurt is a big shot quarterback, and if it comes down to my word against his—well, who are they going to believe? Especially if they talk to the cops in Tyson."

I never got charged for anything there, but I got picked up a few times, and it was pretty much common knowledge that I ran with Frankie Lee's gang.

"I don't know . . . " Mom's saying.

"Did they give you a hard time?" I ask.

This is a little unfair of me, playing on Mom's old hippie distrust of "the Man," but I was telling her the truth. I know I have to face up to what I did to Brent. I just want the rest of the night to be something resembling normal.

"Of course they gave me a hard time," Mom says. "That's what they're here for, isn't it? Why chase real criminals when they can harass single mothers and their daughters who were only trying to defend themselves. You *were* defending yourself, right?"

"Totally. And the guy's girlfriend. I took her to the hospital."

"Won't she vouch for you?" Mom asks.

"She's pretty much hated me for a year and a half at school," I say, "so I doubt that one bit of Good Samaritanism's going to do much to change her mind."

"But you said you rescued her."

"And she was grateful. But it seems she has a history of having this guy bang her around, and you know how that works."

Mom gives me another sigh. "I swear . . . "

"Yeah, it's a crappy world," I say before she can go off on a tangent about how she doesn't know which is worse, the fact that people get abused, or that we live in a society where the abused go right back for more. "So what do you say, Mom? Can I have tonight and turn myself in tomorrow?"

"There will be no turning yourself in," she says. "Go see Jared play and then come home. If they want to talk to you, they can do it here with your mother and a lawyer present."

"We can't afford a lawyer."

"Anna from down the hall's a paralegal."

I have to smile, but of course she can't see that.

"Works for me," I tell her. "What did you tell them when they asked where I was?"

"I said you'd gone to a party with a girlfriend. I was hoping it was true."

I look around the paint-splattered basement. There's Maxine. A corporeal ghost. A whatever-Pelly-is. And me, still blue.

"Close enough," I say. "And when they asked you her name . . . "

"I told them it was a friend from school, but I didn't know which one. And I didn't tell them about Jared's gig."

"So I can go?" I ask, just to be sure.

"After the way you've turned things around this year? Of course you can."

"You're the best, Mom."

"Just promise me you're okay."

"I totally promise. Except for a hint of the blue skin, everything's okay now."

She gives me one last sigh.

"Have a good time," she says. "And try not to find any new trouble."

"I love you, too, Mom," I say before I hang up.

I hand the phone back to Maxine.

"We're still going to the show?" she says.

"Of course we are. Weren't you listening?" I look at the others. "We all are."

"But I don't have a costume," Maxine says.

I smile and point at the last pail of blue paint, which didn't get used.

"We'll be the Blue Girls," I say.

"Who are they?"

"Whoever we want them to be."

I ask the boys to step outside. "And no peeking, ghost boy," I tell Adrian, "or we leave you behind."

"What about my costume?" he asks.

"You can be a ghost."

"I already am a ghost."

"I know. And a pretty convincing one, too."

"And me?" Pelly asks while Adrian just shakes his head.

I laugh. "You'll be just fine the way you are."

"But I can really go with you out into the world?"

"Absolutely. Now, shoo. I need to get Maxine ready."

Once they're gone, she takes off her shirt, and I use one of the T-shirts she bought for the fairies to smear paint all over her arms, neck, and face.

"Close your eyes," I say when I get to them.

It doesn't take long for the poster paint to dry. It flakes around her eyes and mouth, neck and elbows, but it'll work well enough in the club.

"You should turn your coat right side out," she says as we start for the doorway.

"Excellent point. Although maybe wearing our clothes inside out could be a Blue Girl trademark."

"I don't think so."

We gather up the boys outside in the hall and make it back upstairs to Maxine's locker without running into Mr. Sanderson. I turn to Adrian while she gets her coat.

"You know I've got a boyfriend," I tell him.

He nods, then looks a little nervous as I step over to him.

"I just don't want you to make more of this than what it is," I say.

And then I kiss him. On the lips. He gets this goofy look like he's never kissed a girl before. Maybe he hasn't.

"Thanks," I tell him. "I know you didn't mean to get us all into this. And I'm sorry I didn't believe you in the first place."

He doesn't say anything. He just stands there, then slowly lifts his fingers to touch his lips.

"Earth to ghost boy," I say. "Yes, it really happened."

"What happened?" Maxine asks, closing her locker.

"Imogene kissed the ghost," Pelly says.

"News flash," I say. "Girls kiss boys all the time. Now let's go party."

NOW: *Imogene*

Mom's so cool. Jared and I don't get home until well past two, but she's still waiting up for us in the living room and all she wants to do is hug us both and then send us off to bed.

"Did you deal with those bad fairies?" she asks.

"Totally. They won't bother us anymore."

She gives me a considering look. "You still look quite blue."

"I'm pretty sure it's fading."

She raises her eyebrows, but doesn't comment except to give me another hug. Then she points me in the direction of my bedroom and gives me a little push. Pelly's waiting there for me, grinning from ear to ear. For a weird little spindly guy, more hedgehog/monkey than boy, he showed excellent dance moves.

He stays long enough now to point to where he's left my knapsack beside the dresser, thank me for the great night he had, and then he's off with a promise to see me tomorrow.

"And if they put you in their prison," he says before he disappears into the closet, "I'll have you out in a moment."

"I don't think it'll come to that, but thanks."

That night my dreams are a rewind of dancing with my friends while Jared's band plays. Of a slow dance with Thomas during which I swear our hearts are beating at the exact same tempo. There's a bit of bittersweetness in there, too, when I think of Adrian, giving me those sad puppy dog eyes of his. But Maxine hooked him up with the sister of Jared's guitarist and he didn't moon over me again until the show was over and she went home with her brother.

I think he scored a few more kisses, though I'm not sure if that really happened, or if it was only in my dream.

* * *

Mom waits until ten o'clock to call the police and then insists that if they want to talk to me, they can come to the apartment. "Unless," she adds, "you're telling me my daughter is under arrest?"

She's obviously confrontational, so either they have nothing on me, or they want to be damn sure they can build a case before they really get her going, but whichever it is, they do come to us. So we gather in the dining room and let me tell you, it all feels very surreal.

On one side of the table are the two detectives: Harry Black, a beefy guy who totally fills out his suit; when you look at him, you feel like you should be hearing the theme music to some cop show on TV. And then there's the other side of the coin, his partner, Juanita Lopez, a tall woman with a kind face but a grave gaze that you know isn't going to miss a thing.

Sitting across from them, there's Mom and me, and Anna from down the hall, a petite brunette with a killer smile.

"Are you a lawyer, ma'am?" Black asks Anna.

"She's representing us, yes," Mom says before Anna can answer. "And she's here to make sure we don't get railroaded."

"We'll keep that in mind, ma'am," Black says. He turns to look at me, and I know exactly what he's thinking as his gaze goes from my hands, up my arms to my neck and face. "Are you always this—"

"Blue?" I finish for him. "No, it was just a dye job for Halloween, but it's totally not washing off the way it's supposed to."

I wonder what Maxine's mom had to say about her own blue daughter last night. I haven't had the chance to talk to Maxine yet this morning, so I have no idea.

"This is what was so important?" Mom says. "My daughter's Halloween costume?"

I'd ask her to tone down the aggression, but I have to admit I'm kind of enjoying Mom in full protective lioness mode. I'm pretty sure Detective Black can't say the same. He gives a weary sigh, but it's his partner who takes up the questioning.

"Don't worry, Ms. Yeck," Lopez says. "We'll make this as brief as possible."

Mom looks like she's also got on opinion on that innocuous comment, but Anna lays a hand on her arm. There's a long moment where the police are waiting to see if Mom's got more to say.

"So, Imogene," Lopez says, finally. "May I call you Imogene?"

I nod.

"You attend Redding High?"

I give her another nod.

"And were you on the school grounds yesterday evening?"

Yet one more nod from me. This is easy. I don't have to say a word.

"Why were you there?"

"Maybe this would go a lot more quickly," Anna says, "if you could just tell us what it is you need to know. Do we really need to establish the obvious?"

That grave gaze of Lopez's pans to where Anna is sitting, but then she gives a short nod.

"You're right," she says. She turns back to me. "What can you tell me about the attack on Brent Calder?"

"Excuse me? Have you not seen the mess he made of his girlfriend?"

"We're investigating that," Lopez says, "but we're also trying to understand how Mr. Calder was injured."

"I don't know," I tell them.

I decided when I got up this morning that this is a situation where a lie's my first best option. Everything depends on what Valerie's told them—and I don't have high hopes on that count—but I figure I'll at least give it a shot at painting myself as the innocent bystander. And no, I'm not trying to deny what I did. Whether the cops charge me or not, I'm going to carry that with me. It's just that doing it from a juvenile detention center's not going to make it any easier.

"I was looking for my friend Maxine," I go on. "We were supposed to hook up after the game, but it turns out she went to the club ahead of me. Only I didn't know that at the time. So I was walking around the side of the school to the football field to see if she was waiting for me there instead of out front. And that's when I saw these two guys fighting."

"Mr. Calder and . . . ?"

"I didn't recognize the other guy. He took off when I called out. I didn't even know it was Brent until I ran over. If I had, I probably wouldn't have bothered."

"You don't get along?"

Here I was going to be honest.

"Not for a moment," I say.

"So you ran over," Lopez prompts me.

"And I see Valerie lying on the ground. She says something about Brent beating her up, so I take her to the emergency room."

"Leaving Mr. Calder bleeding."

I nod. "Look, I told you. We didn't get along. I don't get along with Valerie either, but at least she didn't try to take a swing at me when I helped her up."

"Mr. Calder tried to hit you?"

"Didn't I just say that? He was acting like I was the one who'd knocked him down. So I just got Valerie out of there."

"And left him. Weren't you worried that he might have bled to death?"

I shook my head. "I didn't realize he was bleeding. I mean, there was blood around, but I thought it was from him and the other guy fighting. Was he cut or something?"

"Or something."

Lopez looks at some notes she has on the table in front of her.

"So you took Ms. Clarke to the hospital," she says, "and you left her there."

I shrug. "I told you. It's not like we were friends or anything. I made sure that she'd be looked after."

"But you didn't tell them about Mr. Calder."

"No."

"Why not?"

"Because he'd just finished beating up his girlfriend and then took a swing at me. I figured he could crawl home on his own."

"Bleeding as he was."

"I didn't know it was serious. It was serious, I take it?"

She nods.

"I still don't care," I say.

"I suppose that explains how you could just go to a club after all of this."

"I suppose it does."

Lopez glances at her partner, before she looks back at me.

"Mr. Calder says you attacked him."

I laugh. "Me? Do you think I'm insane? Have you seen the size of him? He'd"—I think of what Brent was always saying to me—"squash me like a bug."

"He said you had a knife."

"Oh, please. I don't get the big deal, anyway. He's the bad guy in this. Whoever took him down was doing everybody a favor."

"Assault with a deadly weapon is hardly doing anybody a favor."

"Oh, I get it," I say. "He's the star quarterback. So just because he beat up one of his own teammates for missing a catch, and then used his girlfriend for a punching bag, you're still going to do your best to keep his sorry ass from doing any time."

"Are you referring to a Kyle Hanley?" Black asks.

I nod. "That's what Valerie told me. I didn't see it. Just like I didn't see him actually beat up on Valerie."

"Well, that helps," Black says. "Mr. Hanley told us that he didn't recognize his attacker."

"Because he didn't want the crap beat out of him again."

The two of them fall silent. Black's looking at his notes. Lopez is studying me.

"Is that it then?" Anna asks. "Or do you have any further questions?"

Lopez shakes her head. I can tell she doesn't believe me, but I guess all she's got to go on is instinct.

"No," she says. "Ms. Clarke's story corroborates what Imogene's told us."

It *does*? I think in surprise, and hope that nothing's showing on my face.

Lopez picks up her notes and stands up.

"Thank you for your help with this," she says to me. "If you think of anything else we should know, please give me a call."

She lays a business card on the table, then she and her partner say their good-byes and leave.

"It sounds like you had an exciting night," Anna says when they're gone.

She doesn't know the half of it, I think.

* * *

"Well, that went about as well as it could," Mom says after Anna has finished her tea and left. "All things considered."

I smile. "Yes, you were very fierce."

"Oh, god, I was, wasn't I? I just get so guilty as soon as I have to talk to a policeman—even when I have absolutely nothing to hide."

"I know the feeling."

"Except you probably *do* have something to be feeling guilty about."

"Mom!"

"You're right. Not anymore."

We look up as Jared mutters a good morning to us from the doorway before he heads into the kitchen to make himself a coffee.

"You took a chance not telling them the truth," Mom says.

"I figured it was worth a shot, but I didn't really think Valerie would leave me out of it."

"Maybe she'll be nicer to you now."

"Right. As if."

"You have to give people the benefit of the doubt."

"Mom, with her you don't get any benefit, only the doubt."

"So why don't you like her? Is it because she's a cheerleader—"

"It's because she's an asshole."

"—or because she doesn't like you?"

"Probably a bit of both," I have to admit. "At least when we first met."

"This must have been a pretty traumatic experience for her," Mom says. "It could well change her worldview."

"I suppose anything's possible."

"And that," Mom says, "brings us to your original problems."

"Which are all settled. Like I told you last night, the shadowy guys are totally going to leave us alone."

"Just like that."

I nod. "They gave their word, and where they come from, that's supposed to be sacrosanct."

"Must be a nice place. Too bad our world can't be more like that."

"I guess. But Pelly says they have all the same stuff going on there—lying and cheating and everything. The only difference is, when they give their word, they don't break it."

Mom nods. She studies me for a long moment.

"And the blue?" she asks.

"I don't know. But I'm *not* going to a doctor and trying to explain how it happened. They'll stick me in a test tube or something."

"I suppose you're right," she says, but it's obvious she's agreeing only reluctantly.

"Besides, it's starting to fade."

I'm pretty sure it is. I studied myself in the mirror this

morning before the police came, and it really does seem less intense. Still undeniably blue, though.

Mom sighs and shakes her head.

"I'm living my mother's curse," she says.

"How so?"

"When I was your age, she wagged a finger at me and said, 'Just wait until you're a mother yourself. You'll find out what it's like when your own child turns on you.' "

"But we're not so bad, right?"

Mom laughs and gives me a hug.

"You and Jared are perfect Imogenes and Jareds," she says, "and that's all I could hope and ask for."

NOW: *Maxine*

The first thing I want to do when I wake up is call Imogene.

I have the phone in my hand and everything, but at the last moment I don't punch in her number. It's so hard not to. I'm dying to know what's going to happen when the police talk to her, not to mention how she's going to explain her new blue look. Mine was easily put aside. The paint washed off, though I did have to do a major rinse of the tub after my shower.

The best part about my "costume" was Mom's face when I came in—that look of shock when the blue registered. But then all she did was shake her head and ask if I'd had a good time. Either she's seriously loosening up or she *really* doesn't want me to go live with Dad, because she's being way less anal these days. She doesn't even come into my room and tidy up anymore. The clothes I was trying on before I left for school Friday morning were still on my bed when I got home last night.

Anyway, I don't call Imogene. I'm sure she's got enough on her mind without my sidetracking her right now. When she's ready to talk, she'll call.

To distract myself, I go online and write Esmeralda a superlong e-mail detailing the whole of our adventure in the school last night. It's both easier and harder than I thought it would be, but I follow Christy's advice. I don't worry about being writerly; I just set the story down in the same words I'd use in telling it to someone if they were sitting here in my room.

When I'm done, I look it over. With it sitting there in black and white on my computer screen, I find I'm not so much worried about its literary qualities as about how implausible it all sounds.

I hesitate a long moment, then finally hit *send*. If anyone's going to believe this besides those of us who were there—which, hello, includes a ghost and Imogene's not-so-imaginary childhood companion—it will be Esmeralda.

I spend a little time tidying up my room after that. It's nice being able to decide for myself how I want things to go. I think I'm going to start bringing home the clothes that I'm storing at Imogene's and in my locker. I'm *definitely* finding a new home for those dolls, even if it has to be a cardboard box. I start thinking of redecorating, making the room more my own and less little-girly, but then decide, why bother? I hope to go on to university next year and I'm totally planning to live in residence. Or maybe Imogene and I will be able to get an apartment, though I'm not sure we could afford it.

I look at the clock. It's almost eleven.

I can't believe how the time's dragging.

Why hasn't Imogene called yet? Maybe the police have taken her into custody and she's used her one phone call to get a lawyer. Maybe I should call Jared or their mom to find out if I need to start baking a cake with a file in it.

I check my e-mail what feels like every fifteen minutes, but in reality is every two or three. There's never anything from Esmeralda.

Once my room's tidy, I reread her old e-mails and the transcript I made of our chat and wonder again just exactly what it is that she does. What I do know is I'm interested in it, just as I'm interested in what Christy does: cataloging and trying to make sense out of all the things there are in the world that don't make sense.

I told Esmeralda that at the end of my e-mail.

Maybe she's not writing back because she thinks I'm

going to turn into some kind of cyber-stalker wannabe-whatever-she-is. And who would blame her? She doesn't know anything about me, but here I've been blathering on and on about my problems and how I've not been dealing at all well with the weirdness that has become my life. That's got to instill all sorts of confidence in her.

I sigh and walk over to my closet. Pushing the clothes aside, I study the back wall, wondering again just how Imogene and Pelly did their trick of simply showing up in there the other night. Not to mention how they also used it to leave.

Then finally, when I check my e-mail for the kazillionth time, there's a response from Esmeralda.

Date: Sat, 1 Nov 2003 10:32:19 -0800
From: efoylan@sympatico.ca
Subject: Re: What we did on our Halloween vacation
To: fairygrrl@yahoo.com

Oh my Goddess, Maxine. If I was with you right now, I'd give you such a smack in the ear for risking your life the way you did. It was so very foolish . . . but so brave as well.

And what do I know? You got results. And your friend is a *very* resourceful young woman. Nowhere in oral tradition, or in any of the historical texts for that matter, is there a mention of this particular weakness in regards to the anamithim. Well done and thank you for that!

As to why they didn't still attack you when they were trapped in corporeal form, you have to understand that such beings, fearsome though they can be, can also be cowards. They don't have souls, so when they die, they simply cease to exist. The group you faced knew that they could be slain in their paint-trapped forms and obviously weren't brave enough to take the chance of engaging you in physical combat.

But whatever else they might be or do, you can hold them to their word, so no worries on that front.

I've had an exhausting night myself—thanks for asking! There were the usual pixie infestations—if they're not haunting the phones or the Internet, then they'll get up to the more traditional tricks, which are just as annoying. There's always an increase in pixie incidents around Halloween—I think half my life is spent cleaning up after pixies and bodachs—but last night we also had to chase down a half-dozen feral eponies. That's a kind of malevolent spirit that attaches itself to human ghosts and can cause enormous amounts of havoc if they're not dealt with immediately. And then there was the giant that almost woke in the middle of a city park. . . .

Who *is* this woman? I think as I'm reading this. Her life sounds like it's been pulled right from the pages of some police-procedural version of a fairy tale.

All of which is to say, I'm in desperate need of some sleep. I hope that, and I'm sure that, we will talk more in the days to come, but to quickly answer a couple of the points you brought up:

Imogene is suffering from vervain poisoning—which, let me quickly add, isn't as terrible as it might sound. I'd already looked into her problem before last night's fun began. Unfortunately, some of the symptoms will be permanent. The dark blue cast to her skin should mostly go away, but a hint of blue will almost certainly remain. The euphoric sense of extreme capability will definitely fade with time. The latter is, no doubt, what had her so readily take on that bully and face up to the anamithim the way that she did.

I don't mean to take away from Imogene's obvious courage by saying this, but without the effect of the vervain in her system, she would surely have let common sense guide her actions.

Which shows how totally Esmeralda doesn't know Imogene, I think.

Vervain, at least the variety found in the otherworld, is also known as a "heal all," and a rare one at that. It's an enormously beneficial component of any number of poultices, spells, and such, but like anything, too much of a good thing can be problematic. When only the pollen is being utilized, it is normally in very minute quantities, hence Imogene's reaction to a cloud of it being thrown upon her and ingested.

Lastly, I'm delighted by your interest in learning more about the fairy realm. If you are of legal age, we can certainly talk more of your coming to the House to study. I'll tell you more about us and what we do when I'm not so tired. But since you've mentioned that you know Christy Riddell—an old colleague of mine—I'd also recommend you express your interest to him. He and the professor are always in need of able-bodied, open-minded folk to help them with their cataloging and studies, and you could learn much from them.

Now I really do have to go to bed. Try not to have any more adventures before we have the chance to talk again.

Blessed be.
Esmeralda

This is so cool. I know last night I spent half the time being scared out of my mind, but I really do want to learn more about all of this. Of course, I want to write back to her immediately to find out what this House is that she's talking about and who the professor is, but she'll be sleeping anyway. Then the phone finally rings, and it's Imogene asking if it's okay if she comes over.

NOW: *Imogene*

Maxine's mother gives me the once-over when she opens the door. Her eyes only widen slightly, but I guess the surprise factor is mostly gone, seeing how her own daughter came home with a similar look last night.

"Hello, Imogene," she says. "I take it you liked your costume too much to give it up after only one night."

I shake my head. "I made the mistake of using dye instead of just blue paint the way Maxine did. I should have listened to her. This stuff just *won't* wash off."

"Somehow, I doubt you dislike the attention it brings."

I raise my blue eyebrows.

"It's not a value judgment," she says. "I'm working very hard at not doing that anymore. It's just that you have your tattoos, you like to put together outfits that are impossible to ignore . . . "

I'm actually looking very normal today—except for all my blueness. Jeans and a sweater and sneakers. A toque, a scarf, and one of Jared's pea jackets that must be small on him because it's really not that big on me.

But, "Point taken," I say. "I do kind of like it. I just wish I could turn it on and off, the way I can change what I'm wearing."

"Tattoos don't come with an on-off switch."

"No, but if you place them strategically, you can make it look like you don't have any, if that's how you're feeling."

"You are *such* an interesting girl," she says. "But come in, come in. I shouldn't be leaving you to stand in the hall like this."

Ushering me into the living room, she calls to Maxine to let her know I'm here.

"Maxine told me what you did last night," she says. "That was very brave of you."

I try to school my face to stay calm, but I can't help but give Maxine a look as she's coming down the hall. I can't believe Maxine told her about the fairies.

But then Ms. Tattrie adds, "I hope they throw the book at that Calder boy," and I realize what she's talking about.

"We can hope," I say, "but I wouldn't hold my breath."

She nods. "Unfortunately, they do seem to get away with it most of the time, don't they?"

"Unless someone convinces them to stop."

Ms. Tattrie regards me for a long moment.

"Yes," she says. "That was a very dangerous thing you did, but I'm proud of you for doing it, and for helping that girl who, I understand, is anything but a friend."

Maxine's mother just gets weirder and weirder. I think she's actually beginning to like me.

"I'm not planning to make a habit of it," I tell her. "Getting into that kind of situation, I mean."

"Sometimes we have no choice," Ms. Tattrie says, which makes me wonder what kinds of things she's seen in *her* life.

"Sometimes the situations are thrust upon us."

"Yeah, it's sure not a perfect world," I agree.

The conversation turns to lighter subjects as Maxine and I sit and talk with her for a little while longer, then finally we get to retreat to Maxine's room.

"So do you still want to trade in your mom?" I ask when we're both sitting on the bed.

"I guess not," Maxine says. "She's actually starting to seem like a normal mom."

"Or maybe we're just getting mature enough to appreciate her perspective."

"Oh, god, do you think? Are *we* the ones who are changing?"

I laugh at thc look of horror on her face.

"Not likely," I assure her.

She gets up and beckons me to look at what she's got on the screen of her computer—another e-mail from that weird woman she met in the fairy-tale forum.

"So you told her everything?" I ask after I've read it through.

She nods.

"And you want to tell Christy, too?"

"But not to go in some book. Just to, you know, increase the body of knowledge on the subject. I'd tell him not to use our names."

"You're really serious about getting into this stuff, aren't you?"

"Do you think it's weird?"

I smile. "Weird is what I like, Maxine."

"I know. But this is personal stuff—your stuff as well as mine."

"Let me tell you something," I say. I stand up so that we're face to face. "Last night you saved my soul."

"What?"

"I'm serious. I was ready to just cut those guys. I didn't see another way to be sure we'd be safe. Maybe it was me talking, maybe it was this vervain overdose your friend wrote about. I don't know. But I was wrong and you were right. I might have saved our asses, but if I'd done it, I'd . . . I don't know. It would have been crossing a line. I never did it back in Tyson. I never *want* to do it. But last night I was ready."

I see Maxine's eyes filling as I talk, and to tell you the truth, I'm feeling a little teary myself. One more word out of me, and we'd both be bawling. So I just step closer and give her a hug.

She hugs me back in a fierce grip, and then we step back from each other.

"That's the main reason I wanted to come over," I tell her. "To say thanks."

She doesn't say anything for a long moment. When she does speak, it's to ask the last thing I expect right now, but it's entirely appropriate, all things considered.

"Will you tell me about Tyson?" she says.

"What do you want to know?"

"Everything."

So we sit on her bed, and I begin.

NOW: *Imogene*

There's one last piece of unfinished business, and Sunday night he shows up: Adrian in all his ghostliness, standing on the fire escape on the other side of my bedroom window. He's got this apologetic look on his face that makes me smile, because I know just what's going on in his head. For whatever reason, he needs to talk to me, but having turned back into a ghost Saturday morning, he can't exactly pick up a phone and give me a call to say he's coming over. And he *knows* what happened the last time he just showed up outside my window.

"It's okay," I tell him as I open the window. "I know you're not peeping."

"You're still blue."

"Is that *all* anybody can focus on?"

"But it's been what, three days now?"

"Four. Not that I'm counting. And it's fading."

He peers at me. "I guess it is . . . "

"So what's up with you?" I say, because I figure it's well past time to change the subject here.

"I . . . can you come with me?" he asks.

"What, right now? It's almost midnight."

"I have a favor to ask of you. I know—you don't owe me anything. It's just . . . I don't want to do this alone."

"Do what? Why are you being so weird and mysterious?"

"Can you just come?"

I look out the window past him. The night lies thick on the streets and it's all shadowy and quiet. Just another Sunday night in Crowsea with everybody already in bed, or nodding off in front of their TV sets. Here and there in the windows of the other buildings I can see that telltale flicker of light.

My gaze comes back to Adrian's face.

I've got school tomorrow—my first day as a blue girl. I still haven't decided how I'm going to handle the questions and comments that I'm sure to get. Even people who never talk to me are going to want to know what's up. I've gone over it with Maxine and Thomas about a million times today, and Pelly just left me to go back into Closetland a few minutes ago, but none of them had any particularly good suggestions. That leaves me stuck with the bad Halloween dye-job excuse.

So all things considered, I thought a good night's sleep would be an excellent idea. A chance to rest up and prepare for what's sure to be a long and tiring day. But Adrian looks so damn hopeful.

"Sure," I say. "Just let me get dressed."

He turns so that his back is to the window, but he didn't have to. I'm just wearing a big T-shirt for a nightie and I'm not taking it off. Still, I appreciate the gesture on his part. I put on a pair of jeans under it, socks, and sneakers. My coat's in the hall, so I dig out a thick wool sweater with a tight knit that should keep me warm.

"Okay," I say, and approach the window.

He moves aside so that I don't have to step right through him, then follows me down the fire escape.

"Where to?" I ask when we get to the bottom.

"Remember when we first met, I told you there were angels as well as shadows?"

I nod.

"Well, we're going to go look for one of those angels."

"How long's that going to take?" I ask.

I have visions of his expecting me to go tramping through the city with him, all night long, and that's not going to happen.

"Not long," he says. "They usually show up pretty quickly when you want to see them badly enough."

"What do you want to see one for?"

I'm trying to remember what he told me about them, but I'm coming up blank.

"I need to know something," he says. "Did someone tell you how the blue paint would incapacitate the *anamithim,* or was it something you figured out on your own?"

"The truth?"

"No, tell me a lie."

"Now you're just being smart."

"Maybe I'm picking it up from you."

I grin. "That's good. There are two things that'll get you

far in life, so far as I'm concerned: a spunky attitude and a vocabulary of interesting words."

"I should have met you before I went flying with the fairies."

"Except I would've been eight years old or something, and that would just be gross."

"I didn't die *that* long ago."

"Whatever."

"But back to how you dealt with the *anamithim,*" he says.

We're a couple of blocks from the apartment now. I wonder what people would see, if there was anyone around to look our way. Adrian would probably be totally invisible to them, so it'd just be this blue girl, walking along with her hands in her pockets, talking to herself. All I need is a shopping cart and I'd have all the makings of a bag lady in training.

"I was flying by the seat of my pants," I tell him. "Right up until I came into the room where you all were, I was thinking maybe we could use the paint to make a stronger warding circle—just to protect us. You know, something that wouldn't get scuffed or blown away like salt."

"So why did you throw it on them?"

"I don't know. I guess because if they weren't going to come near me with my blue skin, I just figured throwing it on them would really screw them up."

"And your backup plan was . . . ?"

I shake my head. "No backup plan. I tend to run on instinct, which is why I threw out all the earlier plans we had and went with my gut when I thought of the paint."

He gives a slow nod.

"Instinct," he repeats.

"It's not going to be everybody's choice, but it works for me."

"Even when following it seems crazy, or maybe a little scary?"

"I guess. It would depend on the situation."

He nods again.

"I'm afraid to die," he says.

"But you're—"

"Already dead. I know. So it's completely weird. Except I'm not completely dead, because I never went on to wherever it is that we go next."

"You said that when we first met. I don't really blame you for hanging around—not if you've worked a deal where you can put it off. Who wants everything to be over?"

"Except they say that dying's just the start of another, even more interesting journey."

"Who does? People who haven't died yet, that's who."

He shakes his head. "No, the angels do."

And then I remember what he told me about them.

"You're going on," I say. "You're going to get them to show you the way."

"I'm scared to, but I know it's what I should do. I mean, really, what's left for me here? All I do is haunt the same stupid school I hated when I was alive."

"Yeah, but—"

"But I just didn't want to do it by myself. I know we're not really friends, but you're pretty much the closest thing I've got. That's why I asked you to come."

Which is so sad that I don't know what to say.

"Do you mind?" he asks.

"No. I guess not. I mean, I'm flattered that you asked."

"If it's too freaky, I understand."

"No," I say with more certainty. "I can do this for you. And I do think of you as a friend. You pissed me off some, but we're still talking, right?"

"I should warn you, this is going to get a little weird."

"*Anamithim* weird?"

"No. It's just that when an angel shows up, the world changes a bit. It . . . becomes *less,* you could say. There's hardly any sound, and everything goes black and white like an old movie."

"Ho-kay."

"But it's not dangerous."

"Go for it," I tell him. "I won't wig out on you."

He turns into the next alleyway and stops when we've walked halfway down it.

"This is where your angel lives?" I have to ask.

"No, it's just a quiet place, out of the way. I have to call him to me now—I just need to say his name three times. He said he wouldn't come to me again, no matter how much I called to him, but I'm hoping he will this one last time."

So he does just that. Calls out this name, "John Narraway," three times.

Nothing happens.

"Maybe," he says, "you could call with me?"

"Doing that isn't going to get me all tangled up in some new fairy-tale weirdness, is it? Because trust me, I've learned my lesson."

"The angels aren't like that," he says. "They can't even harm ghosts like me. All they can do is try to convince us that it's time for us to go on, and they wouldn't bother with you, because you're still alive."

"Okay. I'll give it a shot."

Adrian gives us a count so we can start at the same time, and then we call the angel's name, "John Narraway," which is way more prosaic than I would have expected. I'm thinking Gabriel. Now there's a good angel name. Or maybe Raphael, though wasn't he also a Teenage Mutant Ninja Turtle? Jared would know.

We repeat the name. Do it a third time.

I wait a few moments, then turn to Adrian. I'm about to say something like how we gave it a shot, but it looks like the angel's a no-show and maybe we should just try again some other time, only that's when it comes creeping up on us.

It's night, and it's already quiet, but there's no mistaking this silence for anything natural. I'm looking at the far end of the alley and as I watch, the yellowy glow of the streetlight loses its color, which is way eerier than you might think it would be, considering everything's pretty much black and white at night anyway. You don't realize how much color the night holds until it all goes away.

I turn at the sound of footsteps.

He looks like an ordinary guy, nothing special, except he's carrying a fiddle case. Almost middle-aged; just a little older than Mom, I'd guess. He has one of those totally nondescript faces that you'd never think about again, once you turn away, but he does have this stern look down really well. He takes one look at me, then turns his attention to Adrian.

"Thanks for coming this one last time," Adrian says.

The angel gives a brusque nod. I can tell there's bad feeling between them, but I don't want to know about it. I've decided to turn a new leaf and totally be the mind-your-own-business girl. At least when it comes to this kind of thing. You know, angels and ghosts and blue girls, oh my.

"What is she doing here?" the angel says.

"I asked her to see me off."

"Don't worry," I say. "I won't get in the way."

He looks at me again. "How can you see me? Only the dead can see us."

Oh, that's just great.

"I'd better still be alive," I tell Adrian, "or I'm really going to punch you." I turn to the angel, and add, "The dead can punch each other, right?"

"This is Imogene," Adrian says.

The angel nods. "I see. The one who—"

"Sent the *anamithim* packing," Adrian finishes for him.

Except, from the look on the angel's face, that's not what *he* was about to say.

"But that's impossible," the angel says.

"*Impossible* pretty much sums up Imogene."

As the angel gives me a considering look, I try to decide if I should take Adrian's comment as a compliment.

"I see what you mean," the angel says before I can make up my mind. He returns his attention to Adrian, and adds, "So you're really ready?"

Adrian nods. "And Imogene can come, right?"

"If she sent a crowd of *anamithim* packing, how could *I* stop her?"

"Hello?" I say. "I'm standing right here. Maybe you could include me in the conversation instead of just talking about me?"

The angel smiles. "Of course. Follow me."

He sets off back down the alley. Adrian reaches for my hand. I hesitate—I mean, what's there to hold on to?—except when I put my hand out to his, real fingers curl around mine.

"What's going on here?" I ask as we fall in step behind the angel. "How come I can feel your hand?"

"This is a borderworld," the angel says over his shoulder. "Spirits have more substance in a place such as this."

Weird. But these days, what isn't?

* * *

It's a totally disconcerting walk we take. I recognize where we are most of the time, but it's all black and white, and everything's silent except for our footsteps and a faint hum like a wind coming from a few streets over. There's no one else around—I mean, *no one*. Not a late-night straggler. Not a cab or a police cruiser.

I'm about to ask how much farther we have to go, when we turn a corner and my gaze is pulled to the far end of this new street. I no longer know where we are, and *for sure* I've never seen anything like this before. It's an immense stone archway, rearing twenty or thirty feet high, and between its pillars, the air shimmers like a heat mirage. There are all kinds of colors in that light that you don't see at first. It seems mostly gold, but then you realize the gold is flecked with every other color you can imagine and some that I don't even think are supposed to be in the spectrum that can be seen by the human eye. But I can see them right now.

"Wow," I say.

It just gets more amazing, the closer we get. And here's a funny thing. When the gate is finally looming right over us, everything that's touched by the light regains its normal color. There's sound, too, but now it's this indescribable low resonating hum that I can feel in my chest, like when a bass guitar's turned up way loud. Only this is a constant sound, so I feel like I'm vibrating in time with it.

I turn to look at Adrian, but I'm not sure he's seeing and feeling what I am because he's got this scared look in his eyes.

"Are you okay?" I ask.

He nods. "You know, seeing your courage back at the school the other night is what's given me the courage to do this."

I want to say, I wish everybody'd stop talking about how brave and smart and everything I'm supposed to be. What happened on Halloween was just dumb luck. But I know he needs to go through these gates, and I know his thinking I'm brave is what's letting him believe he can do this. So I just squeeze his hand, then draw him close for a hug.

"Send me a postcard," I say.

"Yeah, I . . . "

He hugs me back, then steps away. He looks from me to the angel.

"So I just walk through?" he asks.

The angel nods.

Adrian turns back to me. I can't read what's in his eyes anymore. The light coming through the gates is reflecting too strongly in them.

"I like to pretend," he says, "that if I hadn't died . . . you know, if we'd met when I was alive . . . we might have been friends."

"Absolutely," I tell him.

He looks like he's got something else to say, but then he just smiles and walks away, into the light.

There's a flare as he steps through, so bright that it leaves me blinking with the afterflash. I hear a joyous sound. Then he's gone, and I find I have what feels like this big hole in my chest and I'm crying. I don't even know why.

"It's always hardest for those who must stay behind," the angel says.

But that's not it. I'm not sad that he's really dead now,

or that I'll miss him, even though I've got this empty feeling inside. I'm not sad at all, really, or if I am, it's a bittersweet kind of sadness. It's thinking of him living by himself for all those years, a lonely ghost in a school he hated, with no companions except for the mean-spirited fairies who were responsible for his death in the first place. He went through all of that, when he could have had this.

I wipe my eyes on the sleeve of my sweater and look at the angel. The residue of the bright flash is pretty much gone, and I can see properly again.

"Whatever," I say.

"You are an interesting individual," he tells me. "You're so very *here,* so very present. And you certainly take all of this very much in stride."

"After the week I just had," I tell him, "this seems almost normal." But then I look at the gate again. "Well, except for that . . ."

I turn away again to look at him, because that's way easier.

"You're not exactly my picture of an angel," I say.

"I'm not an angel. I just help the lost dead to move on."

"Like on that show *Dead Like Me*."

"We don't get television here—"

"It's on cable, anyway."

"—and I doubt it's anything the same."

"So how you'd get the job?"

"I was like your friend Adrian. I wasn't ready to go on.

But then, when I was ready, I realized it was more important to help others overcome their fears."

"How'd you die?"

"I was hit by a car."

I don't really know what to say, so I just nod.

He goes on. "I think it's always harder for those of us who were taken before our time. You know, suddenly, in an accident."

Like diving off the roof of a school, I think.

"We don't accept what's happened," he explains, "and so we aren't ready to move on."

"I get it."

"Well, no offense," he says, "but I hope we never see each other again."

I smile. "I plan to be an old, old lady before I go."

"I hope that works out for you."

He steps up to me and puts his hand on the top of my head. Before I can back off, or ask him what he thinks he's doing, I have this moment of vertigo—like when Pelly took me traveling through the back of the closet—and the next thing I know, I'm in my room, standing at the window.

Like it was all a dream, except I'm still dressed in my jeans and sweater.

Okay, I think. That was weird. Maybe the weirdest thing yet out of all of this.

I check my reflection in the dresser mirror.

Still blue-skinned and blue-haired.

Maybe I should dye my hair orange before I go to

school. I mean, if you're going to stand out, you might as well *really* stand out.

Instead, I get ready for bed.

Lying there, I think about that light that Adrian walked into. I think about people dying, lost and alone like he did. I think about all the people who are like him right now, living somewhere, all by themselves, no friends, no family. Maybe not even a home. Just a cardboard box in some doorway.

There's a lot worse things than being a blue girl.

I want to go into Mom's and Jared's bedrooms and tell them I love them, but they'll just think I'm weird, waking them up at, what? I look at the bedside clock—three in the morning. I can't call Maxine either because I'd probably wake her mom.

But there is someone I can call.

I dial Thomas's number. He's got a roommate, but their bedrooms are on opposite sides of their apartment. The phone rings a couple of times on his end before his sleepy voice comes on the line.

"Hey," I say.

"Imogene?" I can hear him waking up by the third syllable of my name. "Is everything okay?"

"It is now. I just wanted someone to talk to."

I don't say "someone real," but that's what I mean.

"Sorry 'bout waking you," I add.

"No, that's okay. I'm glad you called."

I laugh. "At three o'clock in the morning?"

"Is that what time it is?"

"Mm-hmm."

"Three A.M.'s an especially good time to get a phone call from your girlfriend. So long as she's not breaking up with you. You're not breaking up with me, are you?"

"No, I just miss you."

And see, he's such a good boyfriend that he doesn't say something like, "But we just saw each other this afternoon."

He says, "Me, too."

CHARLES DE LINT is widely credited as having pioneered the contemporary fantasy genre with his urban fantasy *Moonheart* (1984). He has been a seventeen-time finalist for the World Fantasy Award, winning in 2000 for his short story collection *Moonlight and Vines*; its stories are set in de Lint's popular fictional city of Newford, as were those in two previous story collections, *Dreams Underfoot* and *The Ivory and the Horn*.

His novels and short stories have received glowing reviews and numerous other awards, including the singular honor of having eight books chosen for the Modern Library's reader-selected list of the "Top 100 Books of the Twentieth Century."

A respected critic in his field, de Lint has been a judge for several prestigious awards, and is currently the primary book reviewer for *The Magazine of Fantasy and Science Fiction*.

A professional musician for over twenty-five years, specializing in traditional and contemporary Celtic and American roots music, he frequently performs with his wife, MaryAnn Harris—fellow musician, artist, and kindred spirit.

Charles de Lint and MaryAnn Harris live in Ottawa, Ontario, Canada. Their respective Web sites are www.charlesdelint.com and www.reclectica.com.